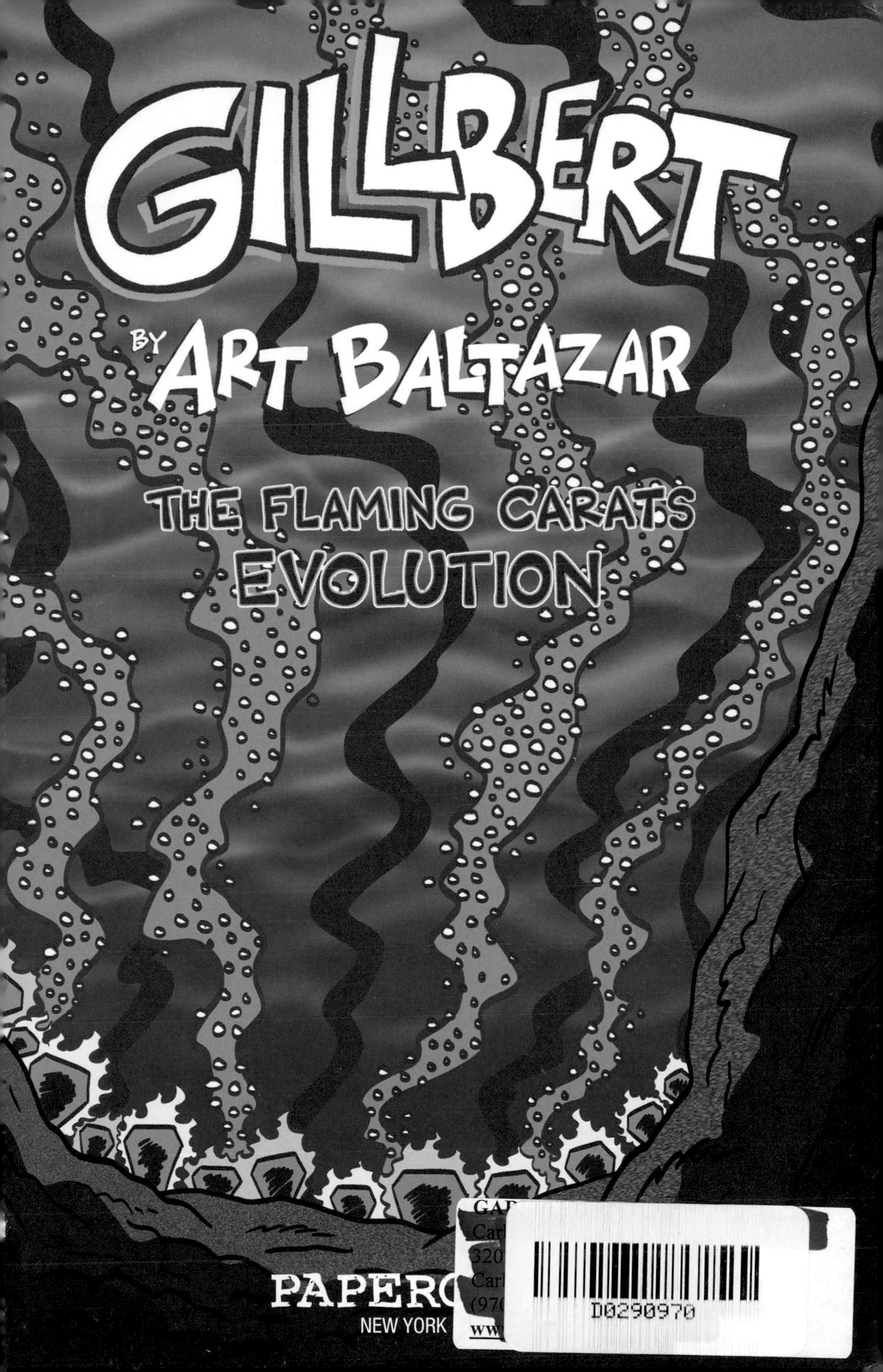
GILLBERT
BY ART BALTAZAR
THE FLAMING CARATS
EVOLUTION
PAPERC
NEW YORK

#3 "The Flaming Carats Evolution"
By Art Baltazar
Production – Big Bird Zatryb
Managing Editor – Jeff Whitman
Jim Salicrup
Editor-in-Chief

Papercutz books may be purchased for business or
promotional use. For information on bulk purchases
please contact Macmillan Corporate and Premium Sales
Department at
(800) 221-795 x5442.

Hardcover ISBN: 978-1-5458-0488-9
Paperback ISBN: 978-1-5458-0489-6

Printed in Lithuania
November 2020

Distributed by Macmillan
First Printing

AW YEAH, PAPERCUTZ PRESENTS...

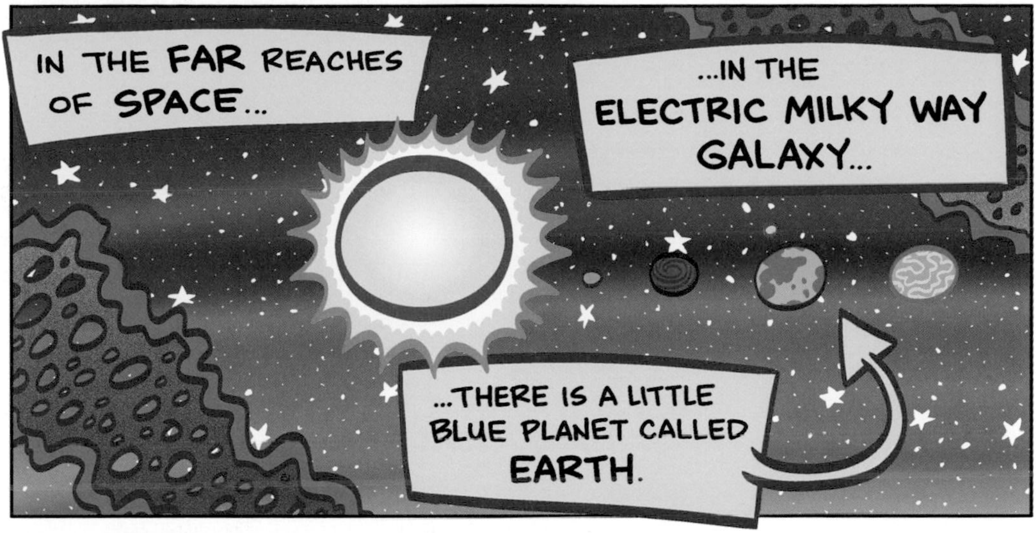
IN THE FAR REACHES OF SPACE...
...IN THE ELECTRIC MILKY WAY GALAXY...
...THERE IS A LITTLE BLUE PLANET CALLED EARTH.

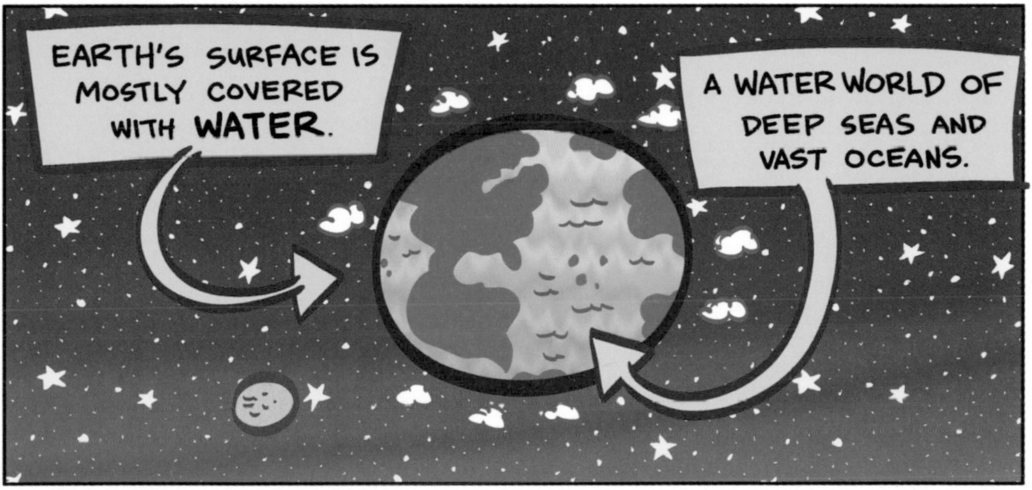
EARTH'S SURFACE IS MOSTLY COVERED WITH WATER.
A WATER WORLD OF DEEP SEAS AND VAST OCEANS.

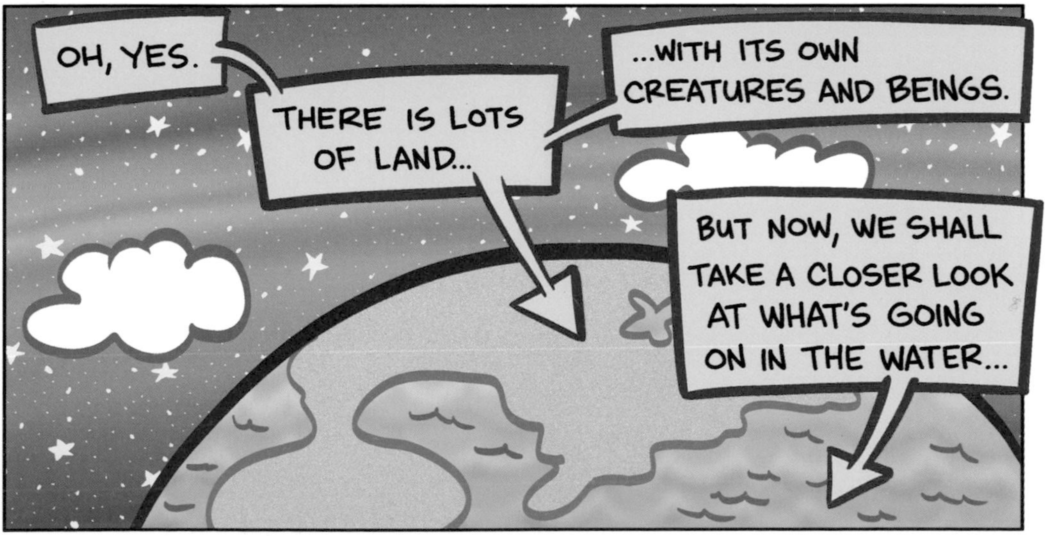
OH, YES.
THERE IS LOTS OF LAND...
...WITH ITS OWN CREATURES AND BEINGS.
BUT NOW, WE SHALL TAKE A CLOSER LOOK AT WHAT'S GOING ON IN THE WATER...

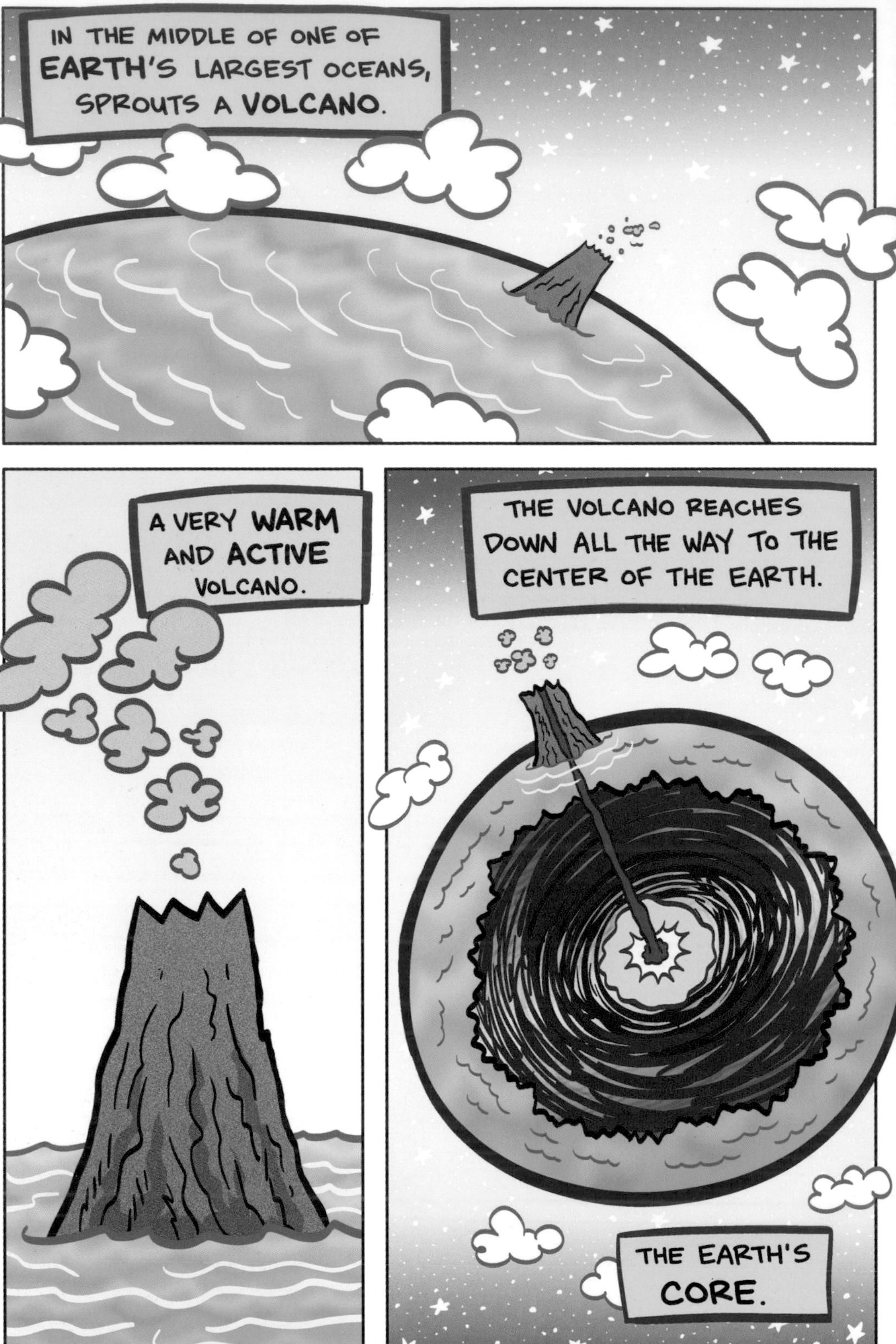
IN THE MIDDLE OF ONE OF EARTH'S LARGEST OCEANS, SPROUTS A VOLCANO.
A VERY WARM AND ACTIVE VOLCANO.
THE VOLCANO REACHES DOWN ALL THE WAY TO THE CENTER OF THE EARTH.
THE EARTH'S CORE.

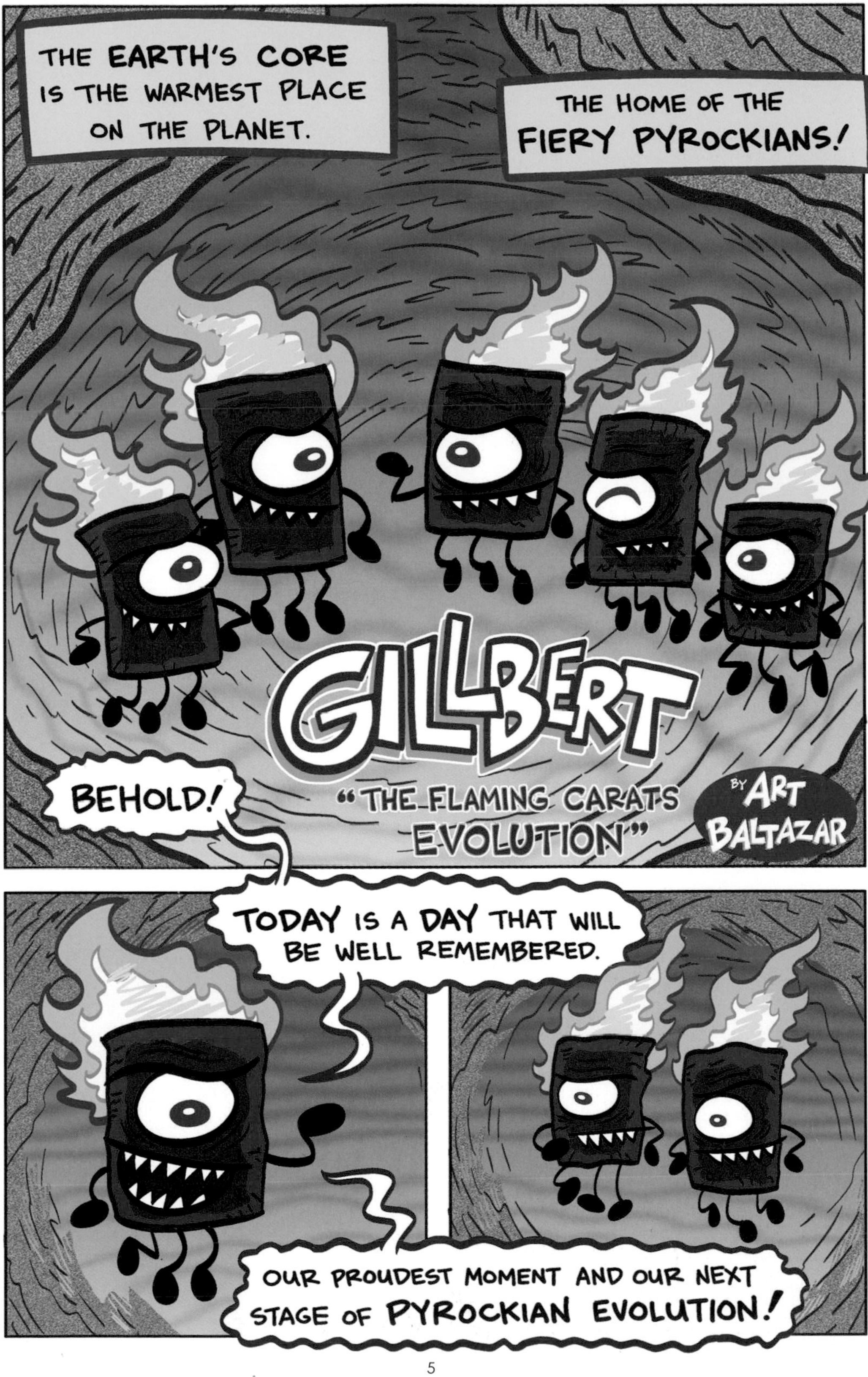
THE EARTH'S CORE IS THE WARMEST PLACE ON THE PLANET.
THE HOME OF THE FIERY PYROCKIANS!
GILLBERT
"THE FLAMING CARATS EVOLUTION"
BY ART BALTAZAR
BEHOLD!
TODAY IS A DAY THAT WILL BE WELL REMEMBERED.
OUR PROUDEST MOMENT AND OUR NEXT STAGE OF PYROCKIAN EVOLUTION!

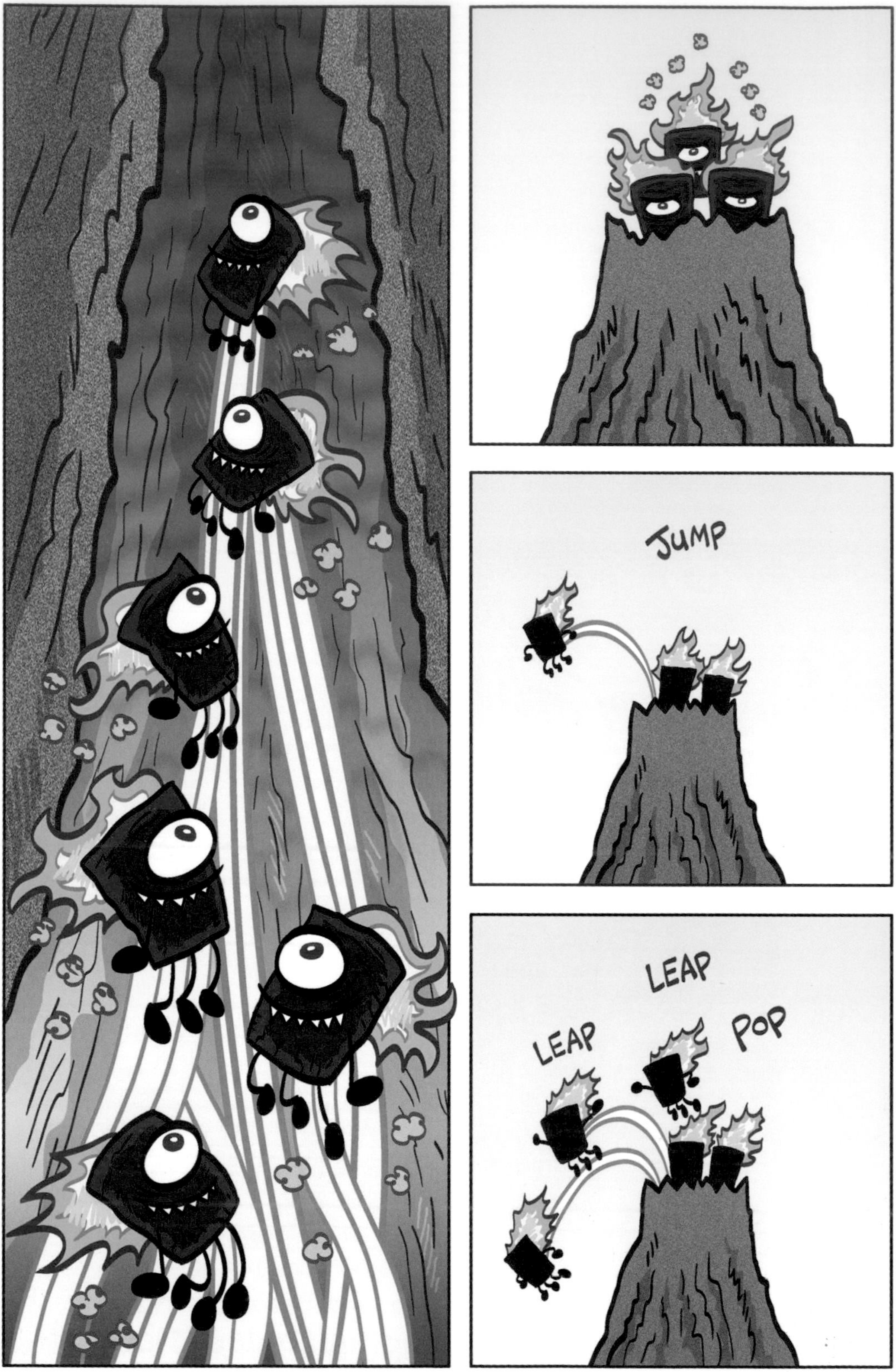
JUMP
LEAP
LEAP
POP

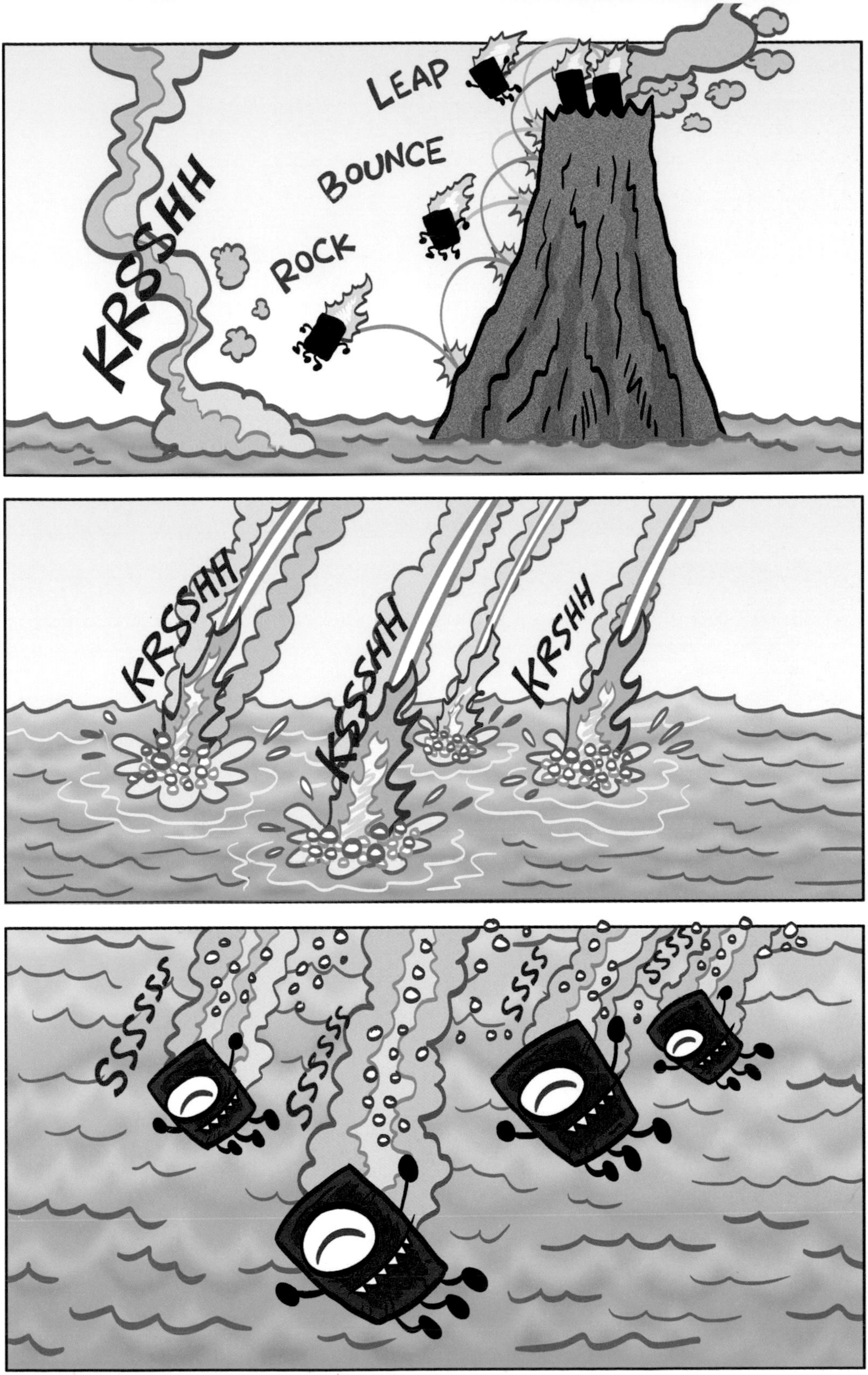
KRSSHH
ROCK
BOUNCE
LEAP
KRSSHH
KSSSHH
KRSHH
SSSSSS
SSSSSS
SSSS
SSSS

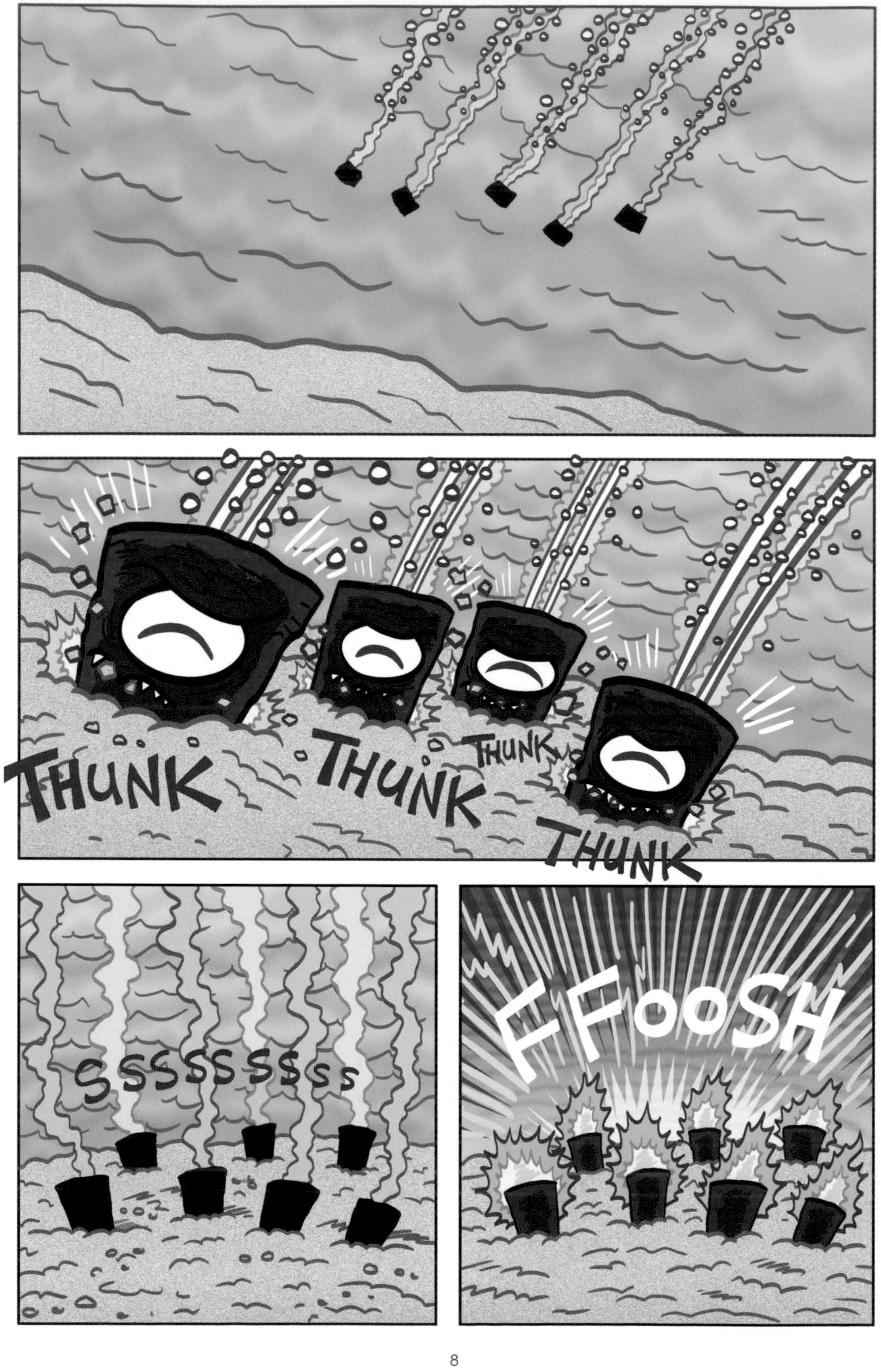
THUNK
THUNK
THUNK
THUNK
SSSSSSSSSS
FFOOSH

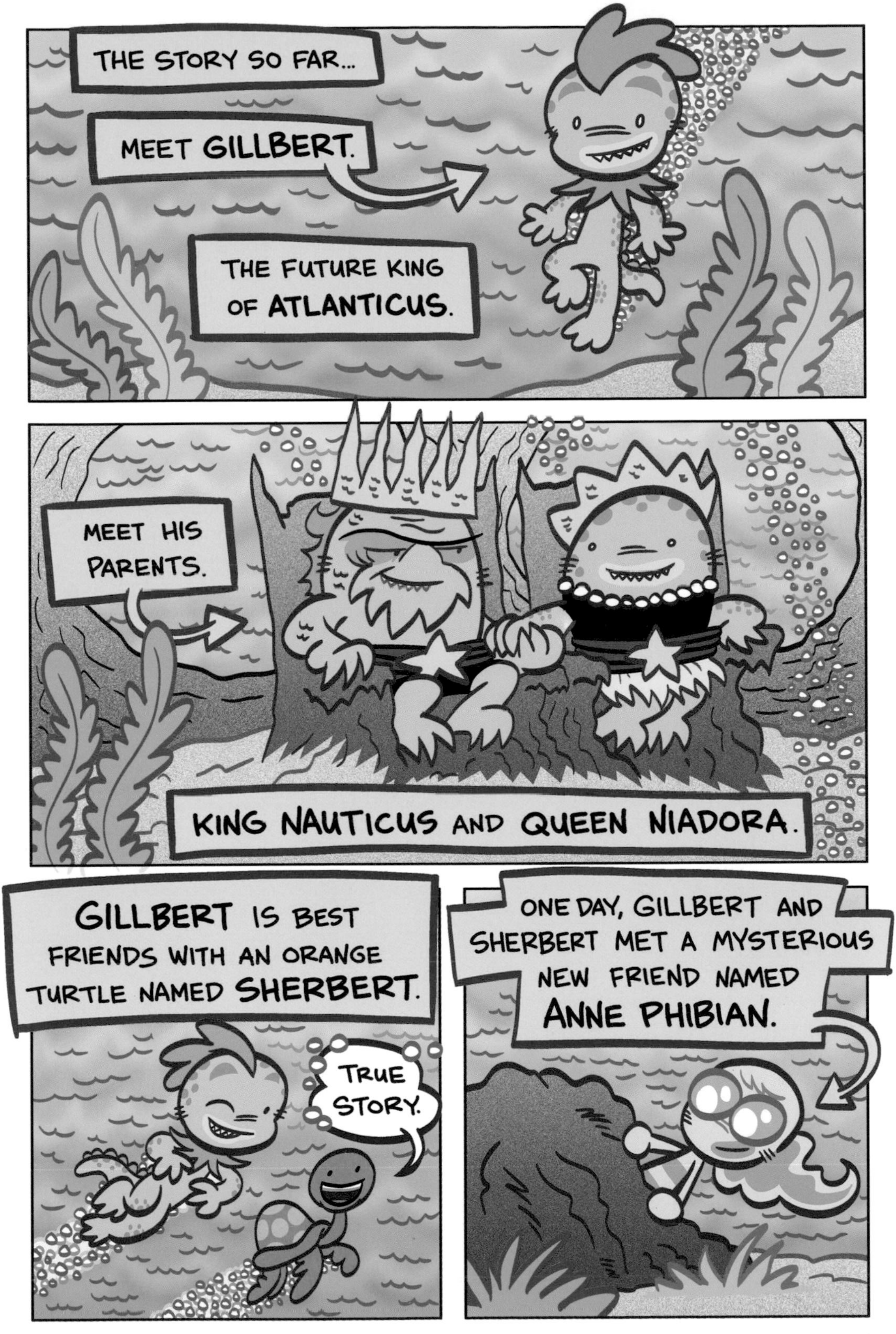
THE STORY SO FAR...
MEET GILLBERT.
THE FUTURE KING OF ATLANTICUS.
MEET HIS PARENTS.
KING NAUTICUS AND QUEEN NIADORA.
GILLBERT IS BEST FRIENDS WITH AN ORANGE TURTLE NAMED SHERBERT.
TRUE STORY.
ONE DAY, GILLBERT AND SHERBERT MET A MYSTERIOUS NEW FRIEND NAMED ANNE PHIBIAN.

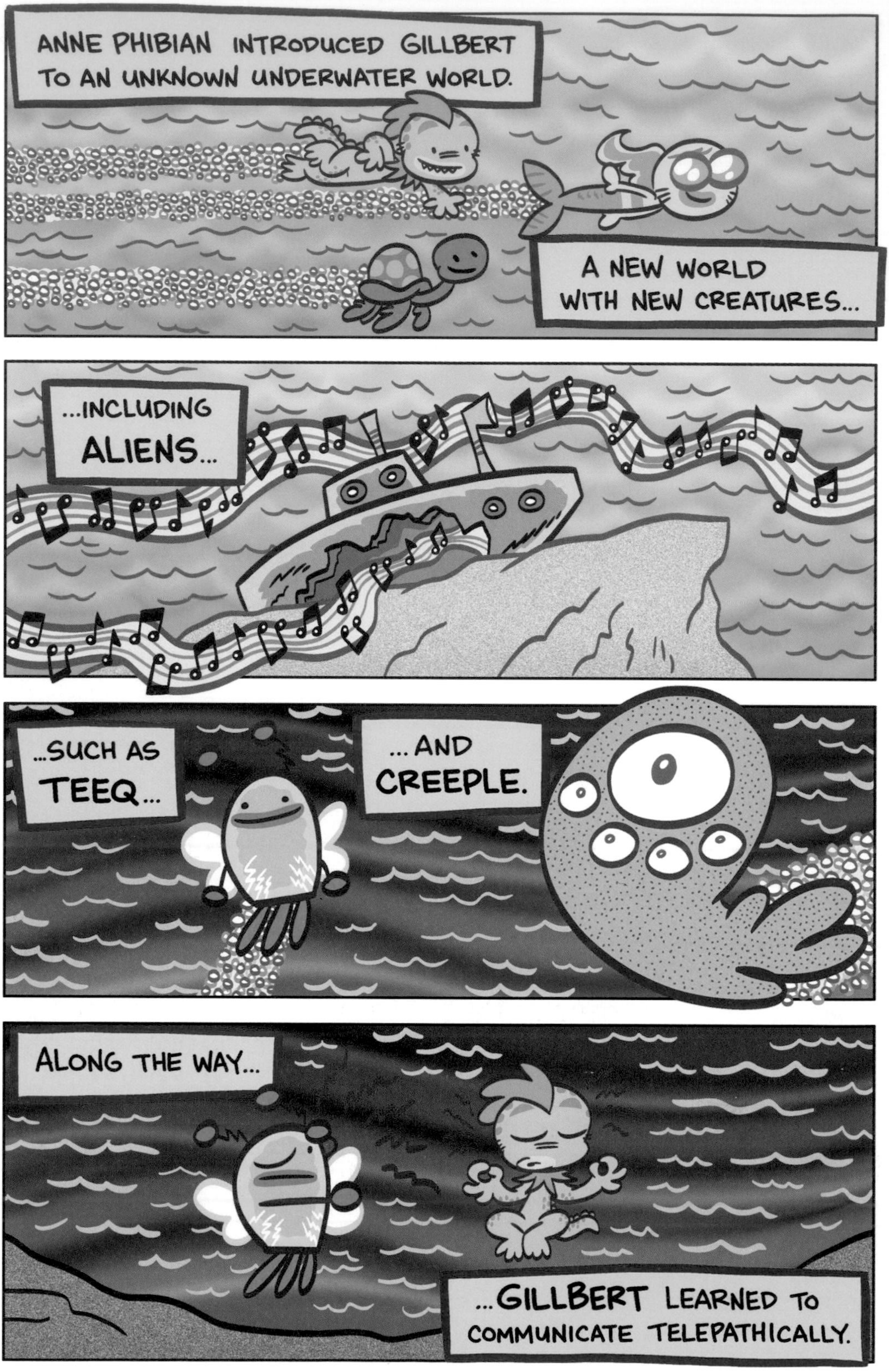
ANNE PHIBIAN INTRODUCED GILLBERT TO AN UNKNOWN UNDERWATER WORLD.
A NEW WORLD WITH NEW CREATURES...
...INCLUDING ALIENS...
...SUCH AS TEEQ...
... AND CREEPLE.
ALONG THE WAY...
...GILLBERT LEARNED TO COMMUNICATE TELEPATHICALLY.

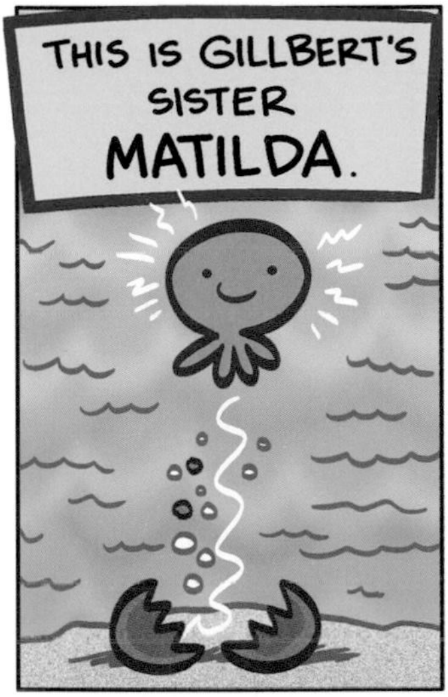
THIS IS GILLBERT'S SISTER MATILDA.

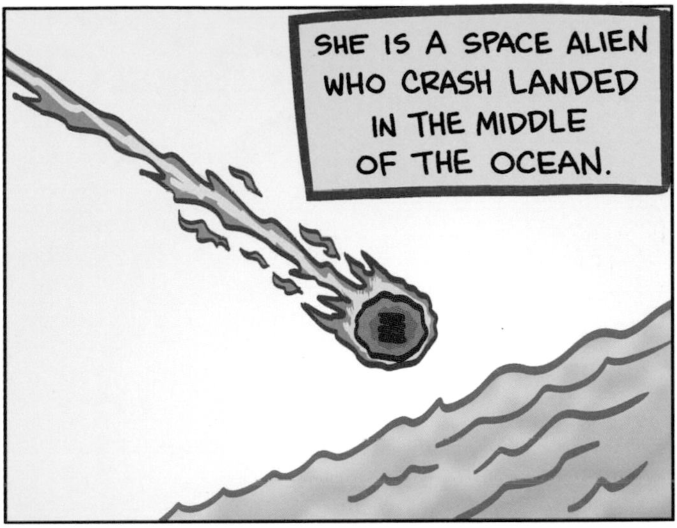
SHE IS A SPACE ALIEN WHO CRASH LANDED IN THE MIDDLE OF THE OCEAN.

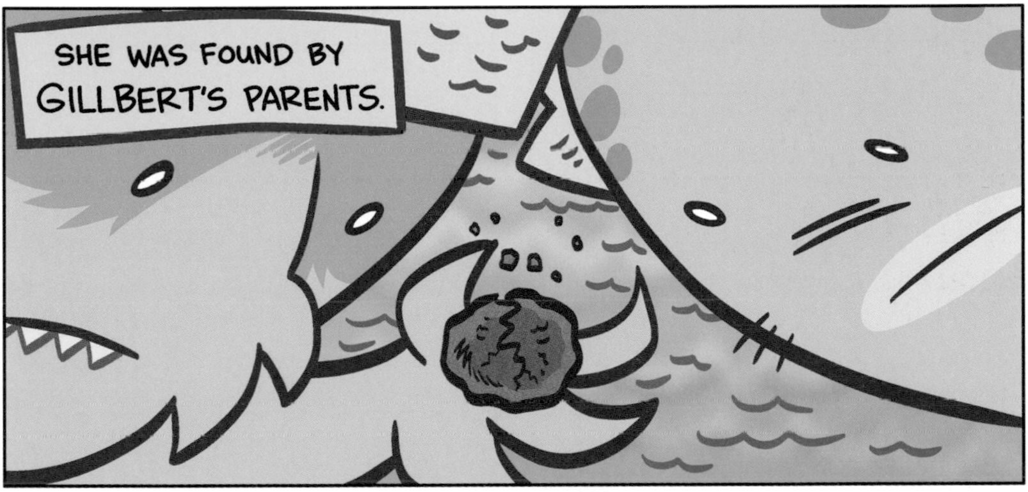
SHE WAS FOUND BY GILLBERT'S PARENTS.

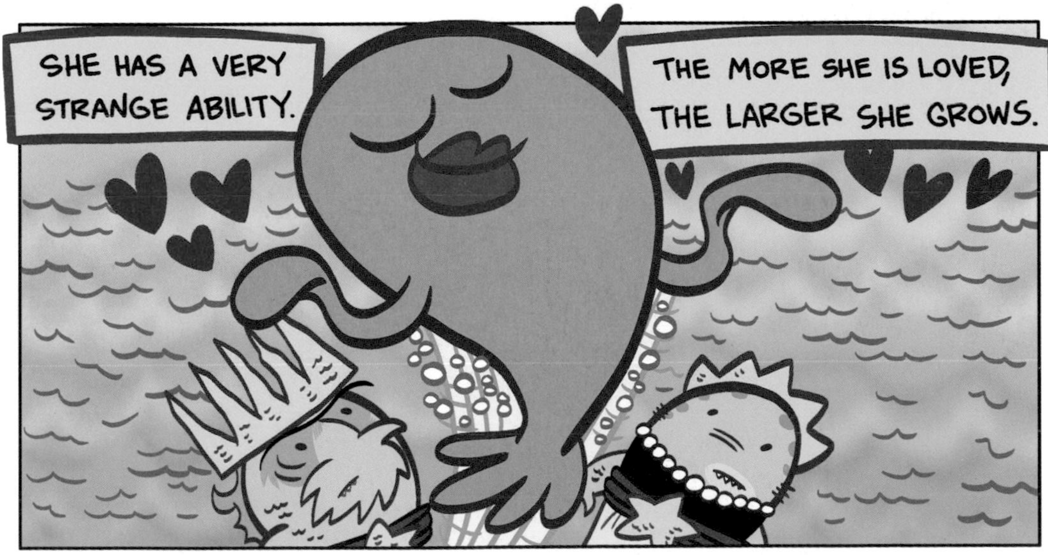
SHE HAS A VERY STRANGE ABILITY.
THE MORE SHE IS LOVED, THE LARGER SHE GROWS.

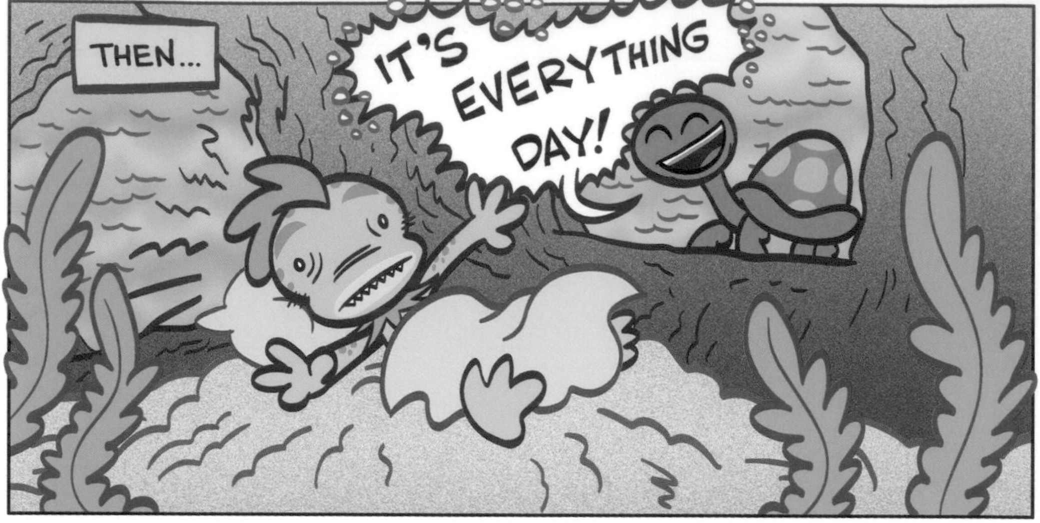
THEN...
IT'S EVERYTHING DAY!

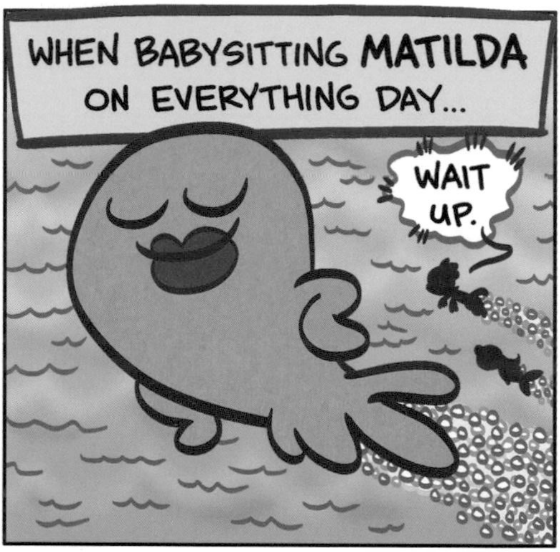
WHEN BABYSITTING MATILDA ON EVERYTHING DAY...
WAIT UP.

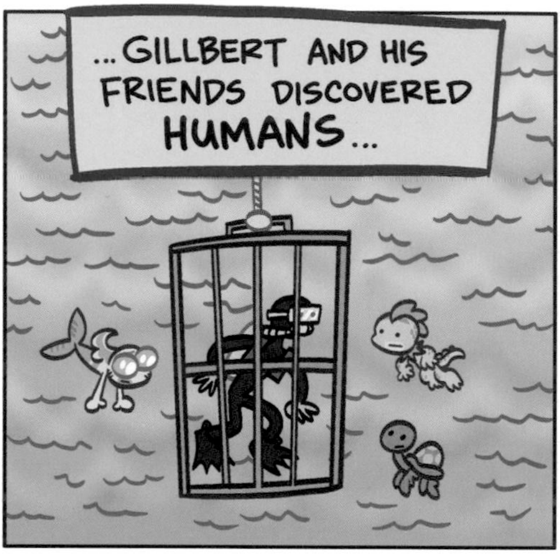
...GILLBERT AND HIS FRIENDS DISCOVERED HUMANS...

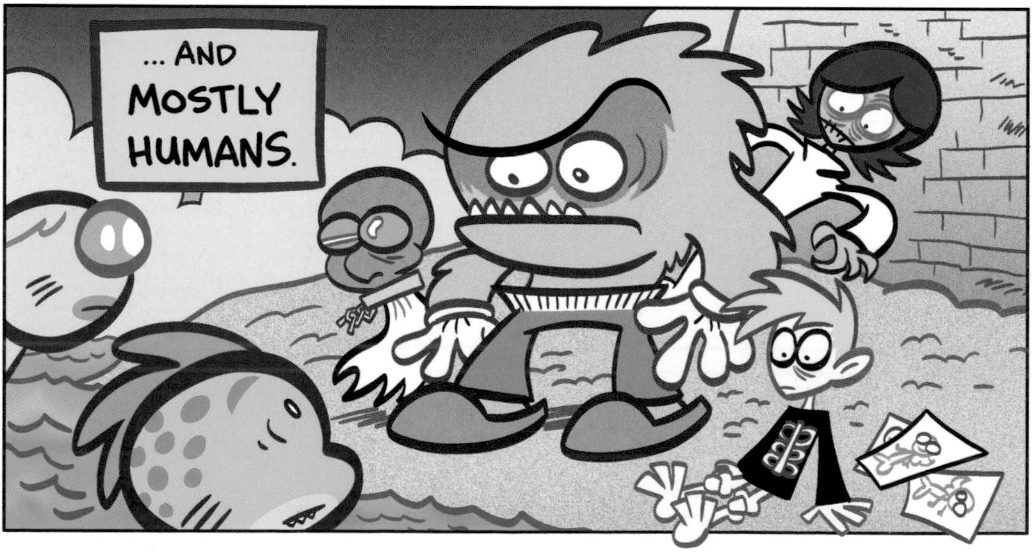
...AND MOSTLY HUMANS.

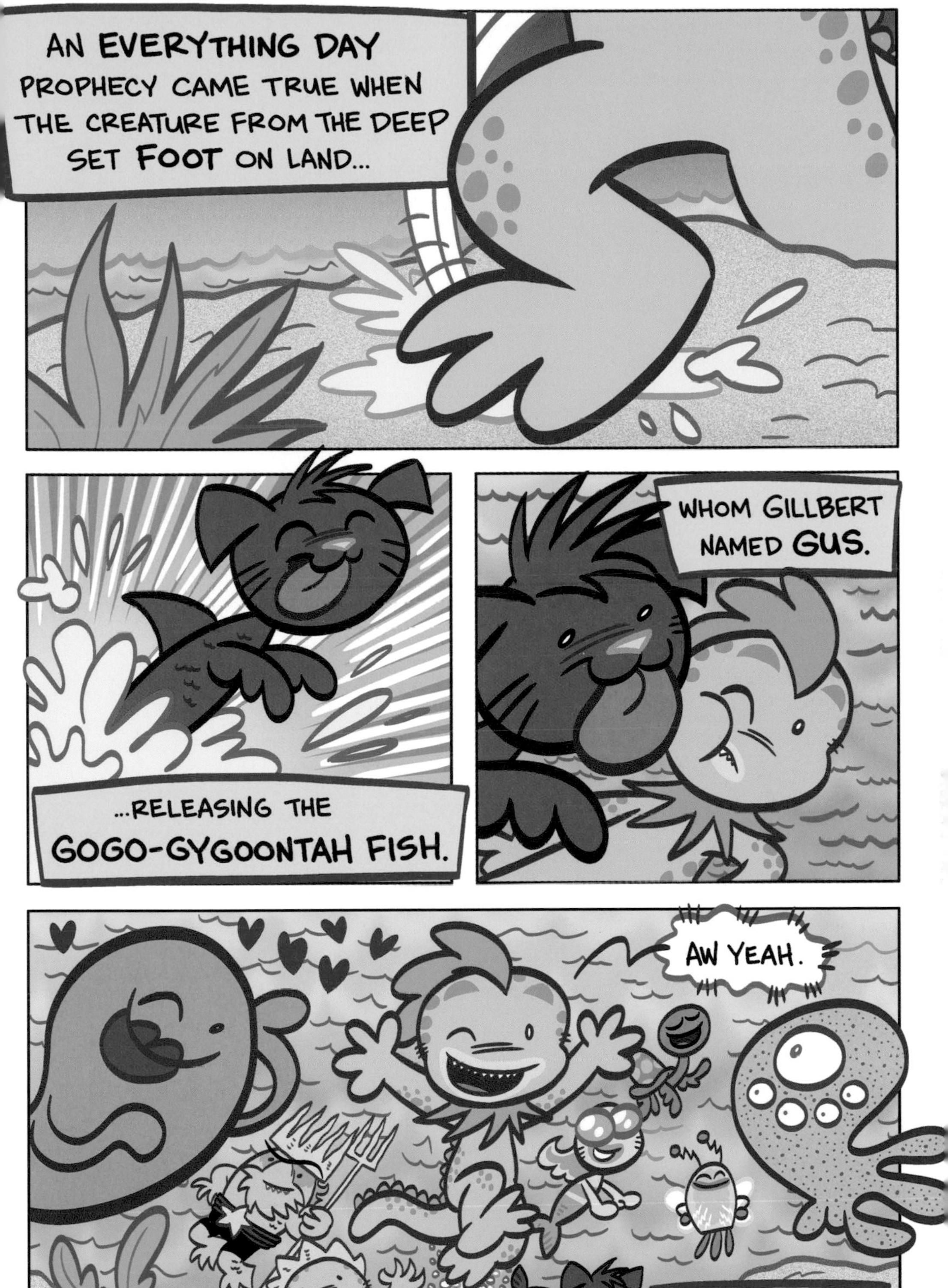
AN EVERYTHING DAY PROPHECY CAME TRUE WHEN THE CREATURE FROM THE DEEP SET FOOT ON LAND...
...RELEASING THE GOGO-GYGOONTAH FISH.
WHOM GILLBERT NAMED GUS.
AW YEAH.
NOW... ON WITH THE STORY.

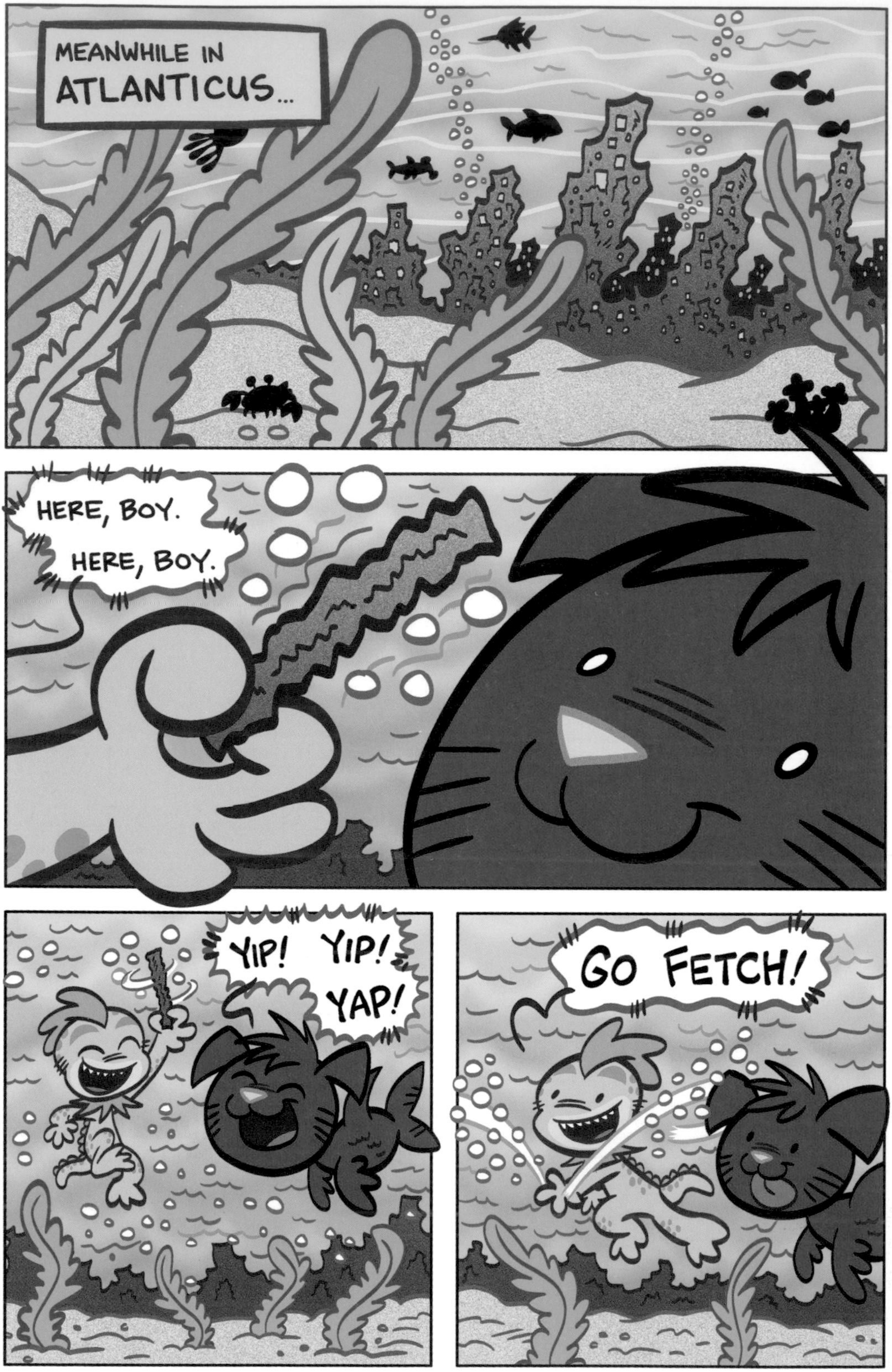
MEANWHILE IN ATLANTICUS...
HERE, BOY. HERE, BOY.
YIP! YIP! YAP!
GO FETCH!

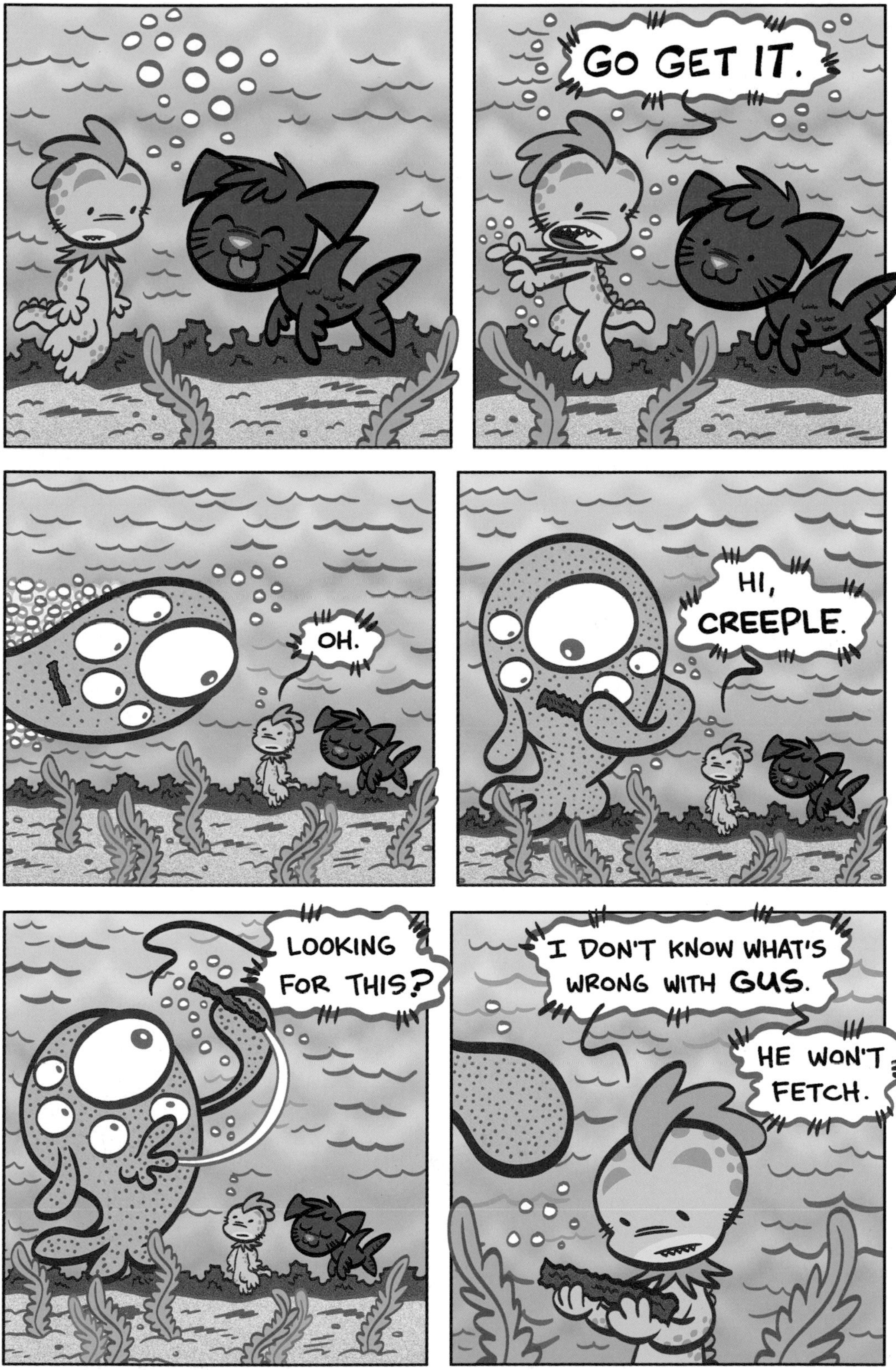
GO GET IT.
OH.
HI, CREEPLE.
LOOKING FOR THIS?
I DON'T KNOW WHAT'S WRONG WITH GUS.
HE WON'T FETCH.

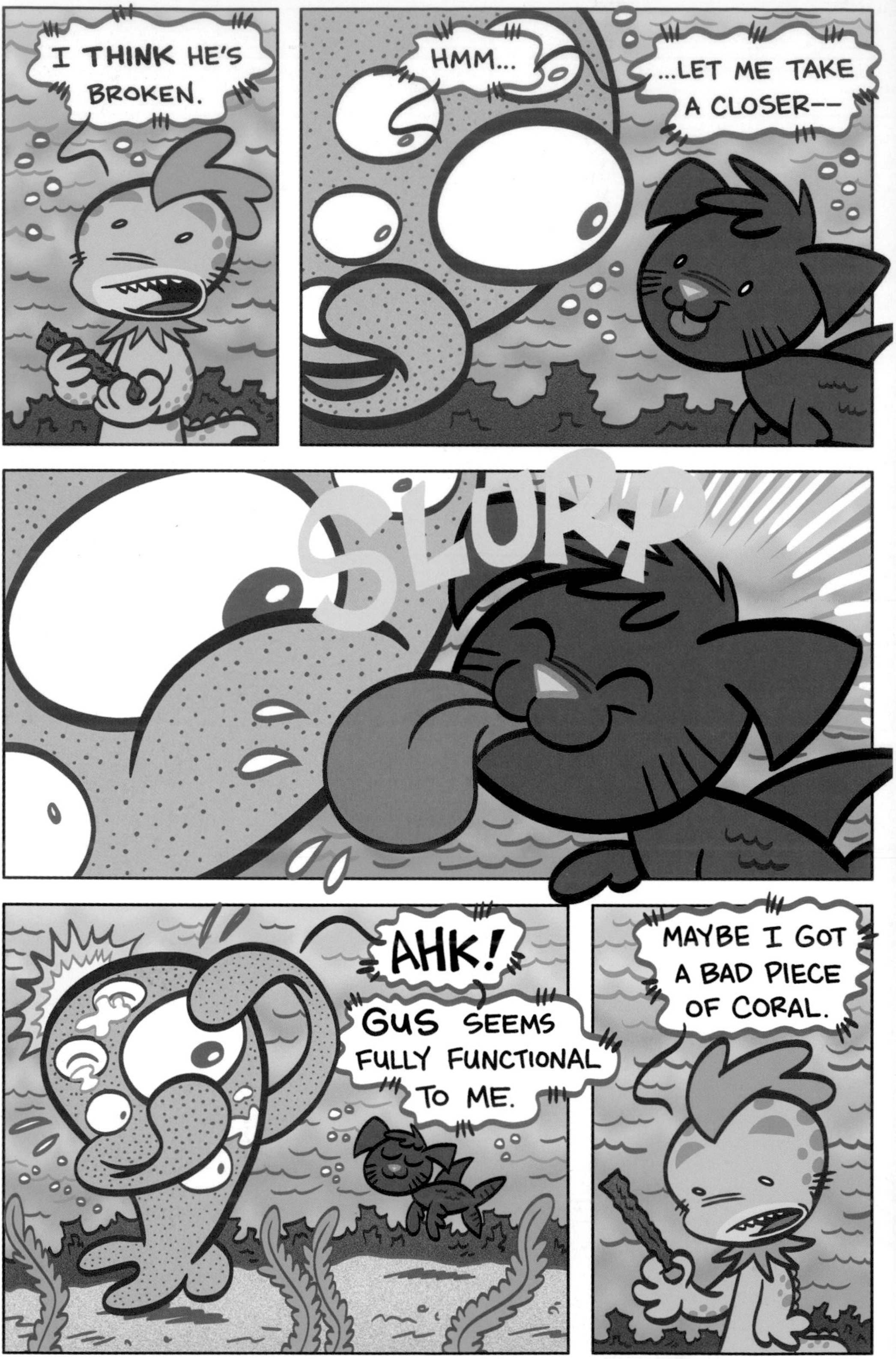
I THINK HE'S BROKEN.
HMM...
...LET ME TAKE A CLOSER--
SLURP
AHK!
GUS SEEMS FULLY FUNCTIONAL TO ME.
MAYBE I GOT A BAD PIECE OF CORAL.

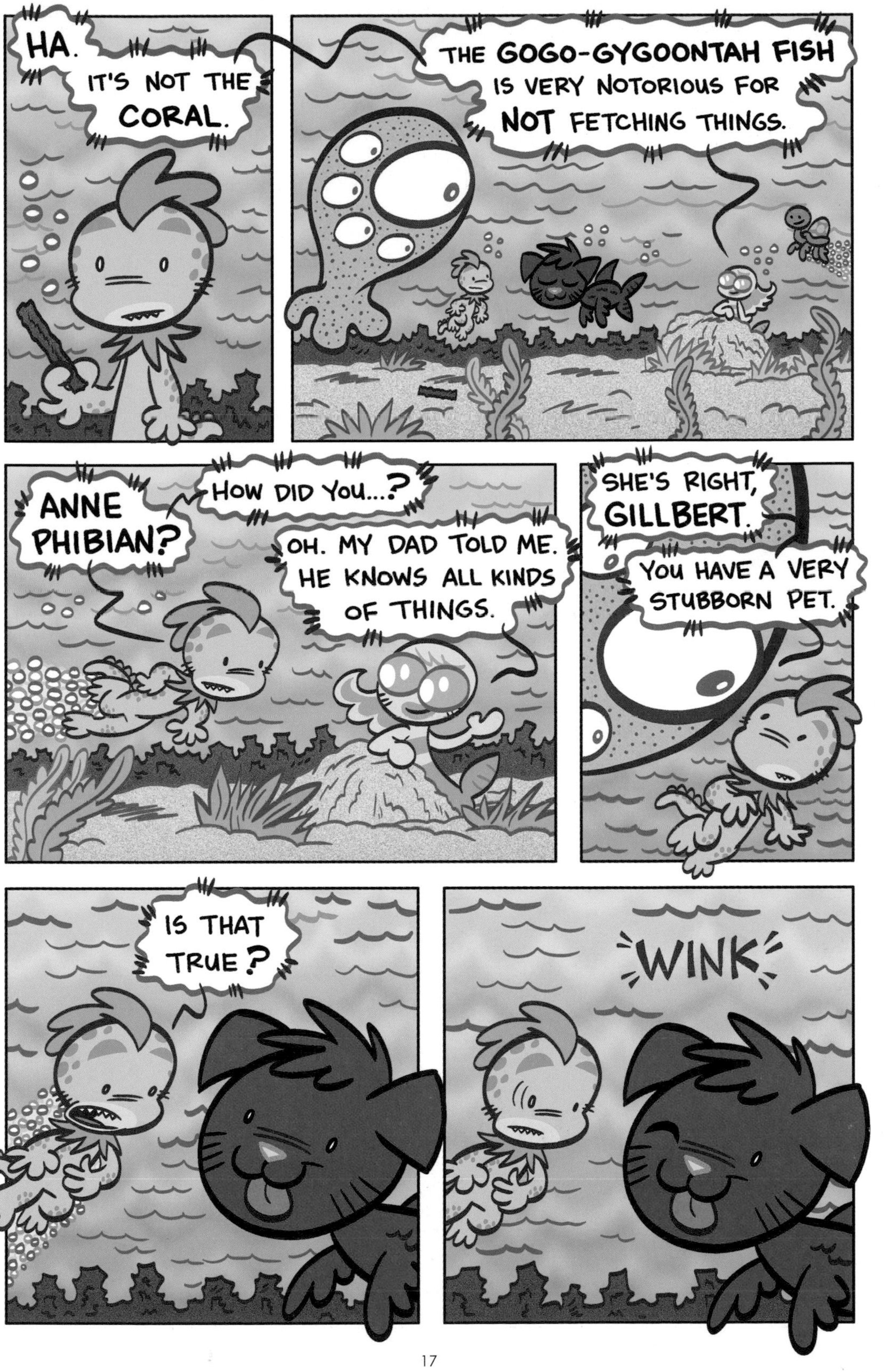
HA.
IT'S NOT THE CORAL.
THE GOGO-GYGOONTAH FISH IS VERY NOTORIOUS FOR NOT FETCHING THINGS.
ANNE PHIBIAN?
HOW DID YOU...?
OH. MY DAD TOLD ME. HE KNOWS ALL KINDS OF THINGS.
SHE'S RIGHT, GILLBERT.
YOU HAVE A VERY STUBBORN PET.
IS THAT TRUE?
WINK

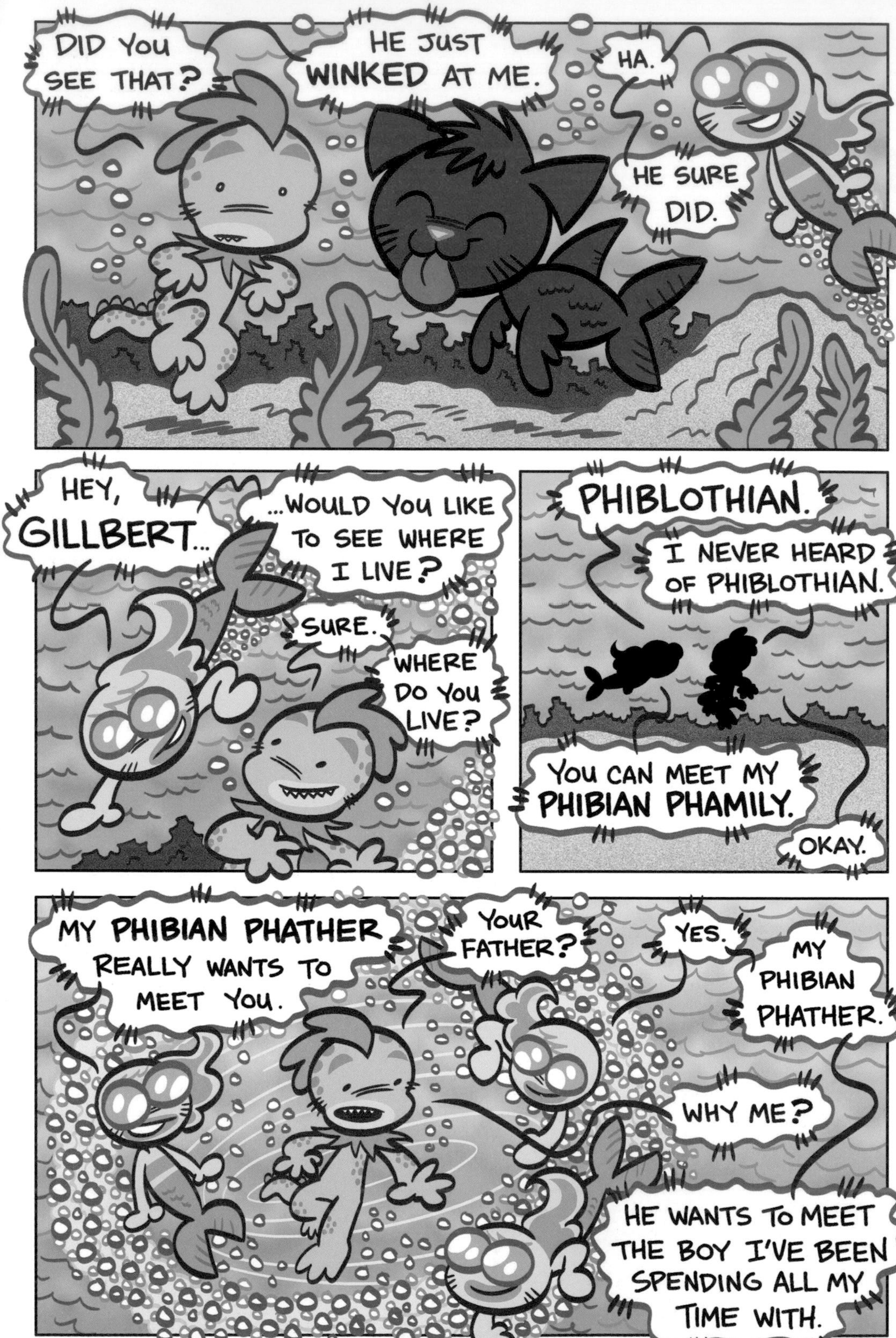
DID YOU SEE THAT?
HE JUST WINKED AT ME.
HA.
HE SURE DID.
HEY, GILLBERT...
...WOULD YOU LIKE TO SEE WHERE I LIVE?
SURE.
WHERE DO YOU LIVE?
PHIBLOTHIAN.
I NEVER HEARD OF PHIBLOTHIAN.
YOU CAN MEET MY PHIBIAN PHAMILY.
OKAY.
MY PHIBIAN PHATHER REALLY WANTS TO MEET YOU.
YOUR FATHER?
YES.
MY PHIBIAN PHATHER.
WHY ME?
HE WANTS TO MEET THE BOY I'VE BEEN SPENDING ALL MY TIME WITH.

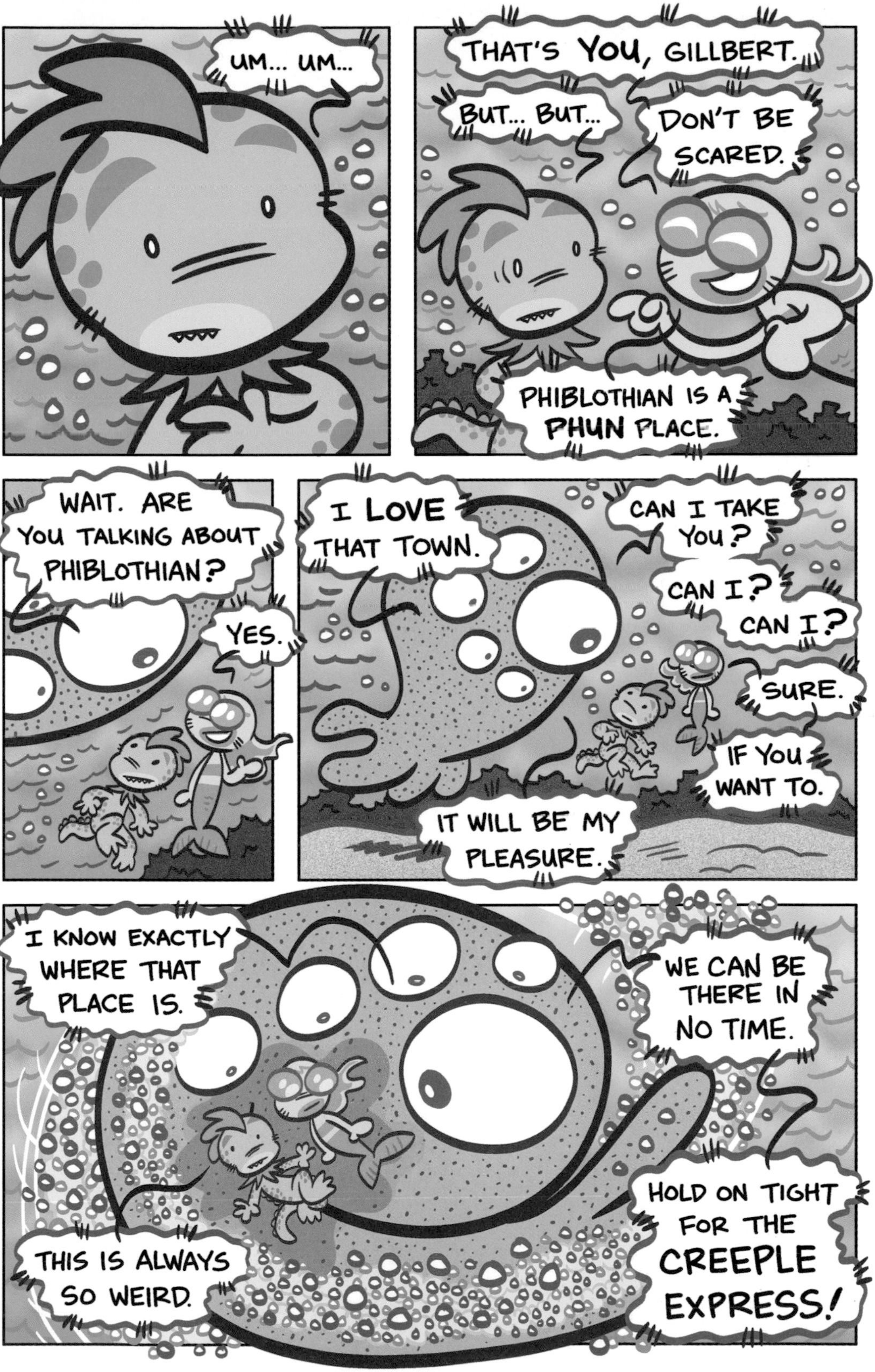
UM... UM...
THAT'S YOU, GILLBERT.
BUT... BUT...
DON'T BE SCARED.
PHIBLOTHIAN IS A PHUN PLACE.
WAIT. ARE YOU TALKING ABOUT PHIBLOTHIAN?
YES.
I LOVE THAT TOWN.
CAN I TAKE YOU?
CAN I?
CAN I?
SURE.
IF YOU WANT TO.
IT WILL BE MY PLEASURE.
I KNOW EXACTLY WHERE THAT PLACE IS.
WE CAN BE THERE IN NO TIME.
HOLD ON TIGHT FOR THE CREEPLE EXPRESS!
THIS IS ALWAYS SO WEIRD.

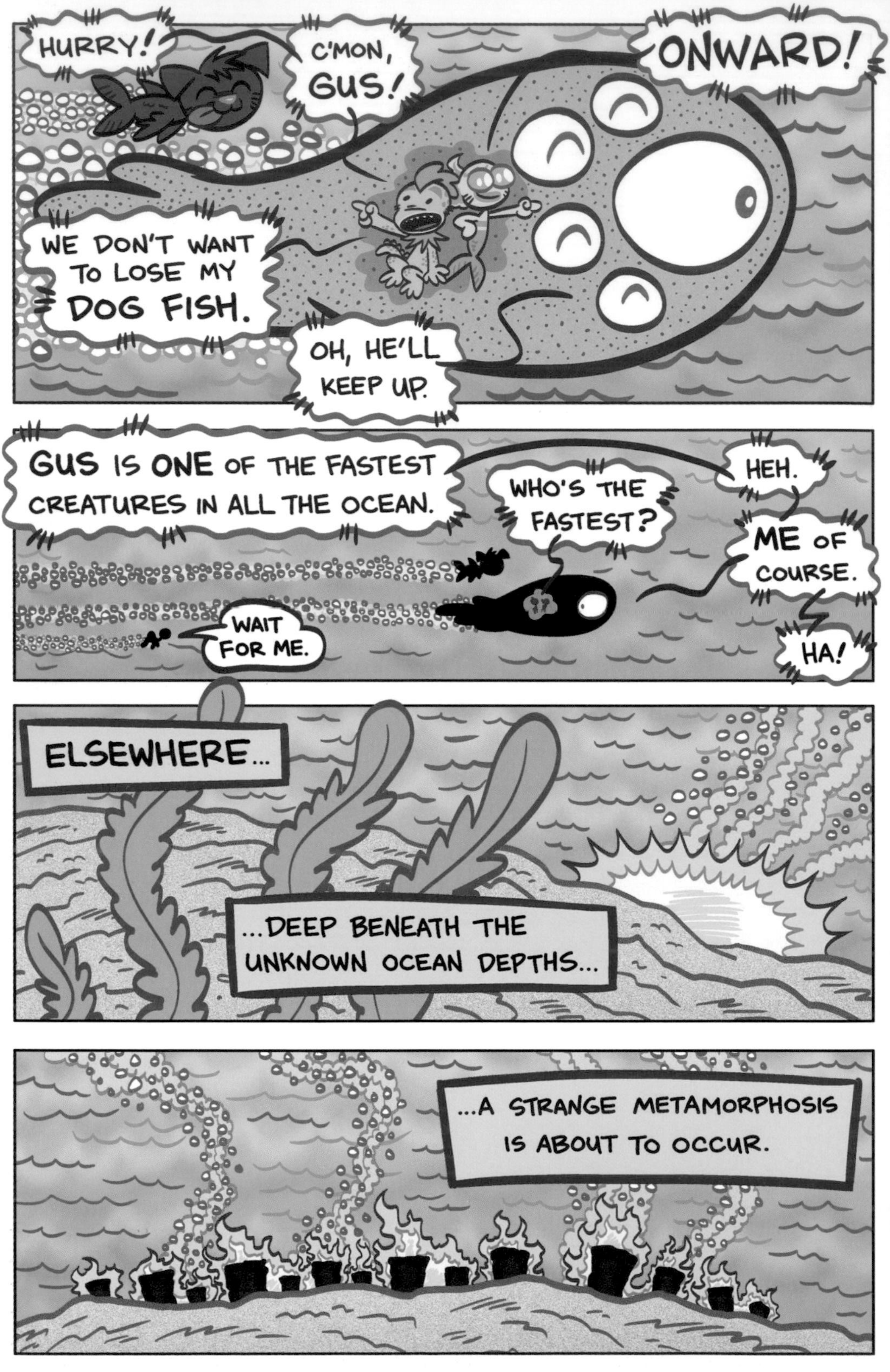
HURRY!
C'MON, GUS!
ONWARD!
WE DON'T WANT TO LOSE MY DOG FISH.
OH, HE'LL KEEP UP.
GUS IS ONE OF THE FASTEST CREATURES IN ALL THE OCEAN.
WHO'S THE FASTEST?
HEH.
ME OF COURSE.
HA!
WAIT FOR ME.
ELSEWHERE...
...DEEP BENEATH THE UNKNOWN OCEAN DEPTHS...
...A STRANGE METAMORPHOSIS IS ABOUT TO OCCUR.

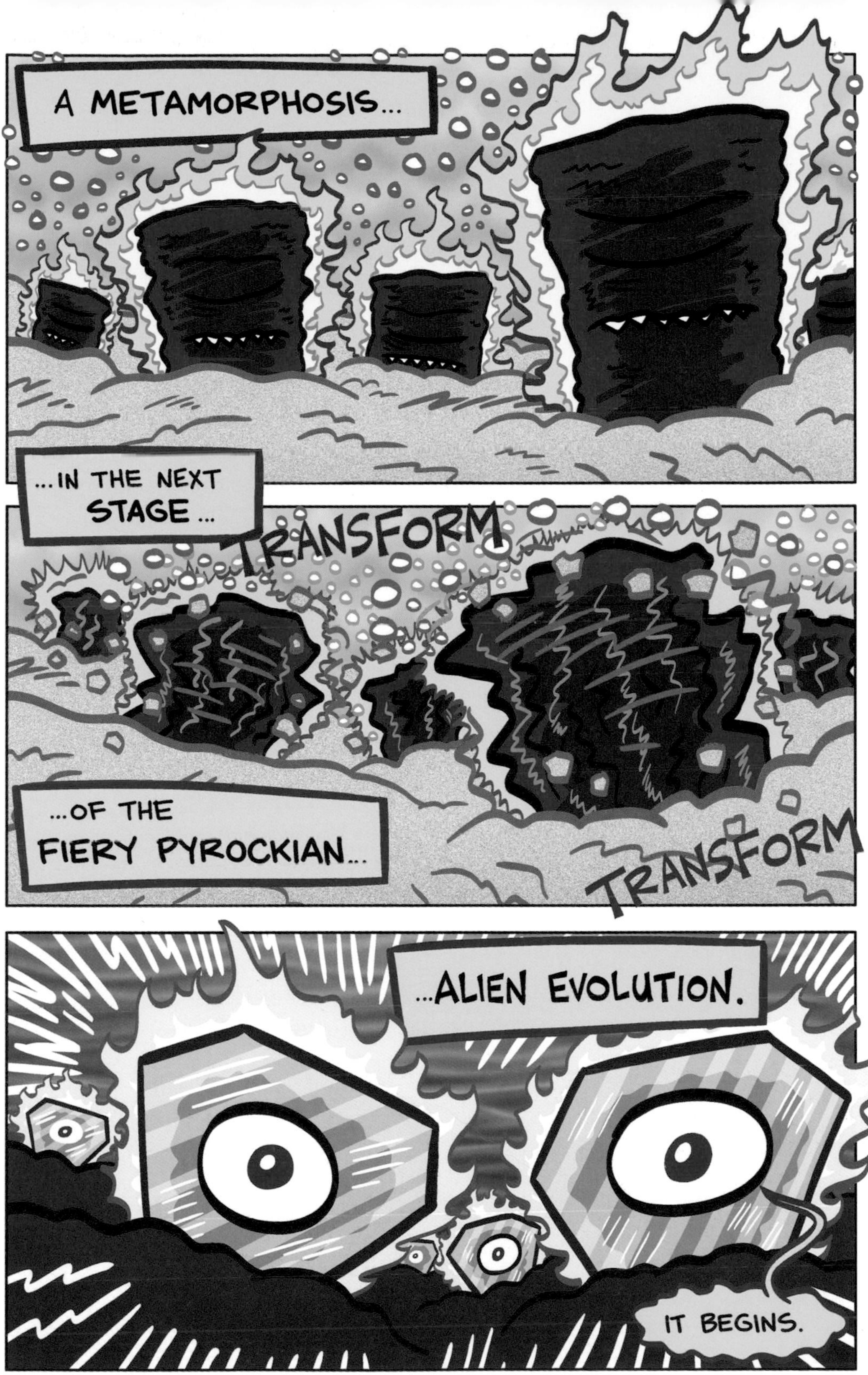

A METAMORPHOSIS...
...IN THE NEXT STAGE...
TRANSFORM
...OF THE FIERY PYROCKIAN...
TRANSFORM
...ALIEN EVOLUTION.
IT BEGINS.

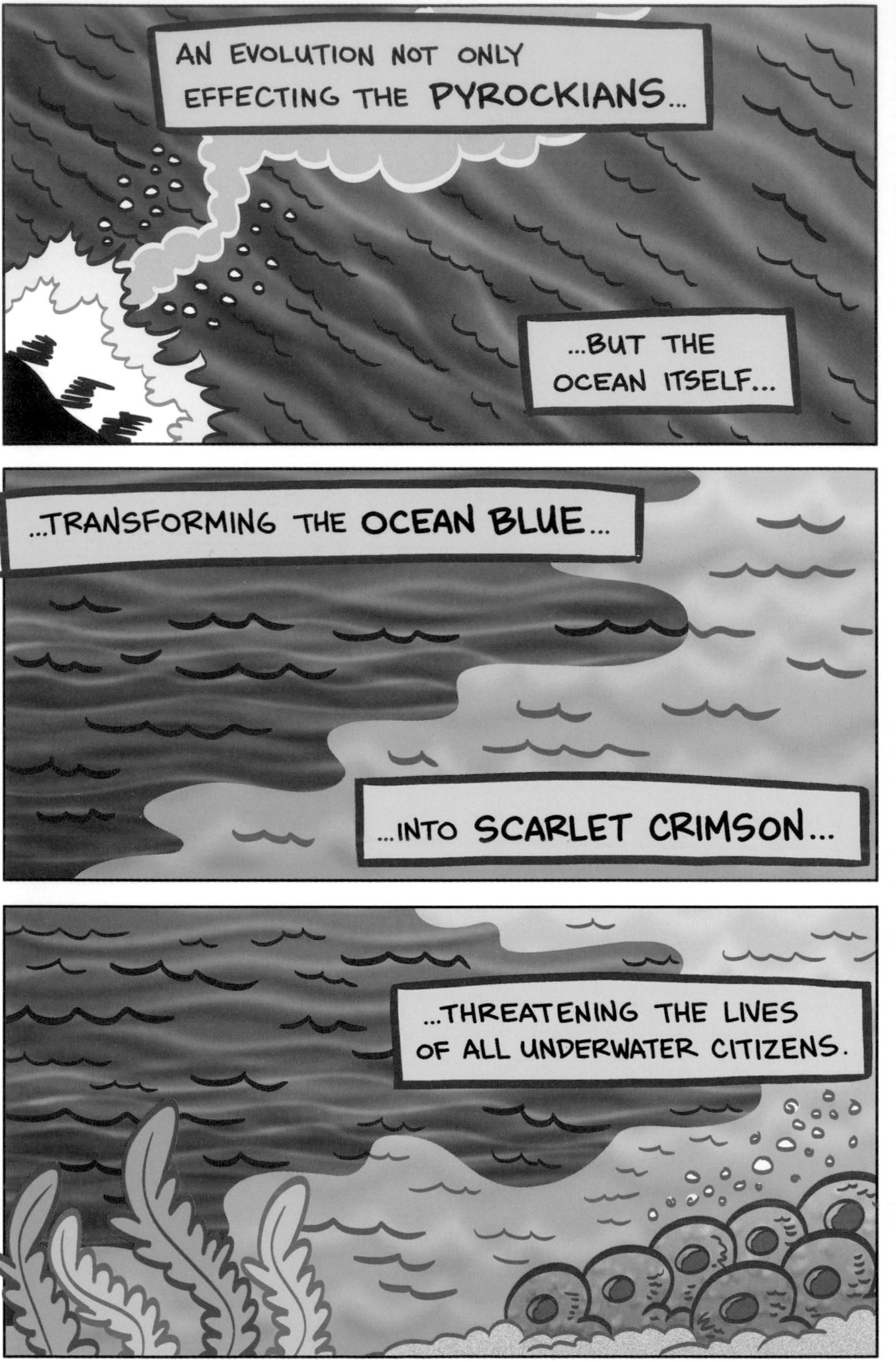
AN EVOLUTION NOT ONLY EFFECTING THE PYROCKIANS...
...BUT THE OCEAN ITSELF...
...TRANSFORMING THE OCEAN BLUE...
...INTO SCARLET CRIMSON...
...THREATENING THE LIVES OF ALL UNDERWATER CITIZENS.

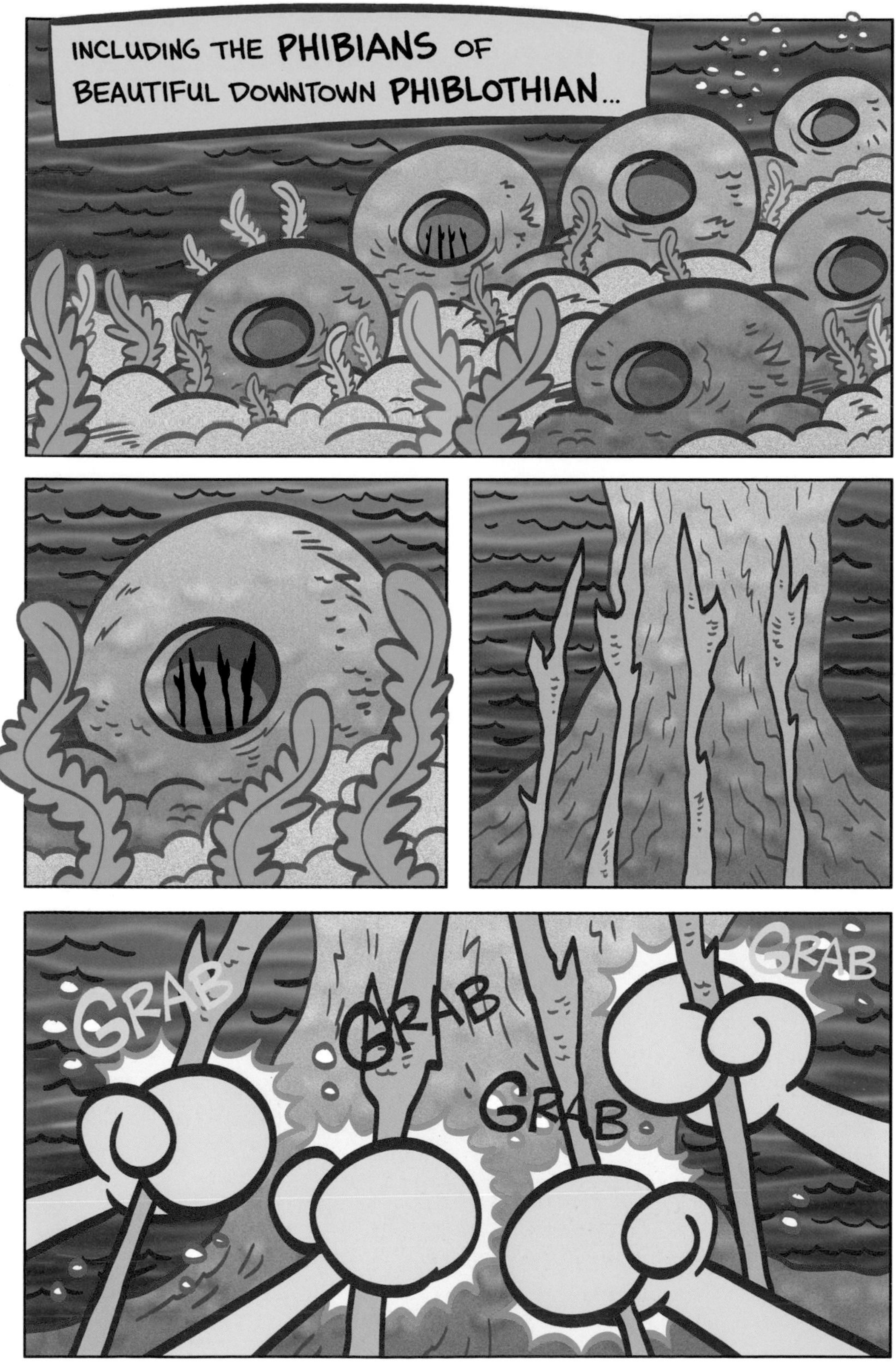
INCLUDING THE PHIBIANS OF BEAUTIFUL DOWNTOWN PHIBLOTHIAN...
GRAB
GRAB
GRAB
GRAB

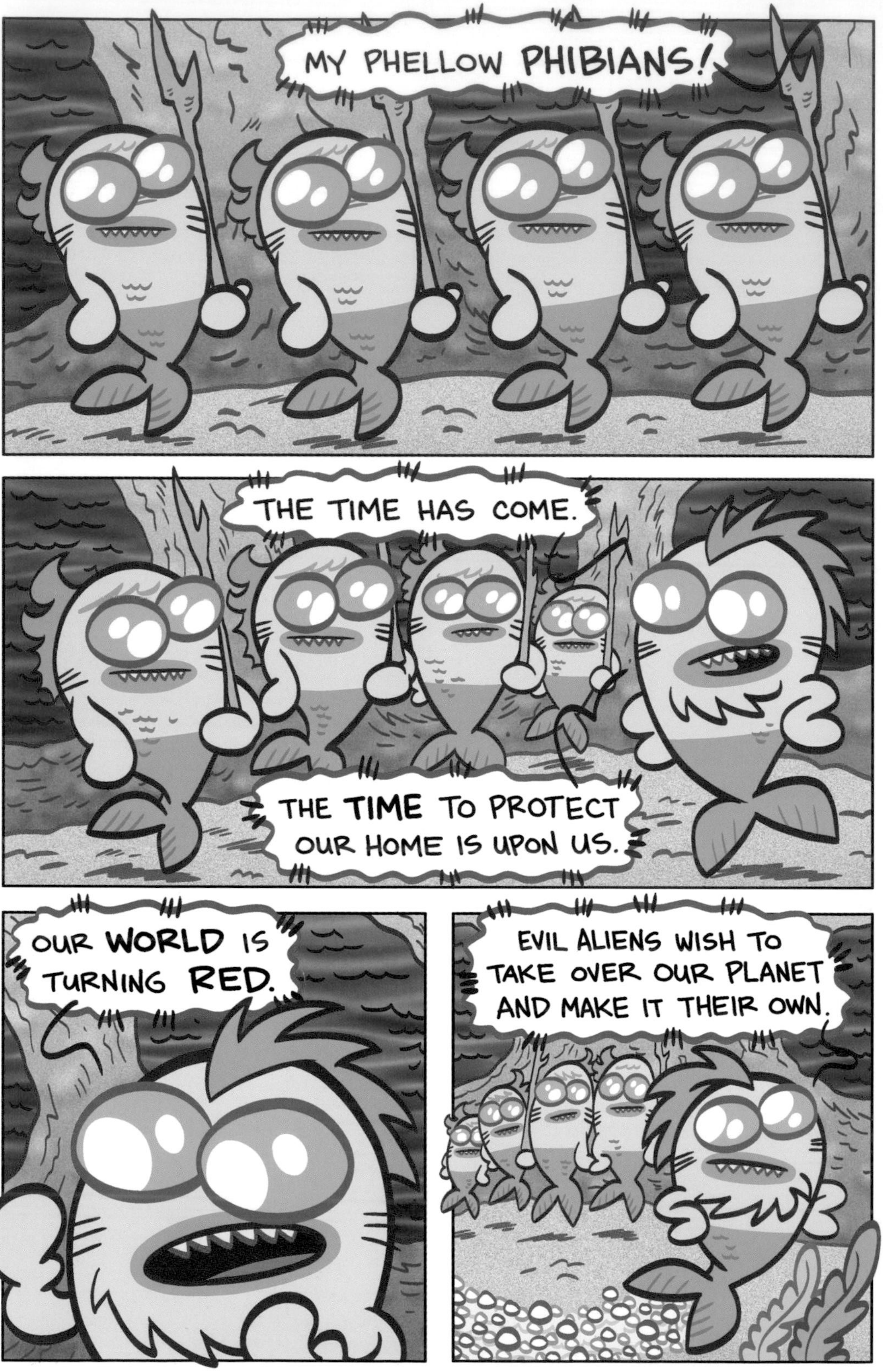
MY PHELLOW PHIBIANS!
THE TIME HAS COME.
THE TIME TO PROTECT OUR HOME IS UPON US.
OUR WORLD IS TURNING RED.
EVIL ALIENS WISH TO TAKE OVER OUR PLANET AND MAKE IT THEIR OWN.

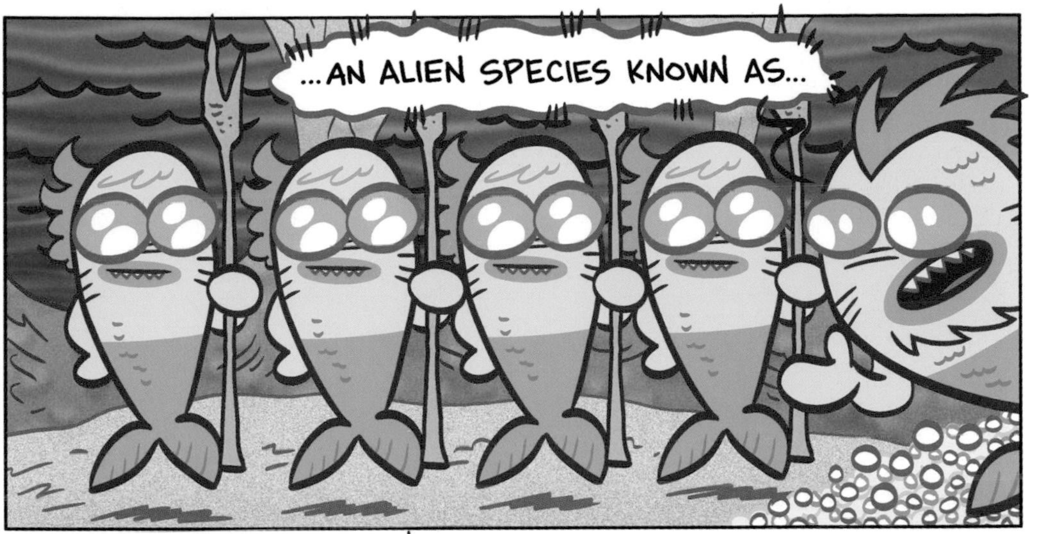
...AN ALIEN SPECIES KNOWN AS...

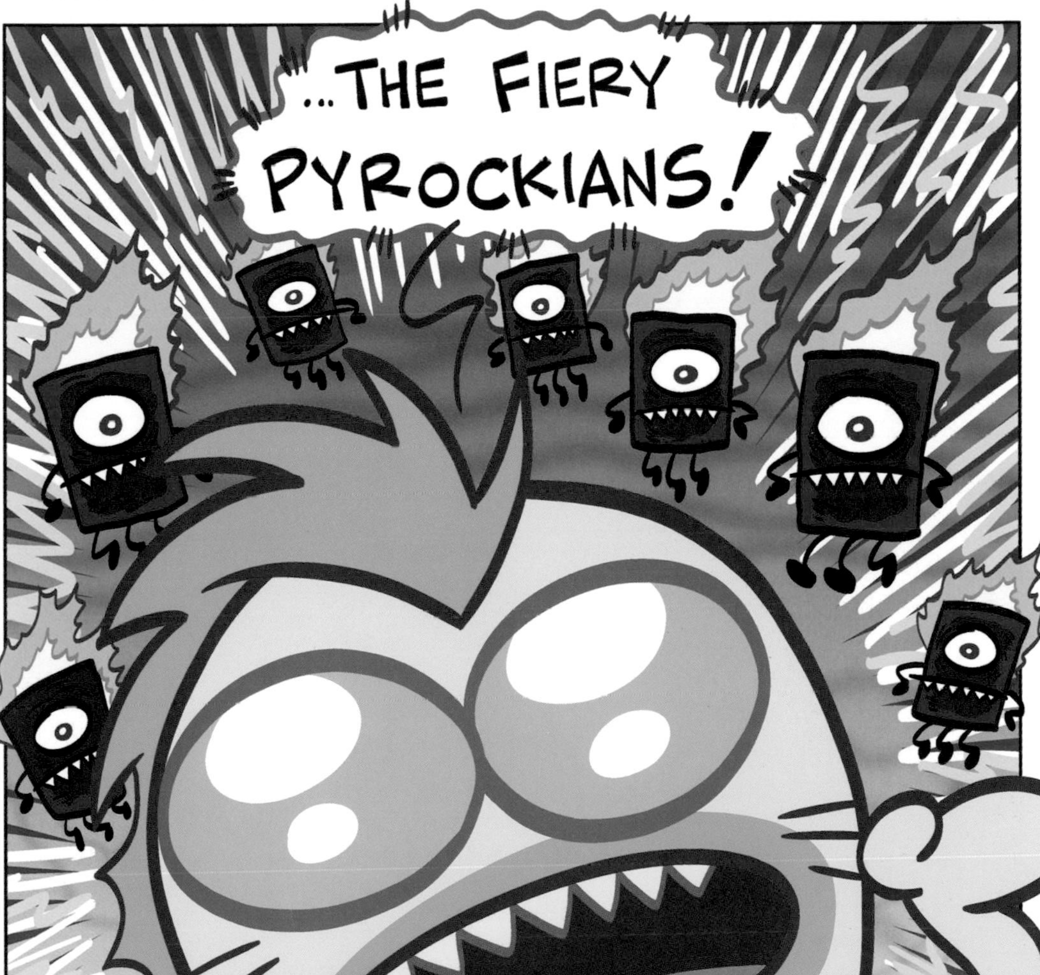
...THE FIERY PYROCKIANS!

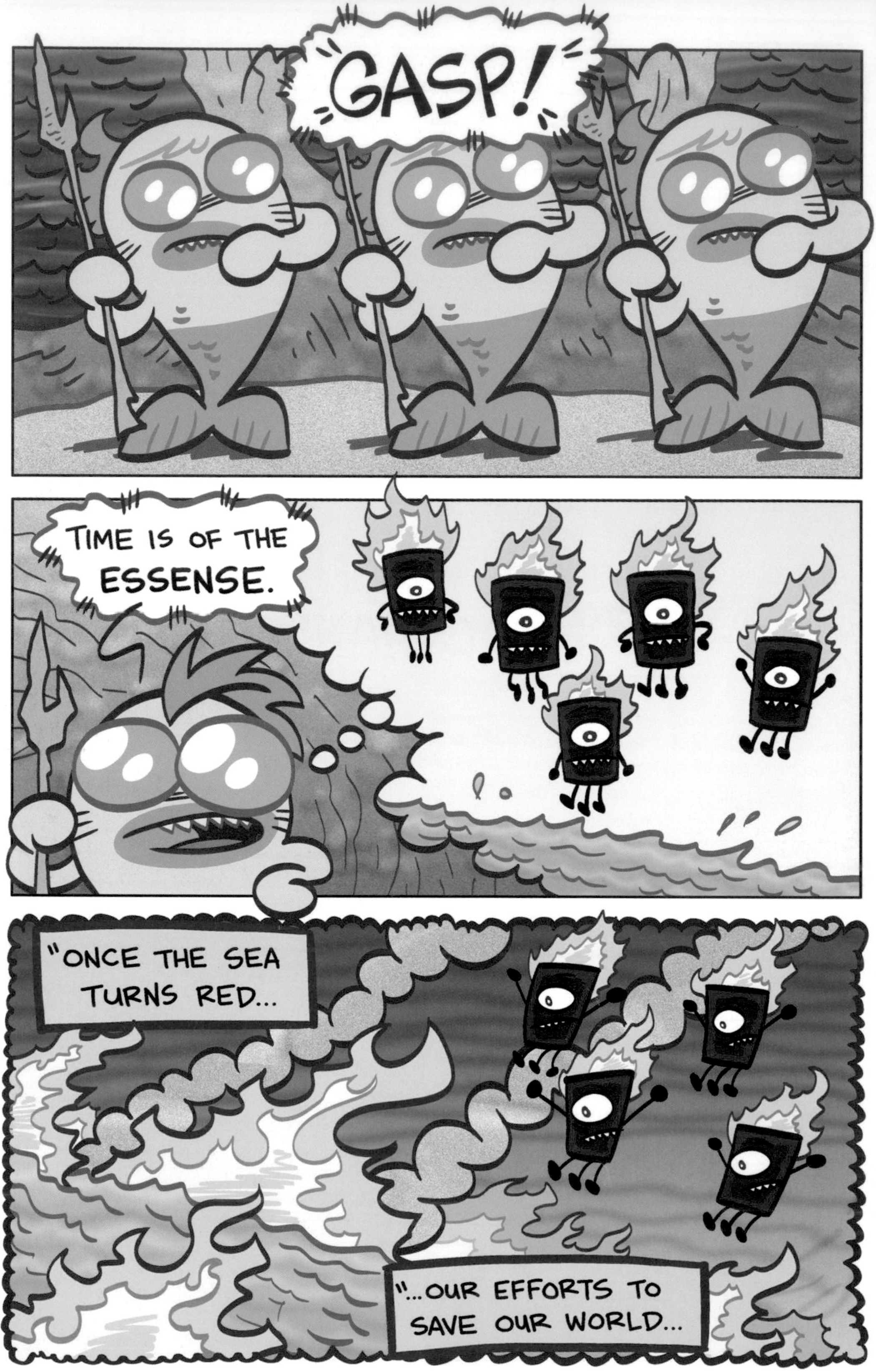
GASP!
TIME IS OF THE ESSENSE.
"ONCE THE SEA TURNS RED...
"...OUR EFFORTS TO SAVE OUR WORLD...

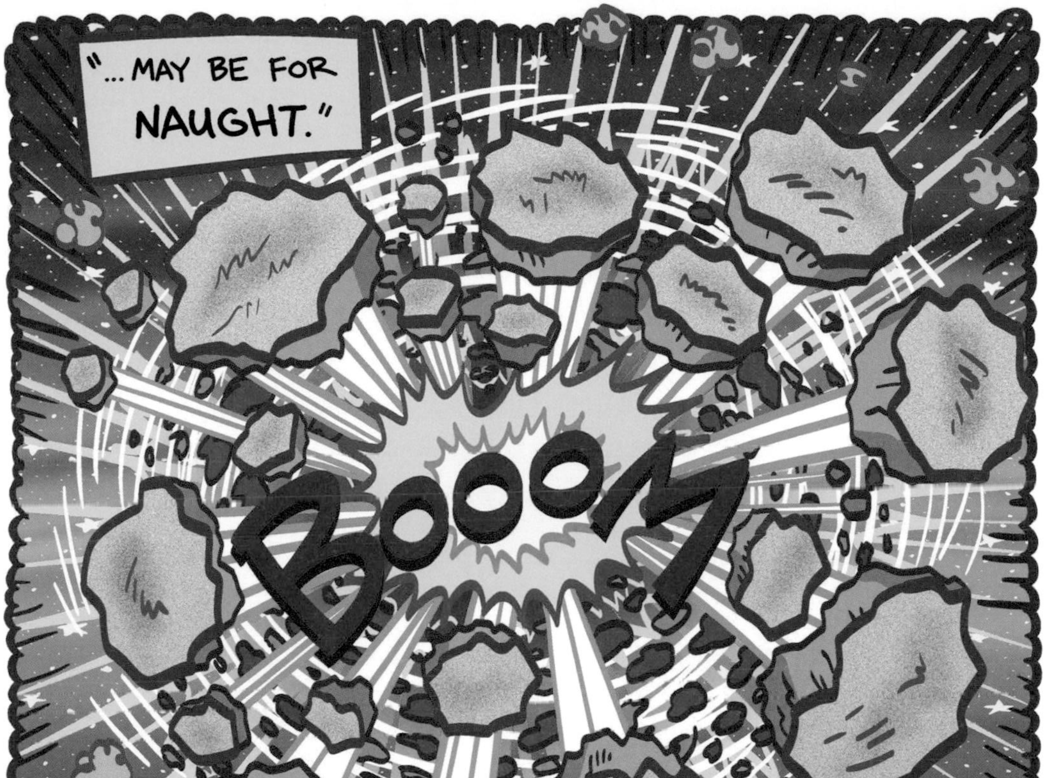
"...MAY BE FOR NAUGHT."
BOOOM

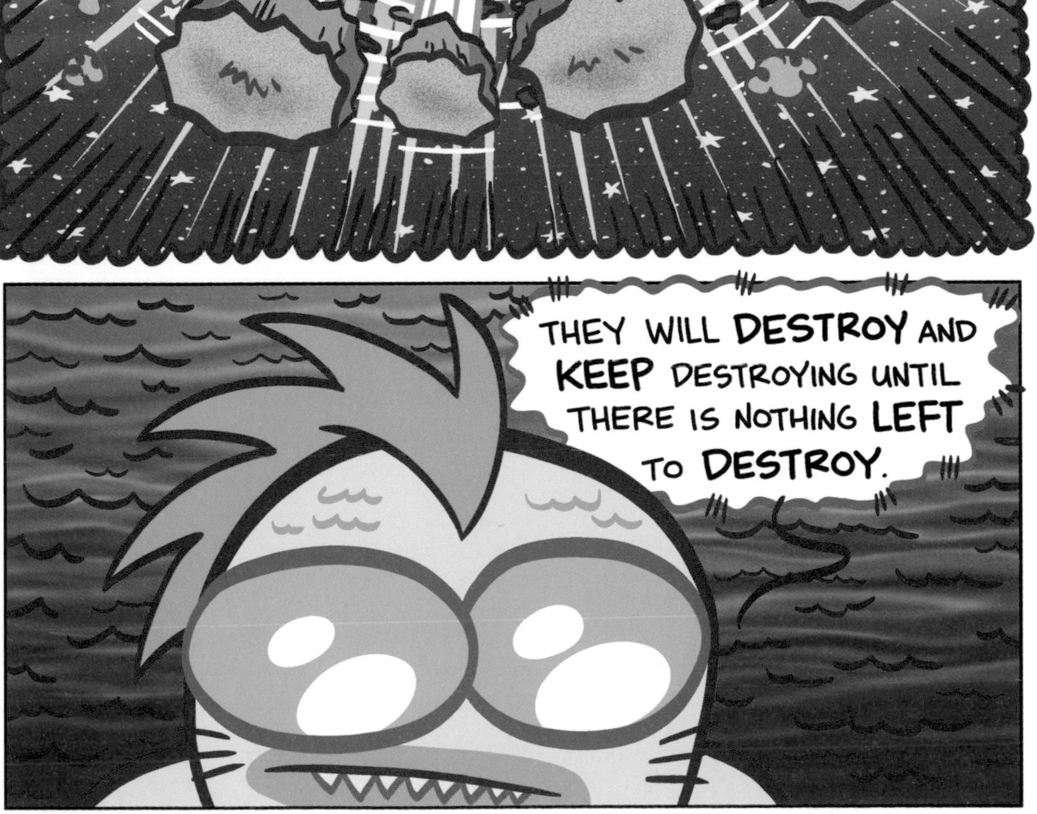
THEY WILL DESTROY AND KEEP DESTROYING UNTIL THERE IS NOTHING LEFT TO DESTROY.

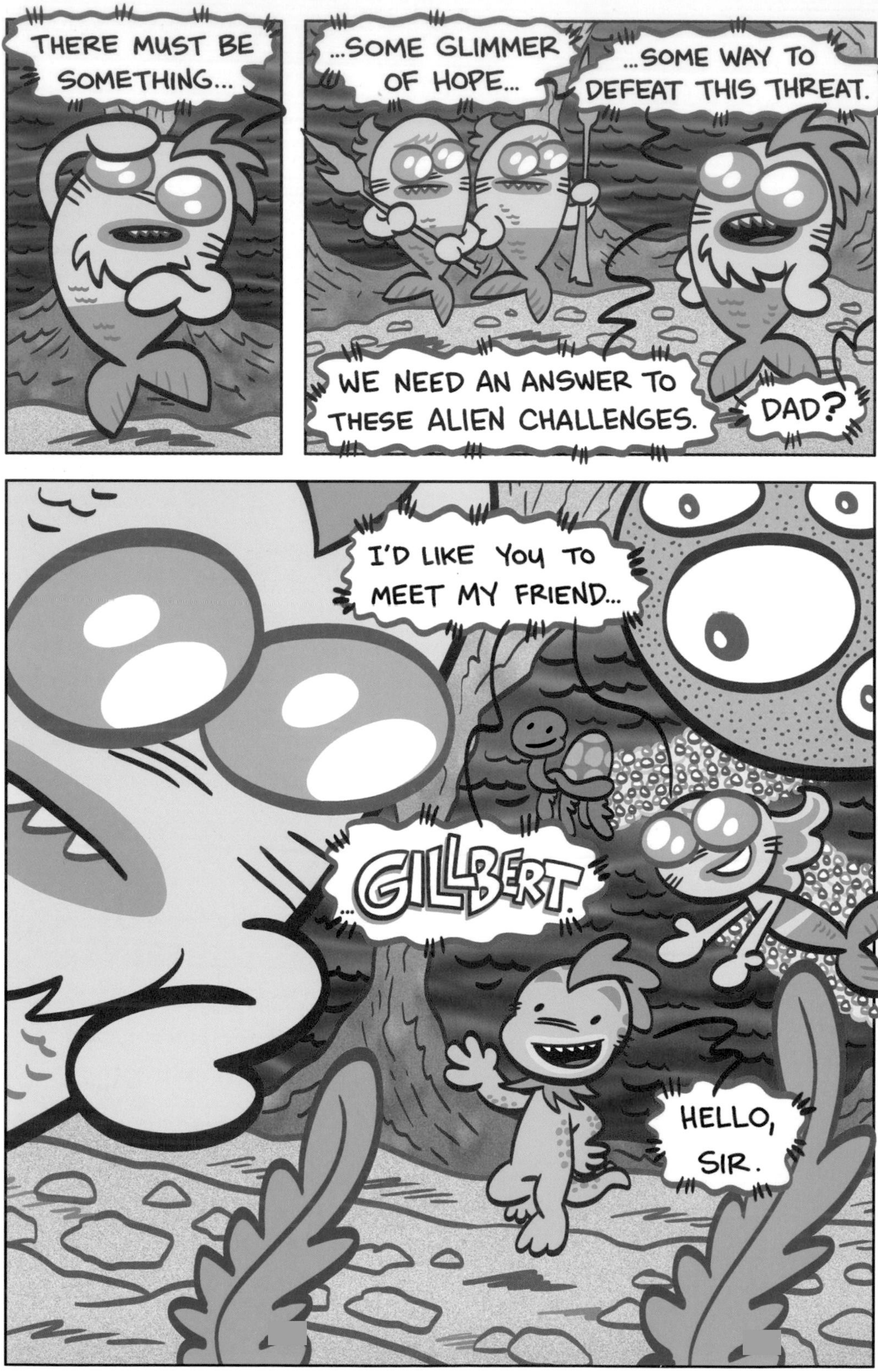
THERE MUST BE SOMETHING...
...SOME GLIMMER OF HOPE...
...SOME WAY TO DEFEAT THIS THREAT.
WE NEED AN ANSWER TO THESE ALIEN CHALLENGES.
DAD?
I'D LIKE YOU TO MEET MY FRIEND...
...GILLBERT.
HELLO, SIR.

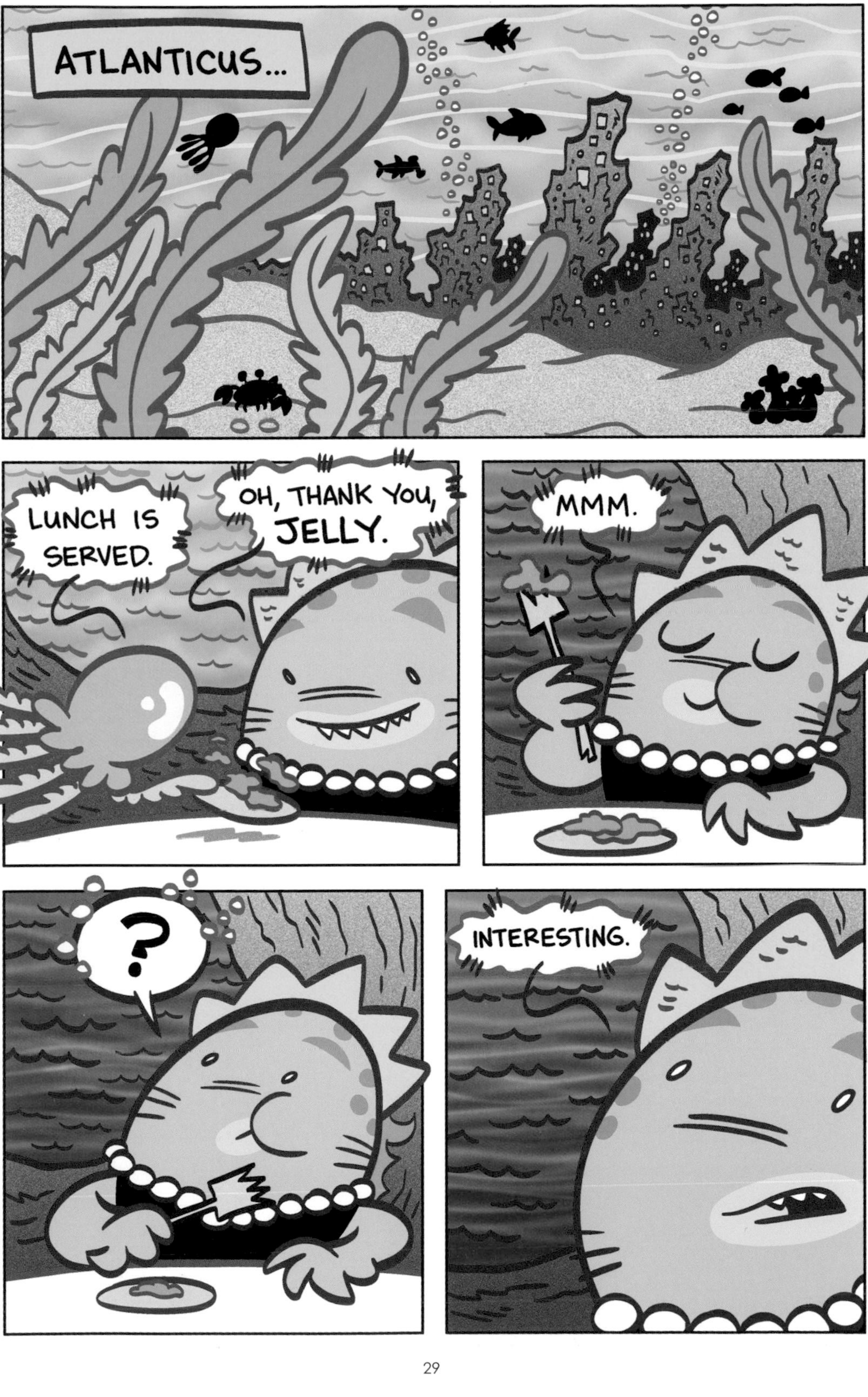
ATLANTICUS...
LUNCH IS SERVED.
OH, THANK YOU, JELLY.
MMM.
?
INTERESTING.

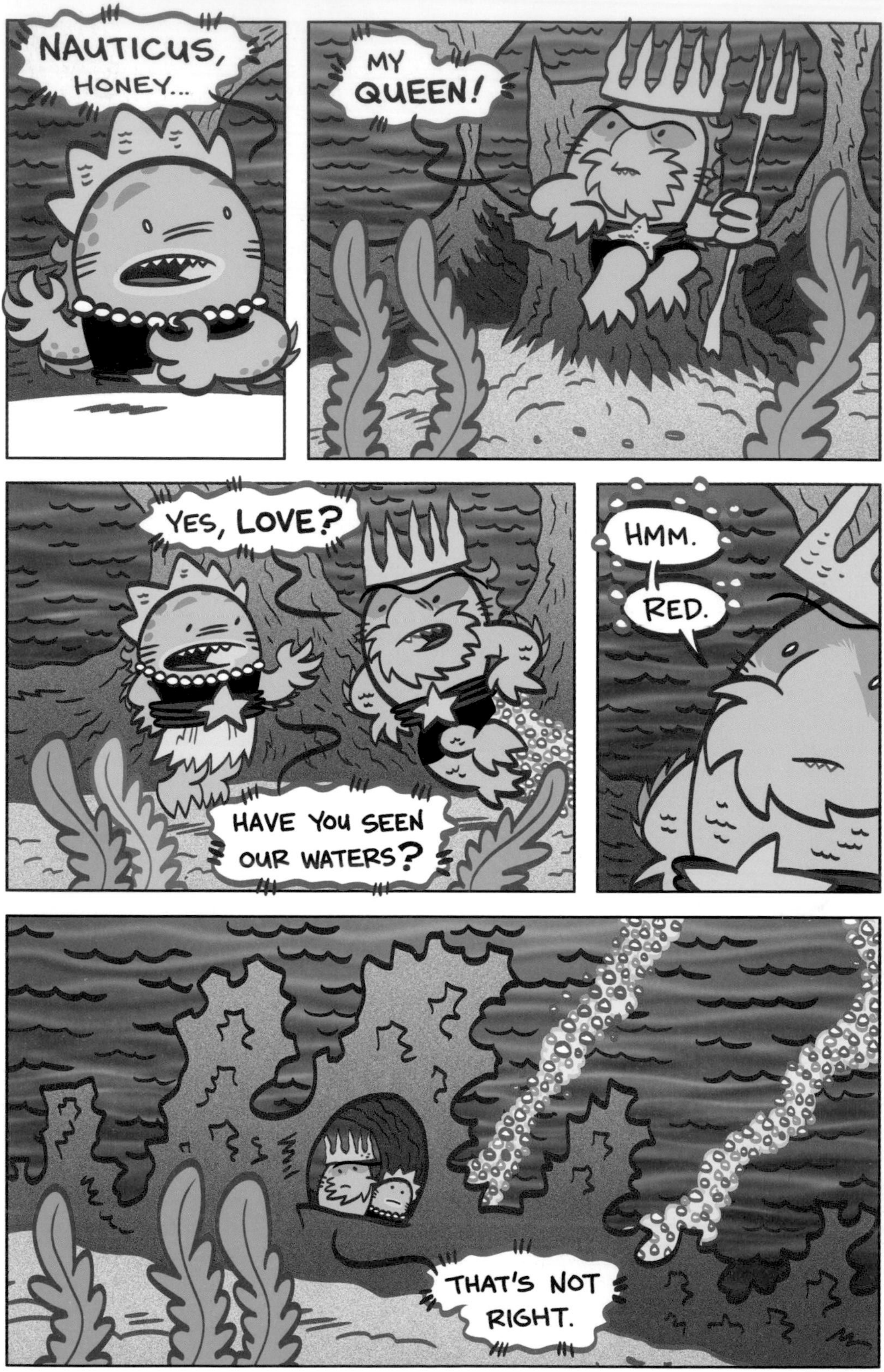
NAUTICUS, HONEY...
MY QUEEN!
YES, LOVE?
HAVE YOU SEEN OUR WATERS?
HMM.
RED.
THAT'S NOT RIGHT.

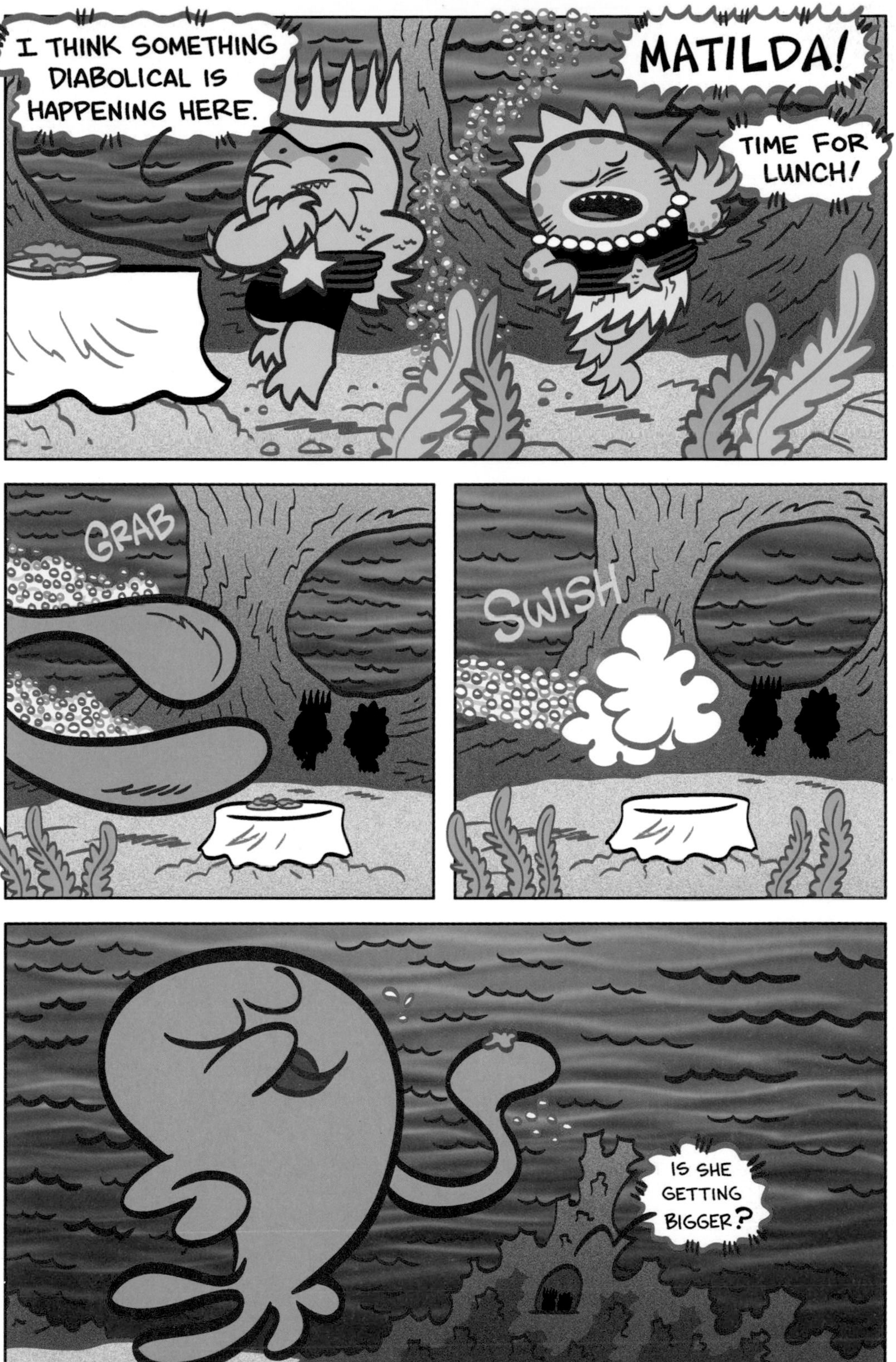
I THINK SOMETHING DIABOLICAL IS HAPPENING HERE.
MATILDA!
TIME FOR LUNCH!
GRAB
SWISH
IS SHE GETTING BIGGER?

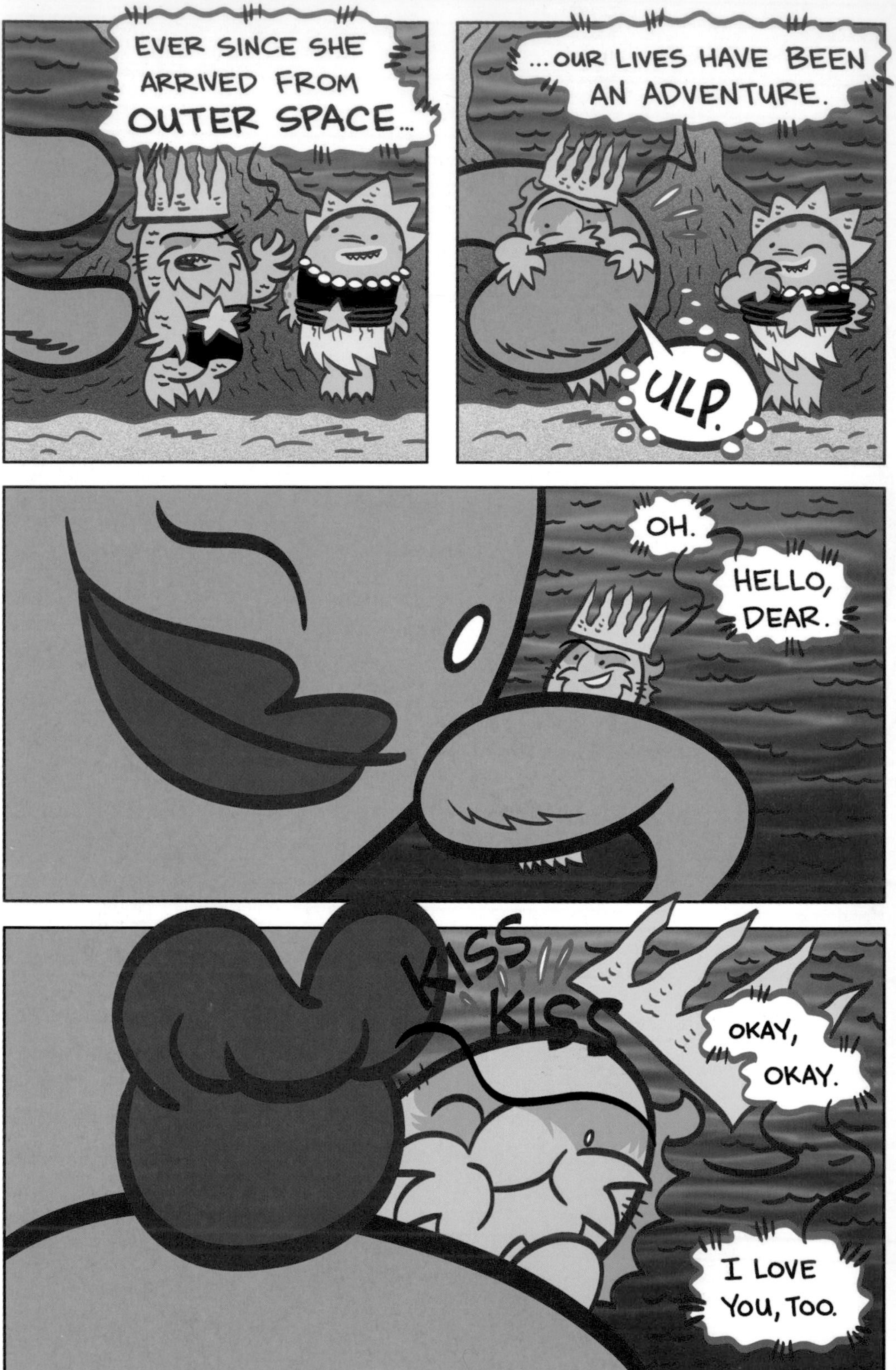
EVER SINCE SHE ARRIVED FROM OUTER SPACE...
...OUR LIVES HAVE BEEN AN ADVENTURE.
ULP.
OH.
HELLO, DEAR.
KISS KISS
OKAY, OKAY.
I LOVE YOU, TOO.

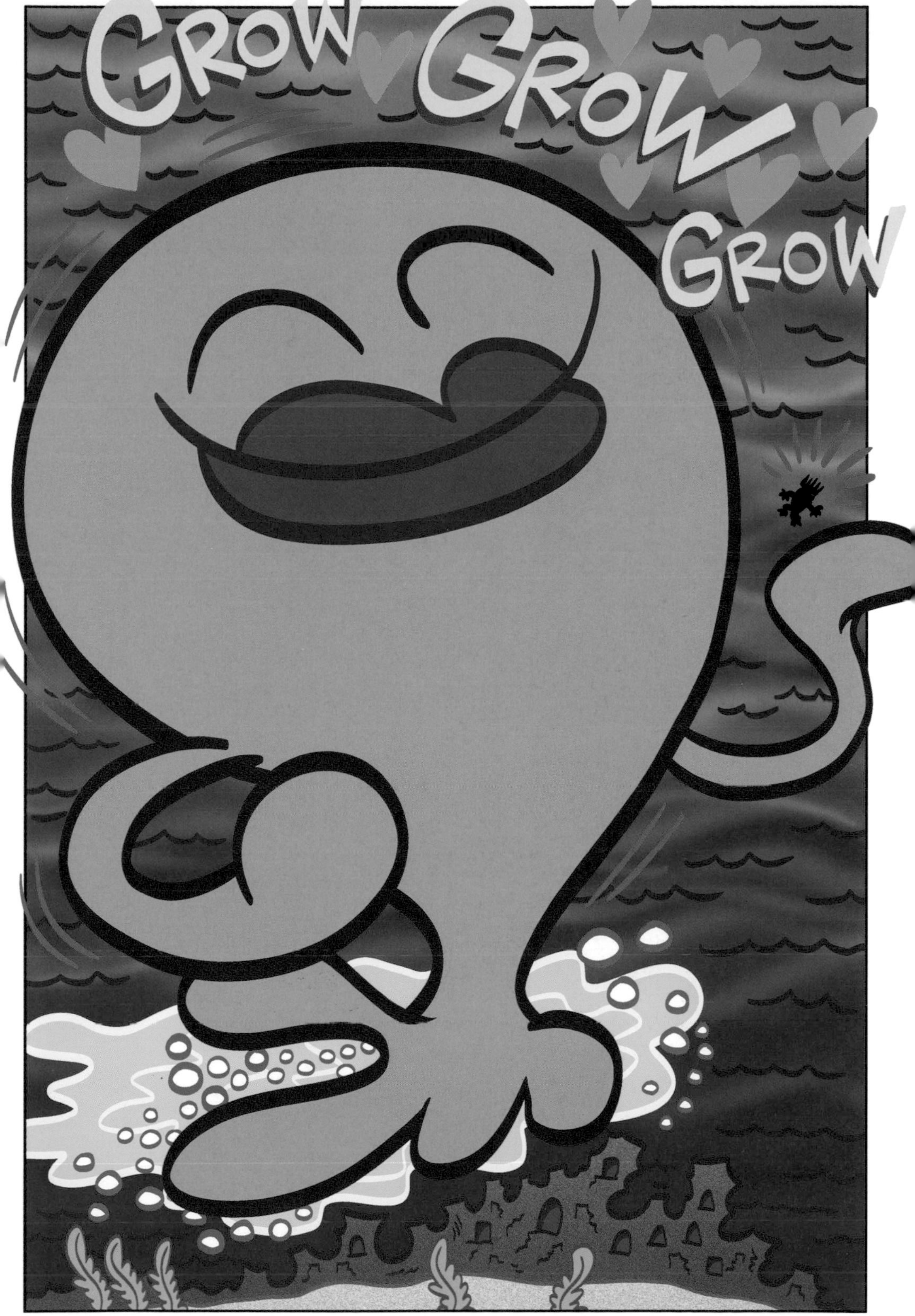
GROW GROW GROW

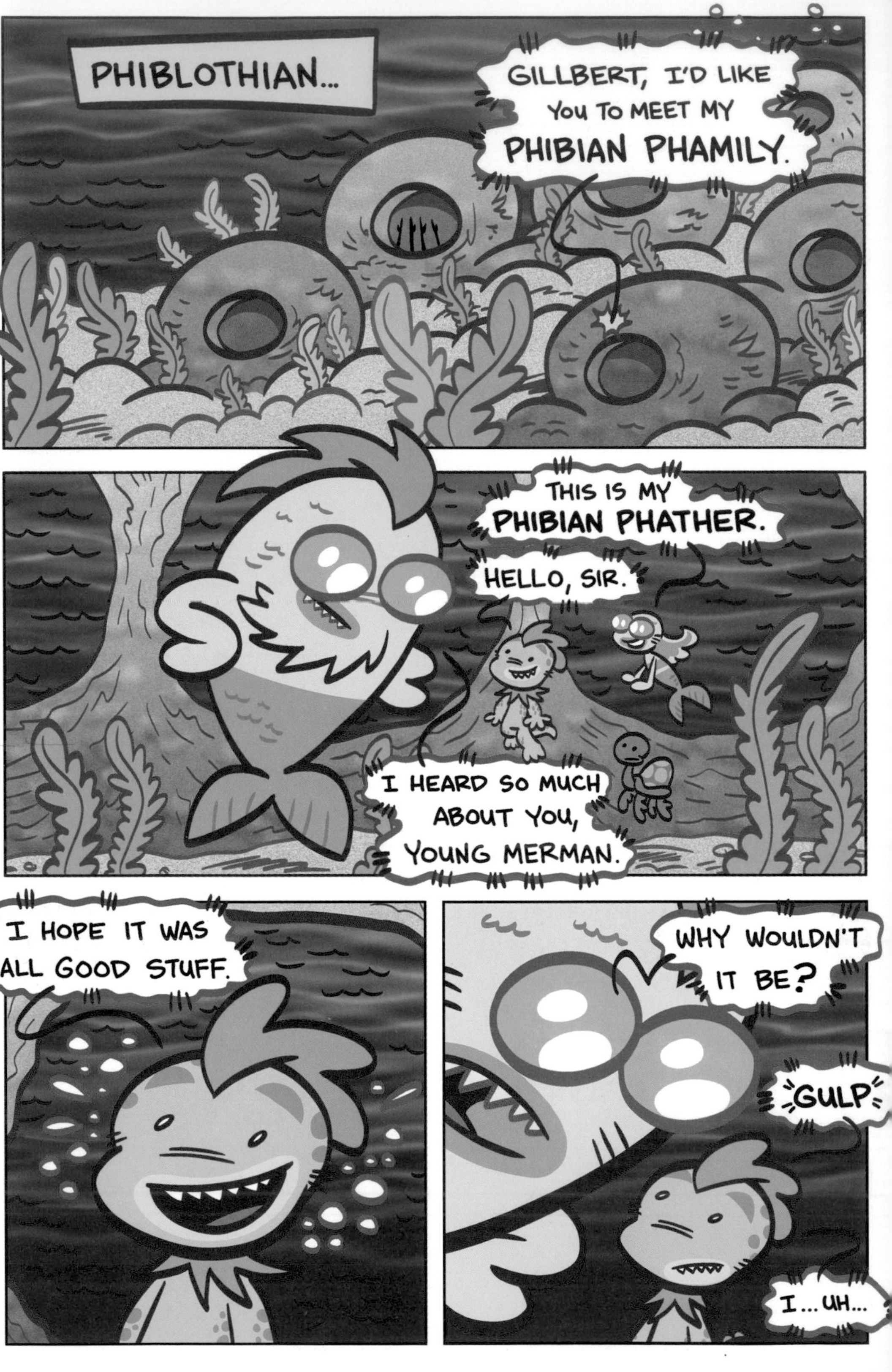
PHIBLOTHIAN...
GILLBERT, I'D LIKE YOU TO MEET MY PHIBIAN PHAMILY.
THIS IS MY PHIBIAN PHATHER.
HELLO, SIR.
I HEARD SO MUCH ABOUT YOU, YOUNG MERMAN.
I HOPE IT WAS ALL GOOD STUFF.
WHY WOULDN'T IT BE?
GULP
I... UH...

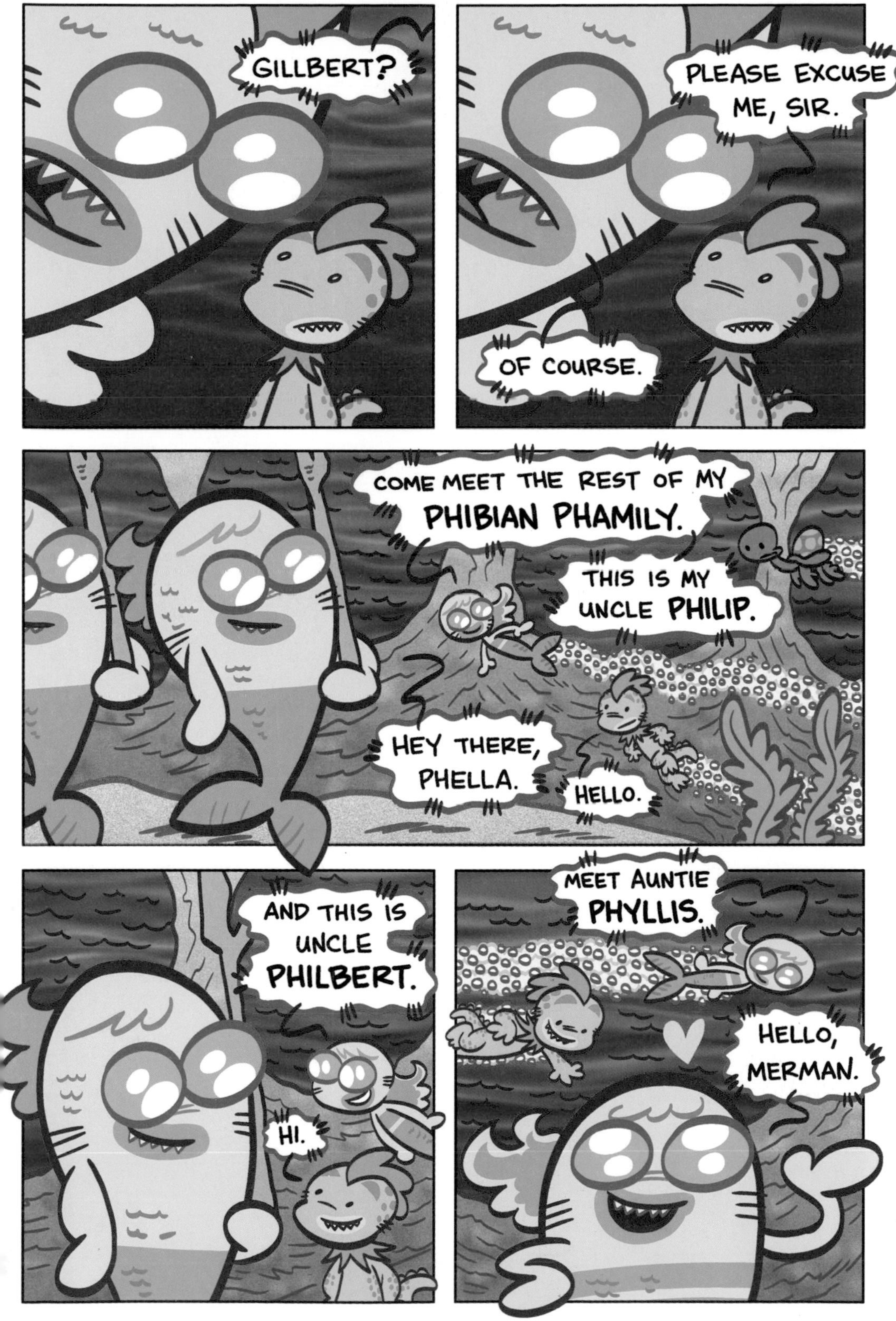
GILLBERT?
PLEASE EXCUSE ME, SIR.
OF COURSE.
COME MEET THE REST OF MY PHIBIAN PHAMILY.
THIS IS MY UNCLE PHILIP.
HEY THERE, PHELLA.
HELLO.
AND THIS IS UNCLE PHILBERT.
HI.
MEET AUNTIE PHYLLIS.
HELLO, MERMAN.

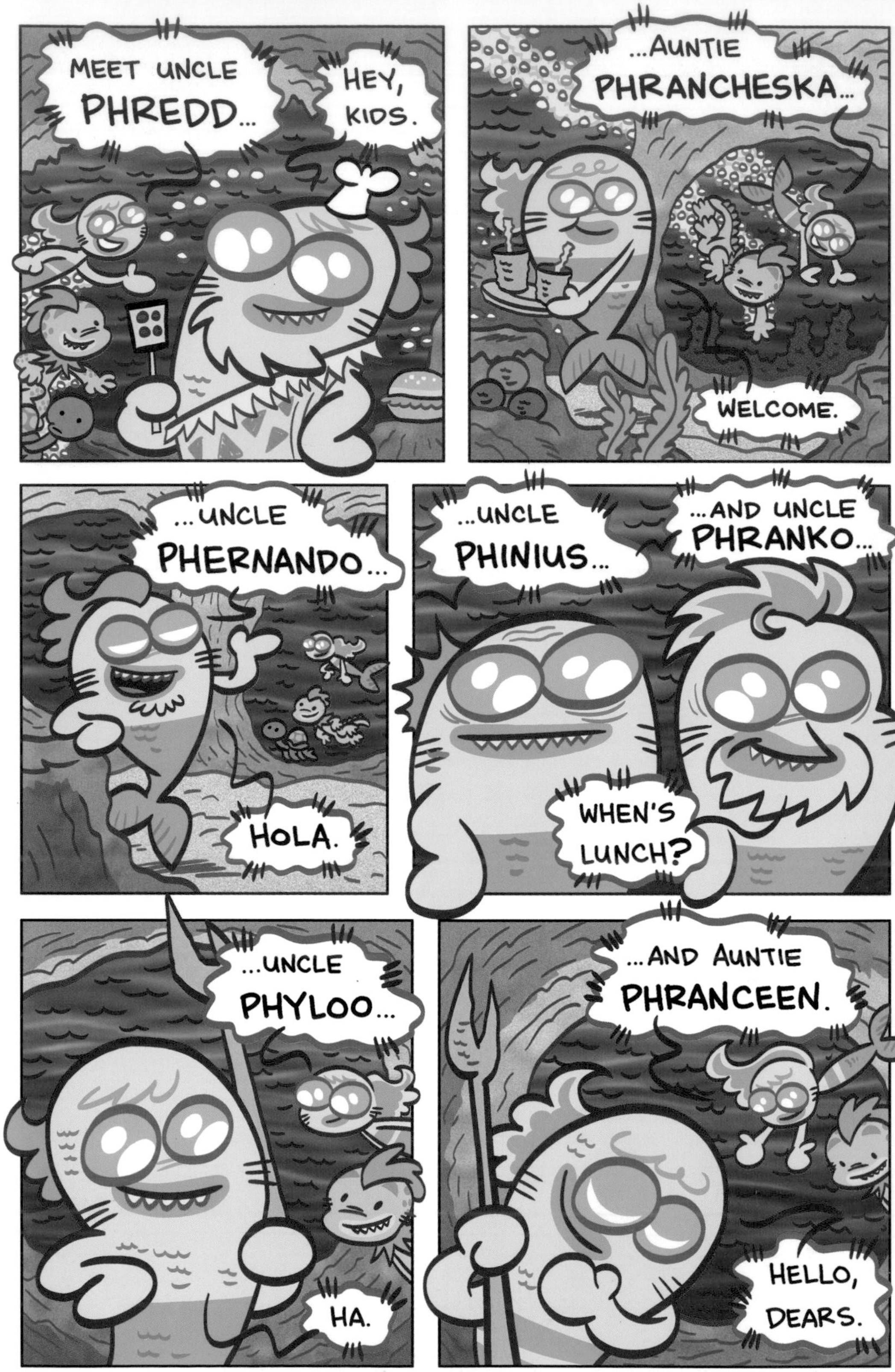
MEET UNCLE PHREDD...
HEY, KIDS.
...AUNTIE PHRANCHESKA...
WELCOME.
...UNCLE PHERNANDO...
HOLA.
...UNCLE PHINIUS...
...AND UNCLE PHRANKO...
WHEN'S LUNCH?
...UNCLE PHYLOO...
HA.
...AND AUNTIE PHRANCEEN.
HELLO, DEARS.

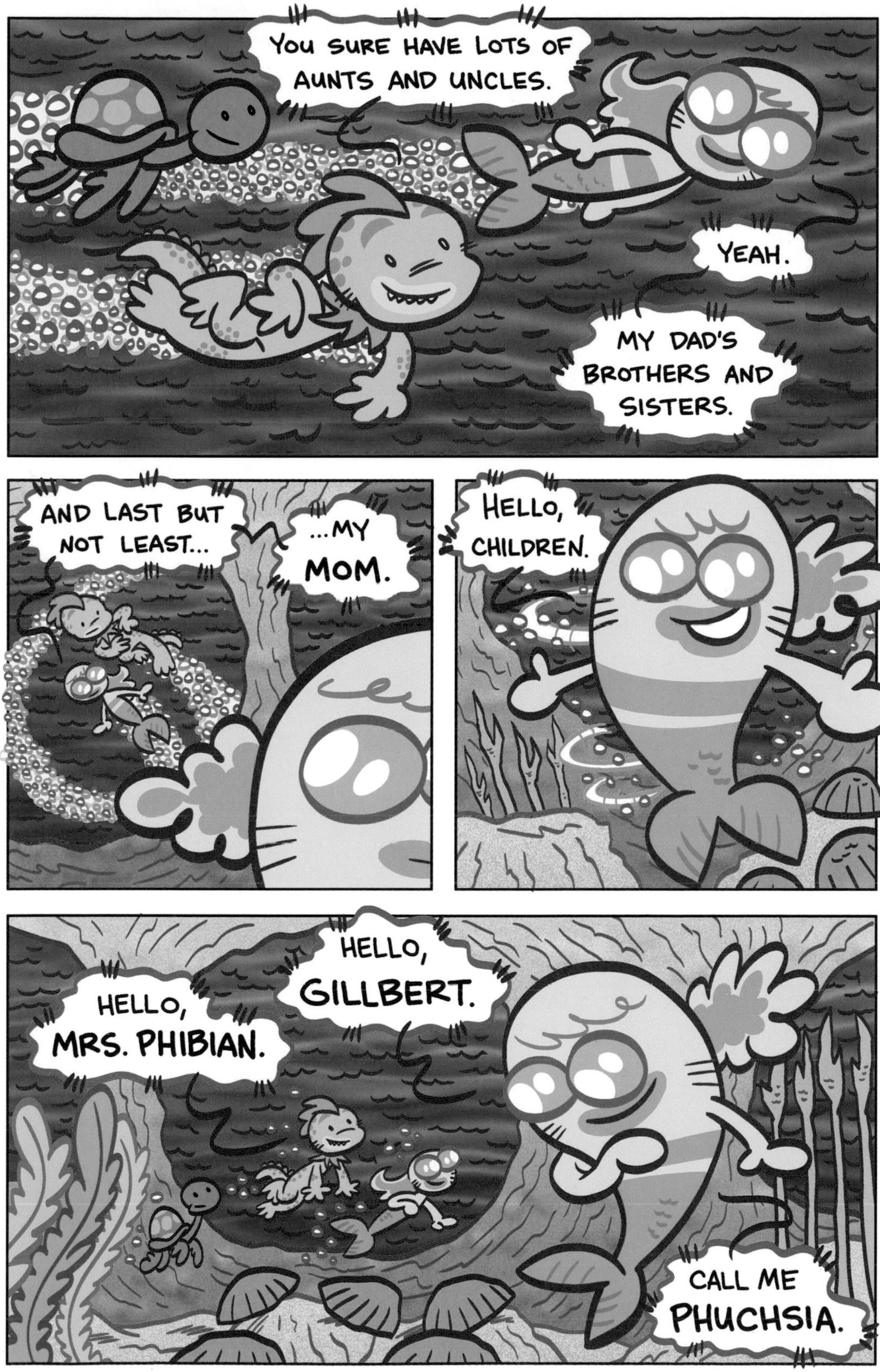
YOU SURE HAVE LOTS OF AUNTS AND UNCLES.
YEAH.
MY DAD'S BROTHERS AND SISTERS.
AND LAST BUT NOT LEAST...
...MY MOM.
HELLO, CHILDREN.
HELLO, MRS. PHIBIAN.
HELLO, GILLBERT.
CALL ME PHUCHSIA.

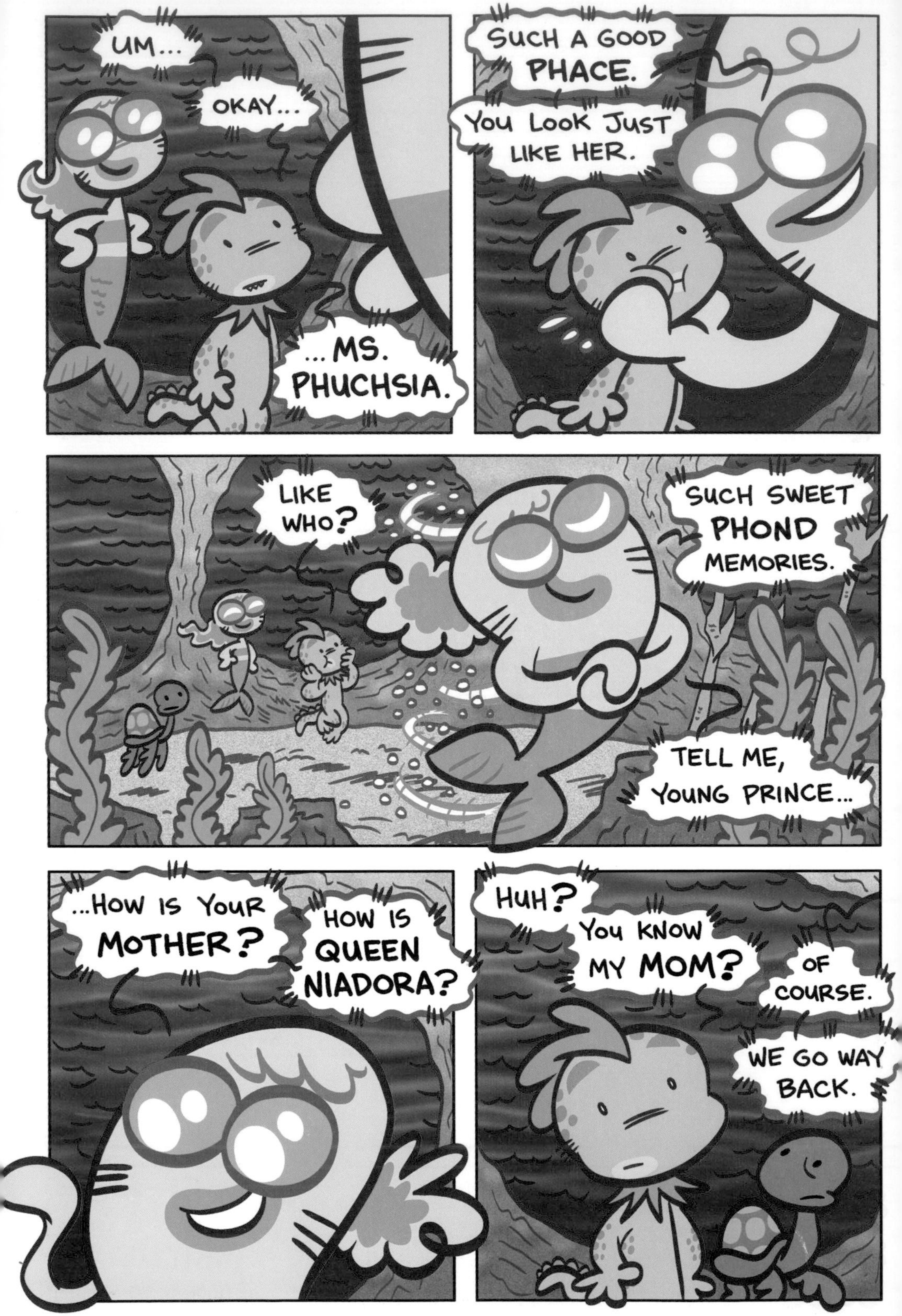
UM...
OKAY...
...MS. PHUCHSIA.
SUCH A GOOD PHACE.
YOU LOOK JUST LIKE HER.
LIKE WHO?
SUCH SWEET PHOND MEMORIES.
TELL ME, YOUNG PRINCE...
...HOW IS YOUR MOTHER?
HOW IS QUEEN NIADORA?
HUH?
YOU KNOW MY MOM?
OF COURSE.
WE GO WAY BACK.

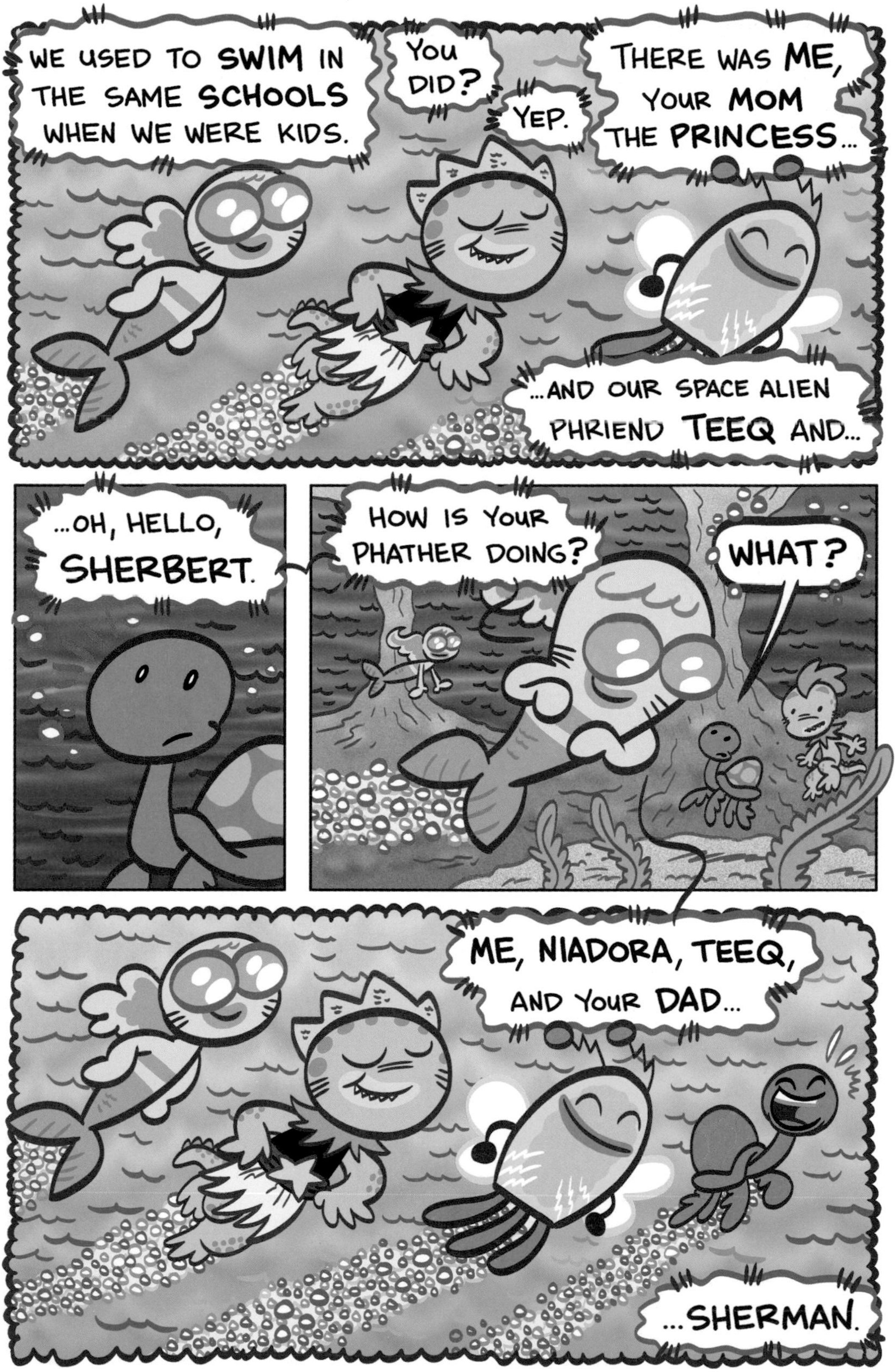

WE USED TO SWIM IN THE SAME SCHOOLS WHEN WE WERE KIDS.
You DID?
YEP.
THERE WAS ME, YOUR MOM THE PRINCESS...
...AND OUR SPACE ALIEN PHRIEND TEEQ AND...
...OH, HELLO, SHERBERT.
HOW IS YOUR PHATHER DOING?
WHAT?
ME, NIADORA, TEEQ, AND YOUR DAD...
...SHERMAN.

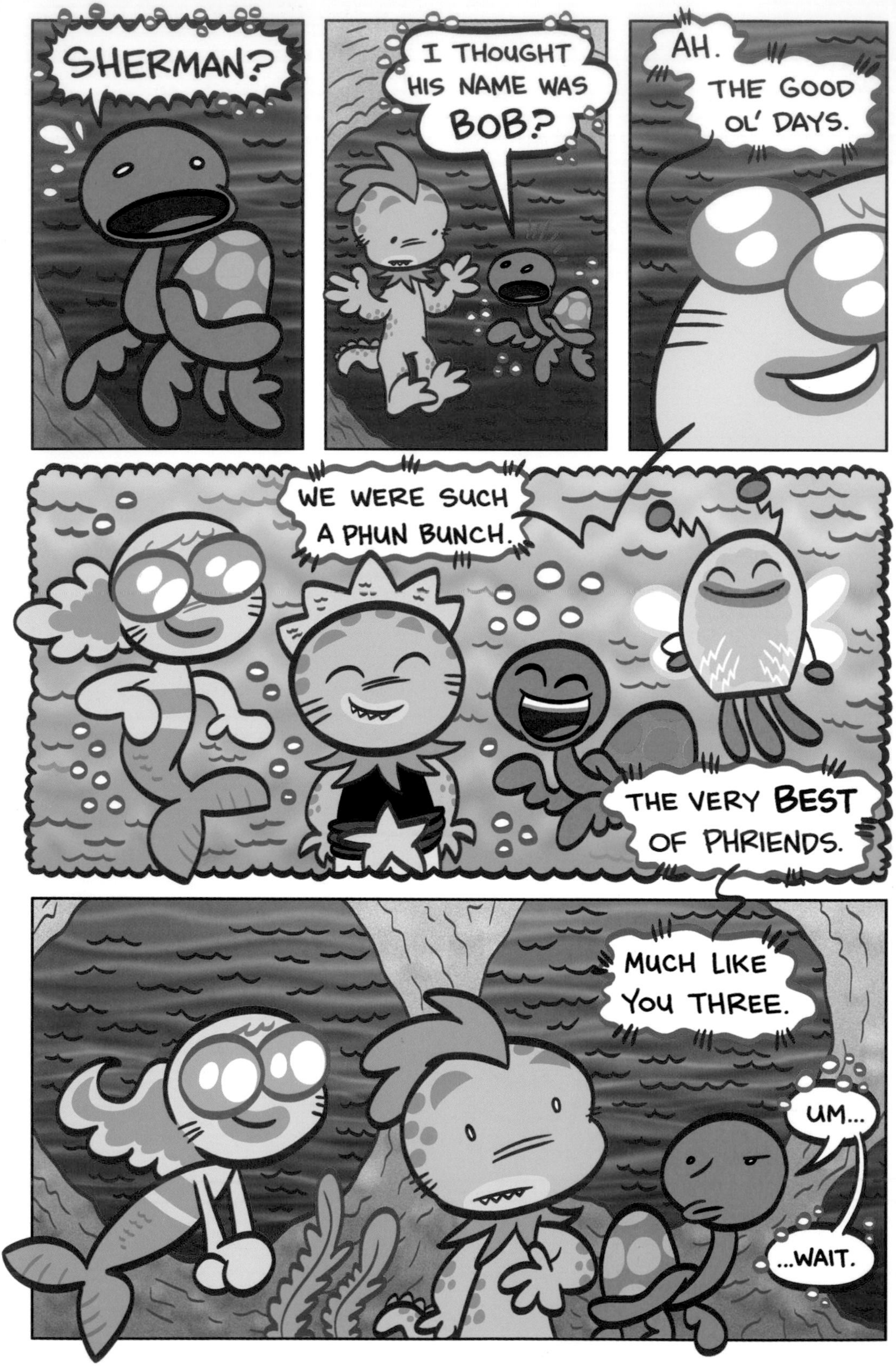
SHERMAN?
I THOUGHT HIS NAME WAS BOB?
AH. THE GOOD OL' DAYS.
WE WERE SUCH A PHUN BUNCH.
THE VERY BEST OF PHRIENDS.
MUCH LIKE YOU THREE.
UM...
...WAIT.

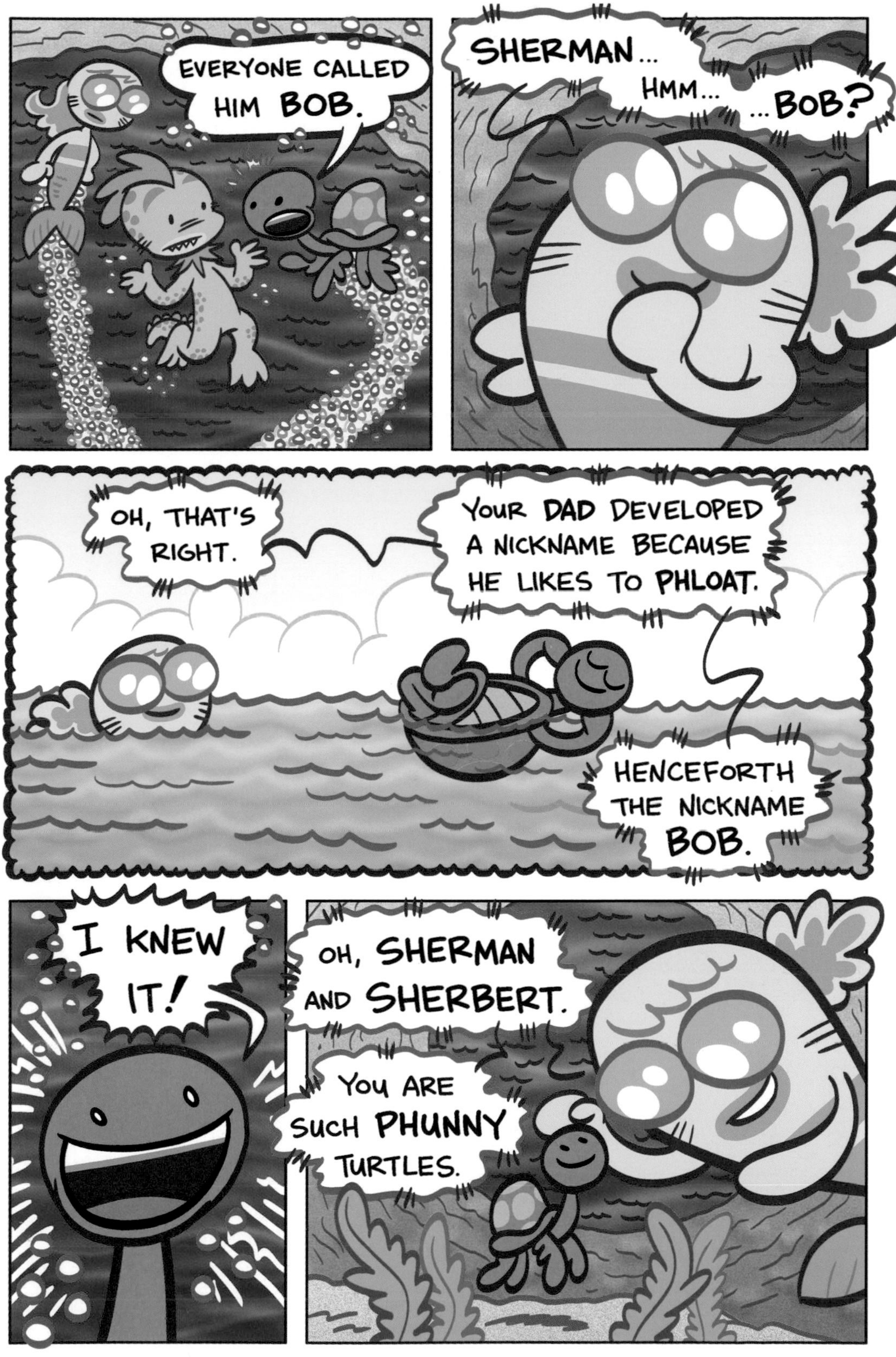
EVERYONE CALLED HIM BOB.
SHERMAN...
HMM...
...BOB?
OH, THAT'S RIGHT.
YOUR DAD DEVELOPED A NICKNAME BECAUSE HE LIKES TO PHLOAT.
HENCEFORTH THE NICKNAME BOB.
I KNEW IT!
OH, SHERMAN AND SHERBERT.
YOU ARE SUCH PHUNNY TURTLES.

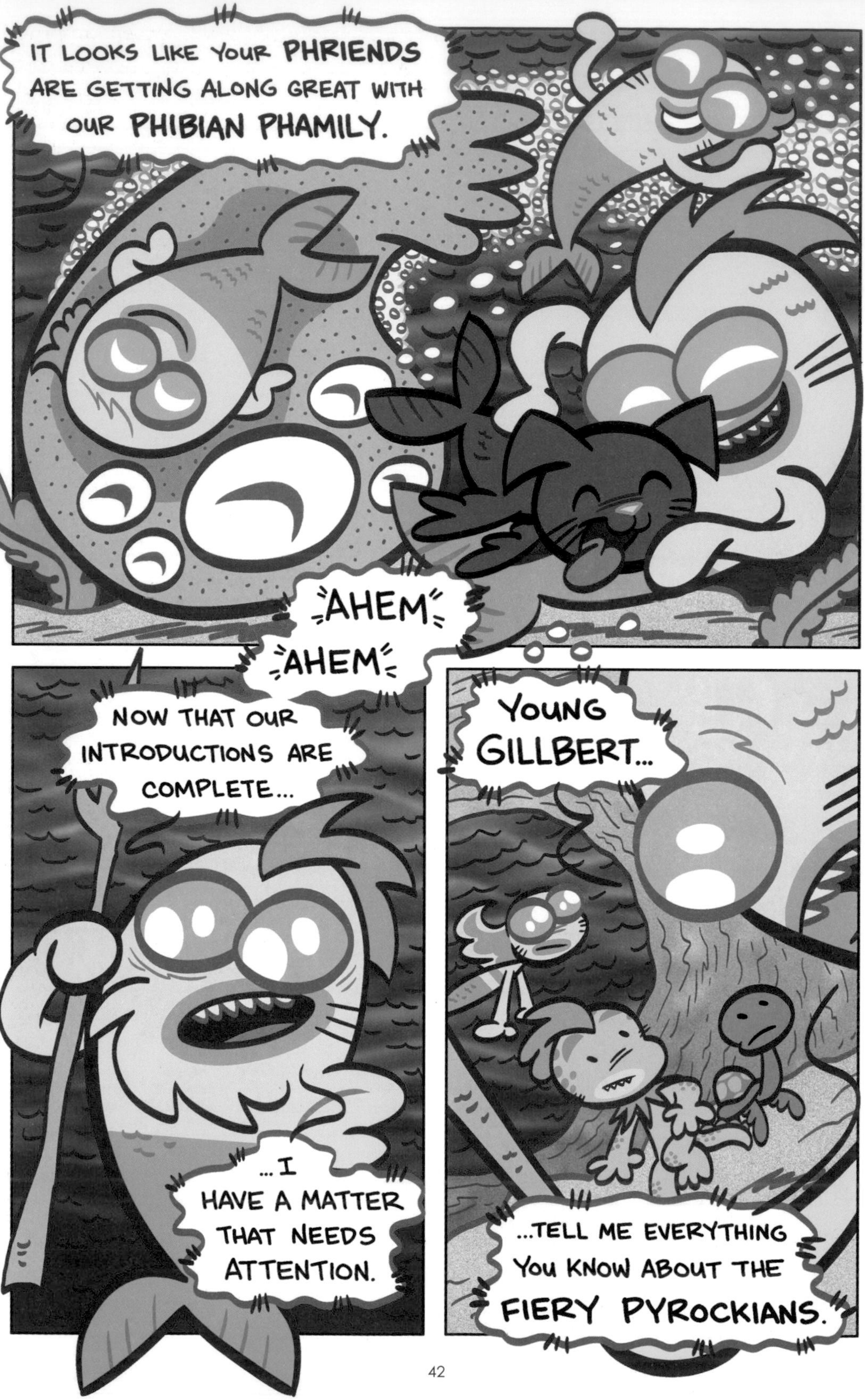
IT LOOKS LIKE YOUR PHRIENDS ARE GETTING ALONG GREAT WITH OUR PHIBIAN PHAMILY.
AHEM
AHEM
NOW THAT OUR INTRODUCTIONS ARE COMPLETE...
...I HAVE A MATTER THAT NEEDS ATTENTION.
YOUNG GILLBERT...
...TELL ME EVERYTHING YOU KNOW ABOUT THE FIERY PYROCKIANS.

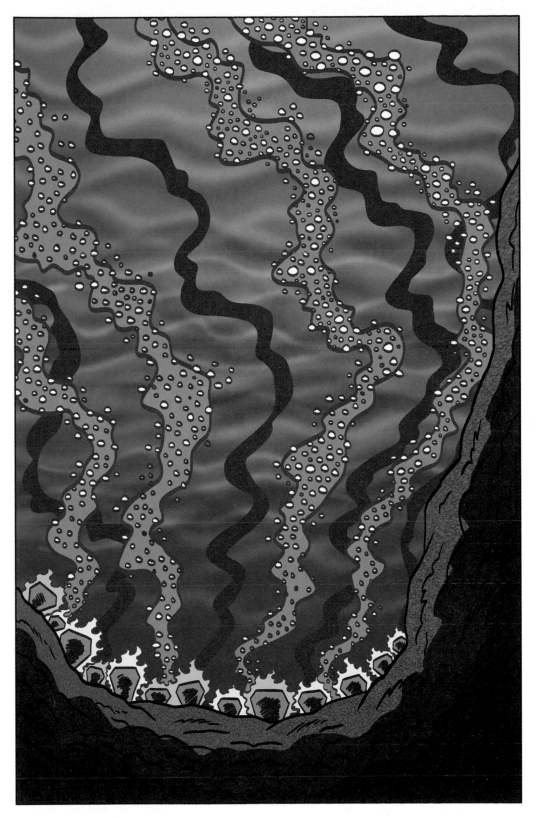

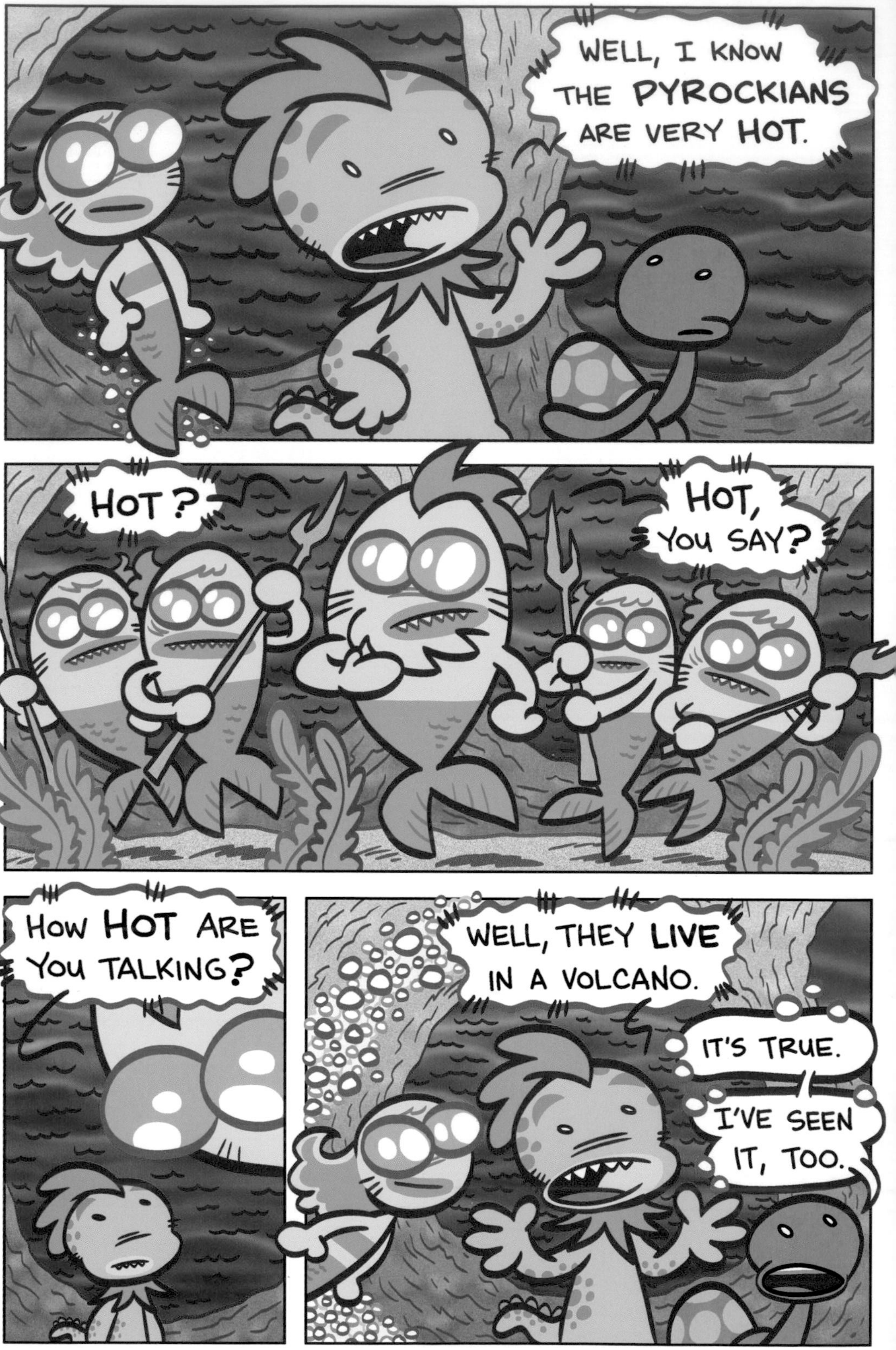
WELL, I KNOW THE PYROCKIANS ARE VERY HOT.
HOT?
HOT, YOU SAY?
HOW HOT ARE YOU TALKING?
WELL, THEY LIVE IN A VOLCANO.
IT'S TRUE.
I'VE SEEN IT, TOO.

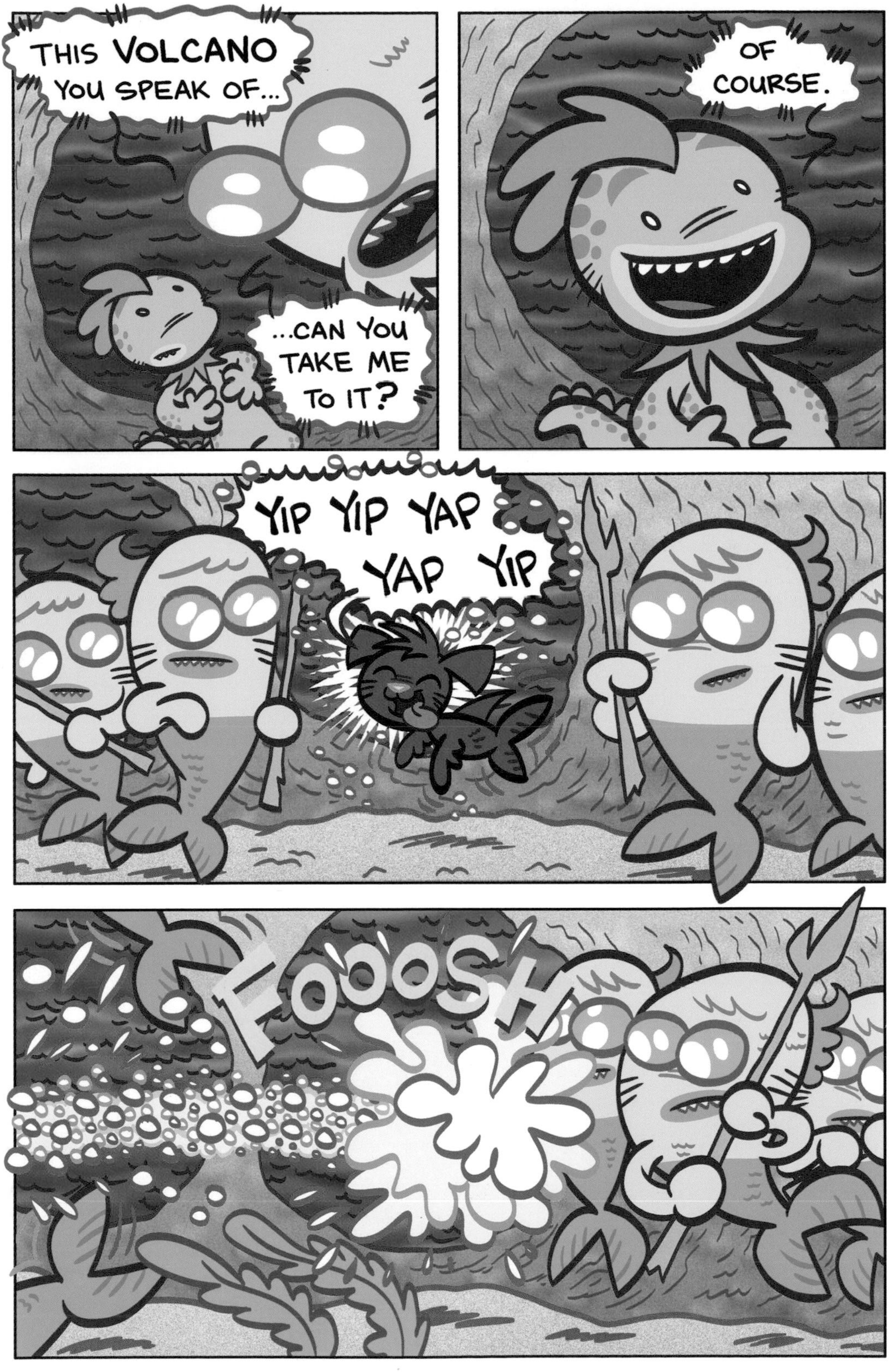
THIS VOLCANO YOU SPEAK OF...
...CAN YOU TAKE ME TO IT?
OF COURSE.
YIP YIP YAP YAP YIP
FOOOSH

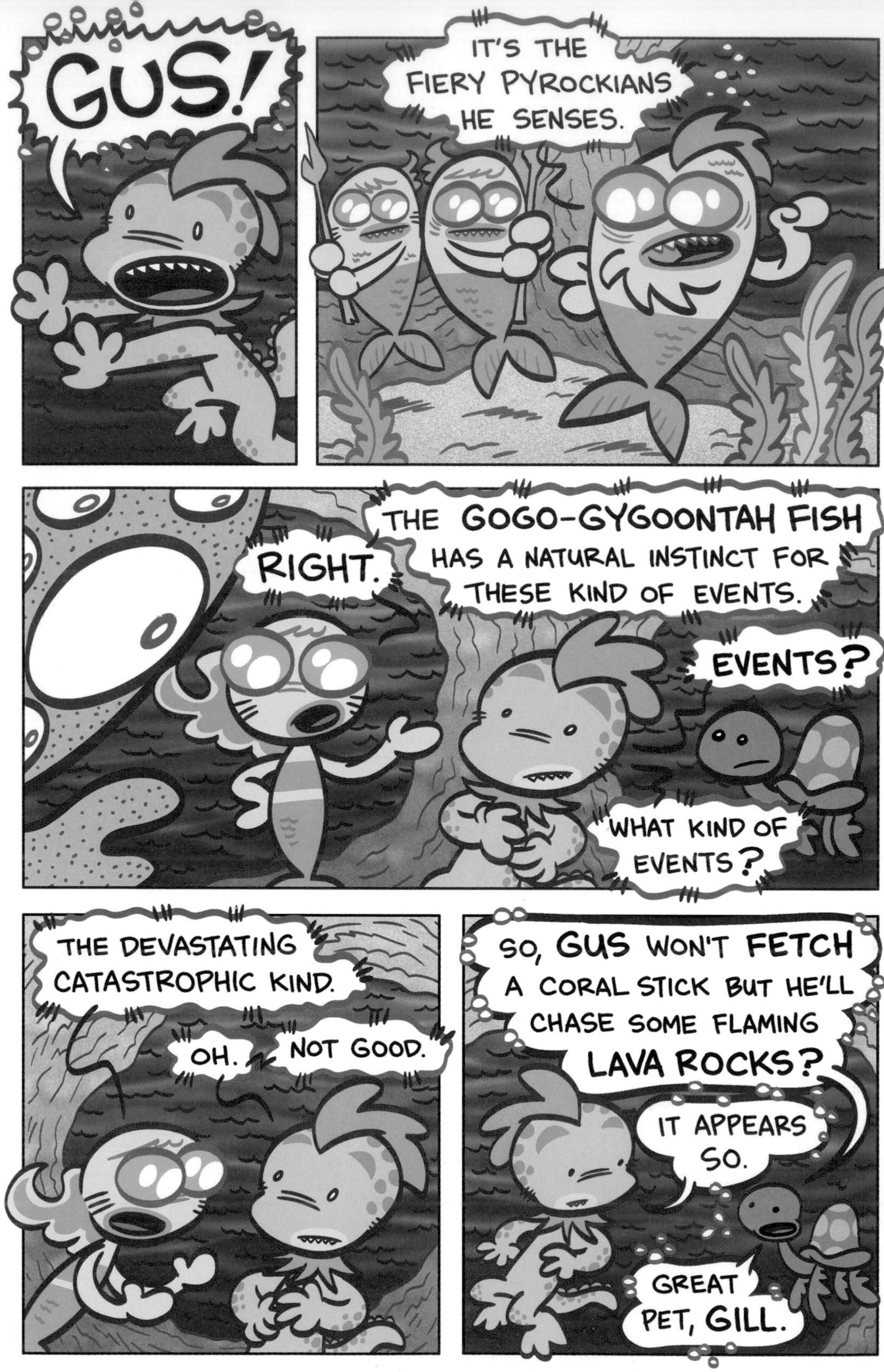
GUS!
IT'S THE FIERY PYROCKIANS HE SENSES.
RIGHT.
THE GOGO-GYGOONTAH FISH HAS A NATURAL INSTINCT FOR THESE KIND OF EVENTS.
EVENTS?
WHAT KIND OF EVENTS?
THE DEVASTATING CATASTROPHIC KIND.
OH.
NOT GOOD.
SO, GUS WON'T FETCH A CORAL STICK BUT HE'LL CHASE SOME FLAMING LAVA ROCKS?
IT APPEARS SO.
GREAT PET, GILL.

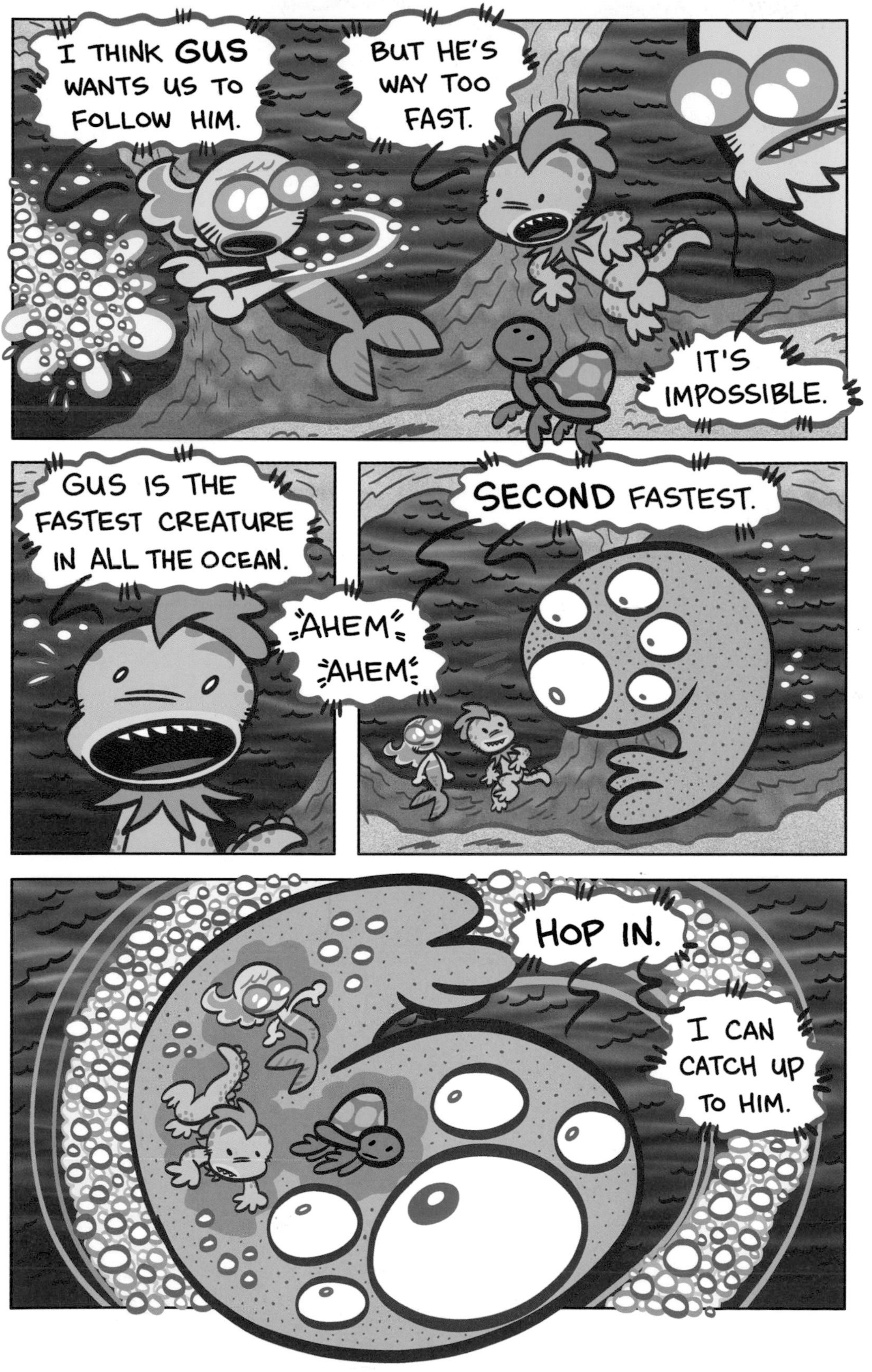

I THINK GUS WANTS US TO FOLLOW HIM.
BUT HE'S WAY TOO FAST.
IT'S IMPOSSIBLE.
GUS IS THE FASTEST CREATURE IN ALL THE OCEAN.
AHEM AHEM
SECOND FASTEST.
HOP IN.
I CAN CATCH UP TO HIM.

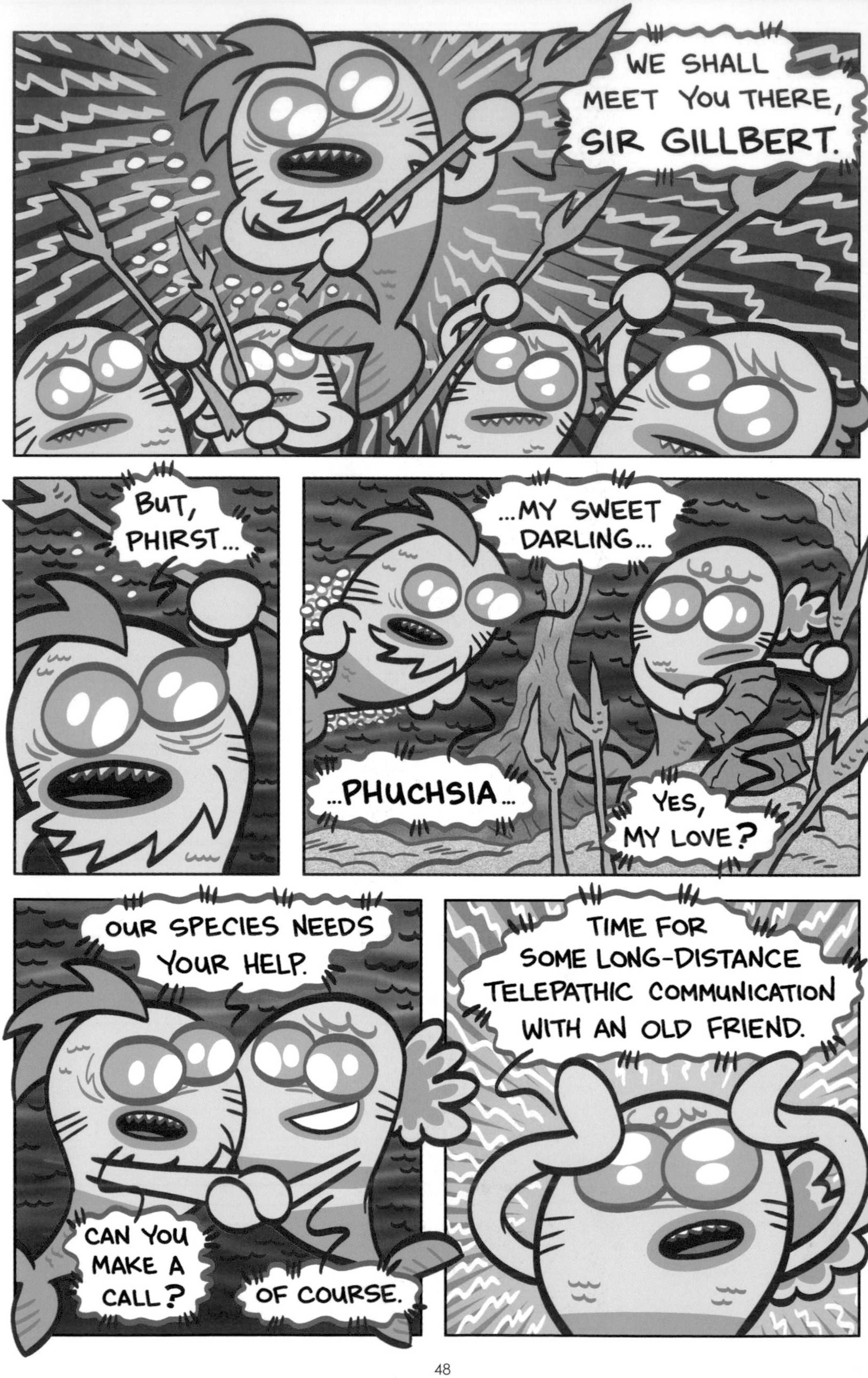
WE SHALL MEET YOU THERE, SIR GILLBERT.
BUT, PHIRST...
...MY SWEET DARLING...
...PHUCHSIA...
YES, MY LOVE?
OUR SPECIES NEEDS YOUR HELP.
CAN YOU MAKE A CALL?
OF COURSE.
TIME FOR SOME LONG-DISTANCE TELEPATHIC COMMUNICATION WITH AN OLD FRIEND.

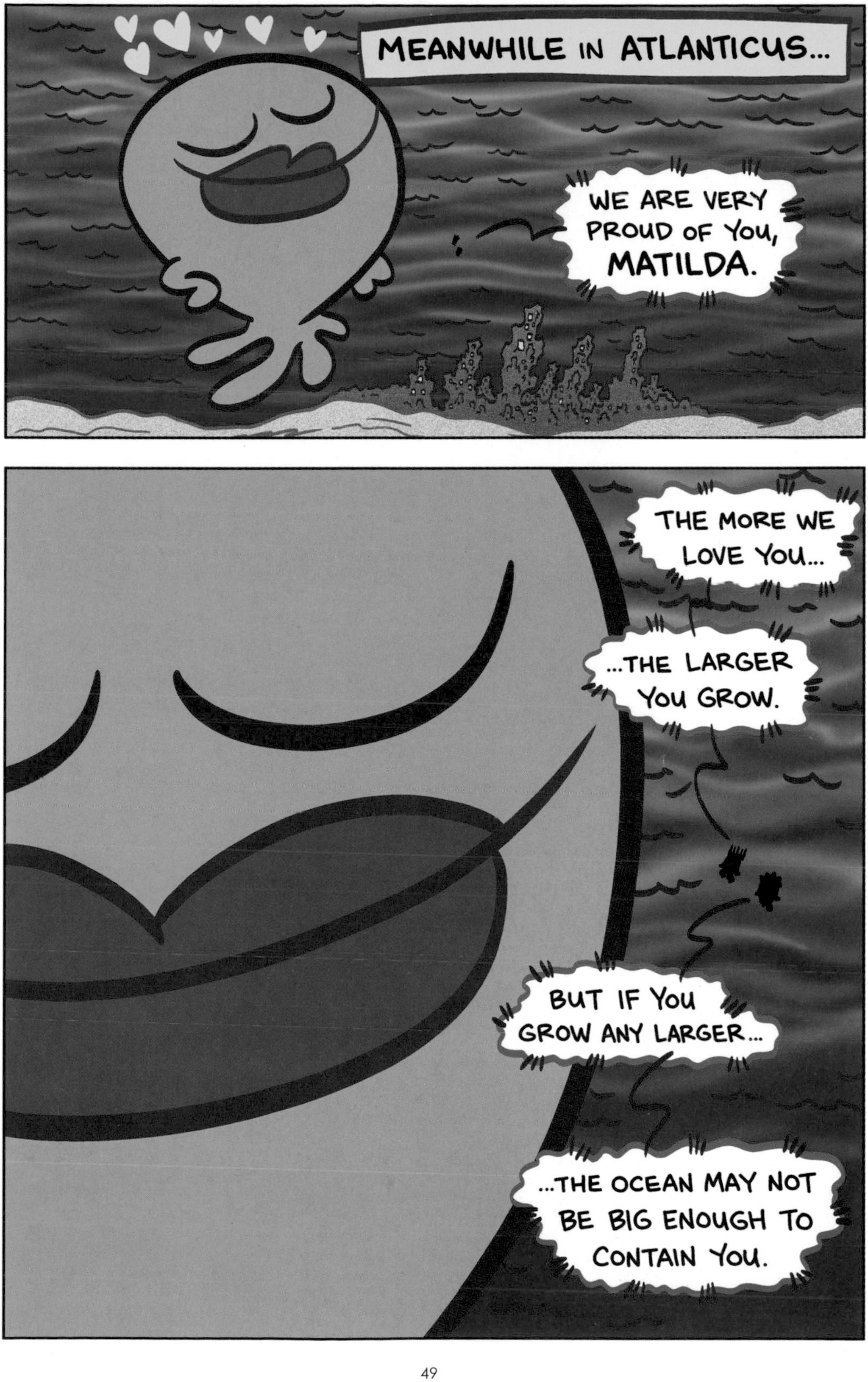
MEANWHILE IN ATLANTICUS...
WE ARE VERY PROUD OF YOU, MATILDA.
THE MORE WE LOVE YOU...
...THE LARGER YOU GROW.
BUT IF YOU GROW ANY LARGER...
...THE OCEAN MAY NOT BE BIG ENOUGH TO CONTAIN YOU.

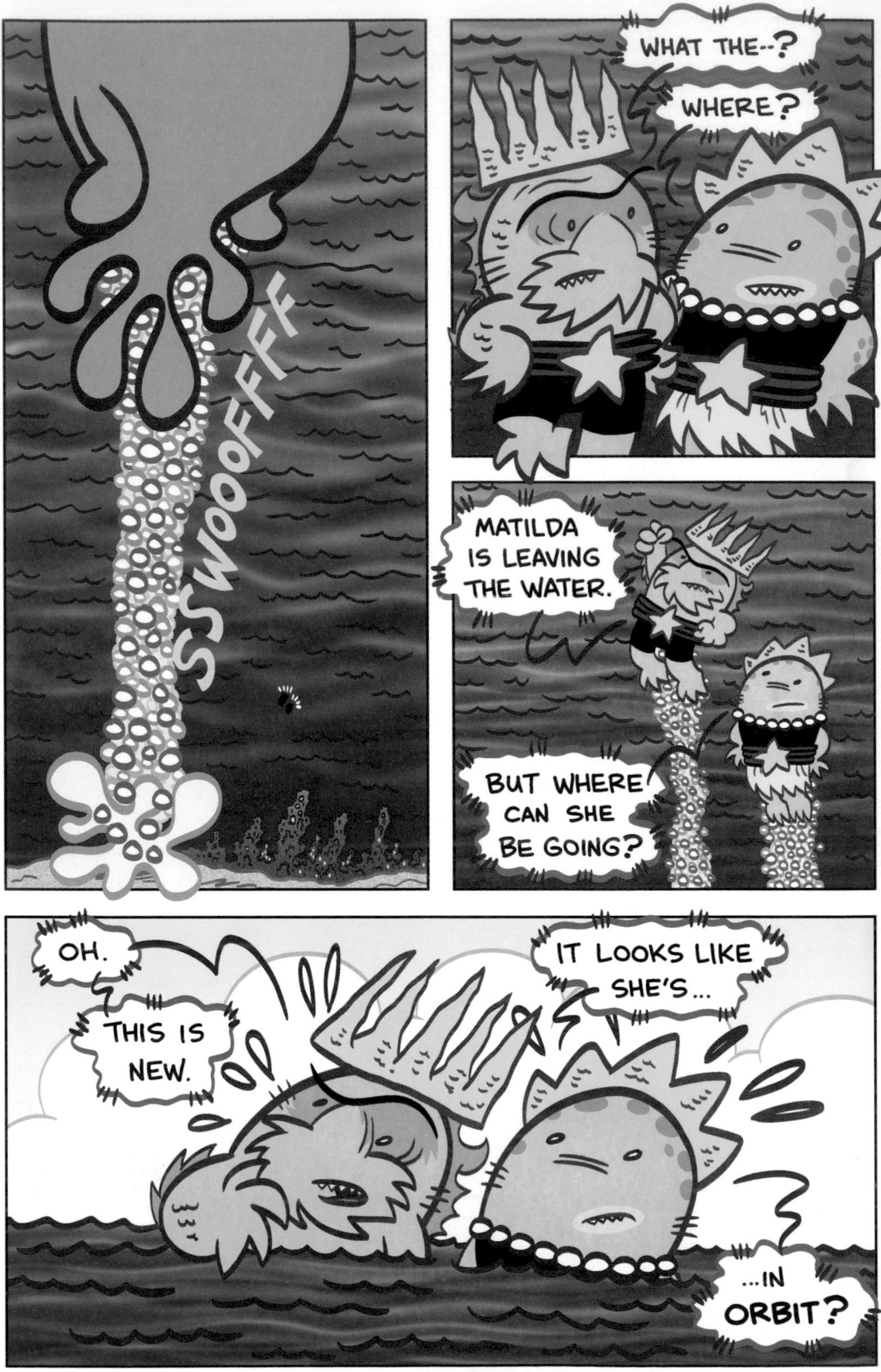
SSWOOFFFF
WHAT THE--?
WHERE?
MATILDA IS LEAVING THE WATER.
BUT WHERE CAN SHE BE GOING?
OH.
THIS IS NEW.
IT LOOKS LIKE SHE'S...
...IN ORBIT?

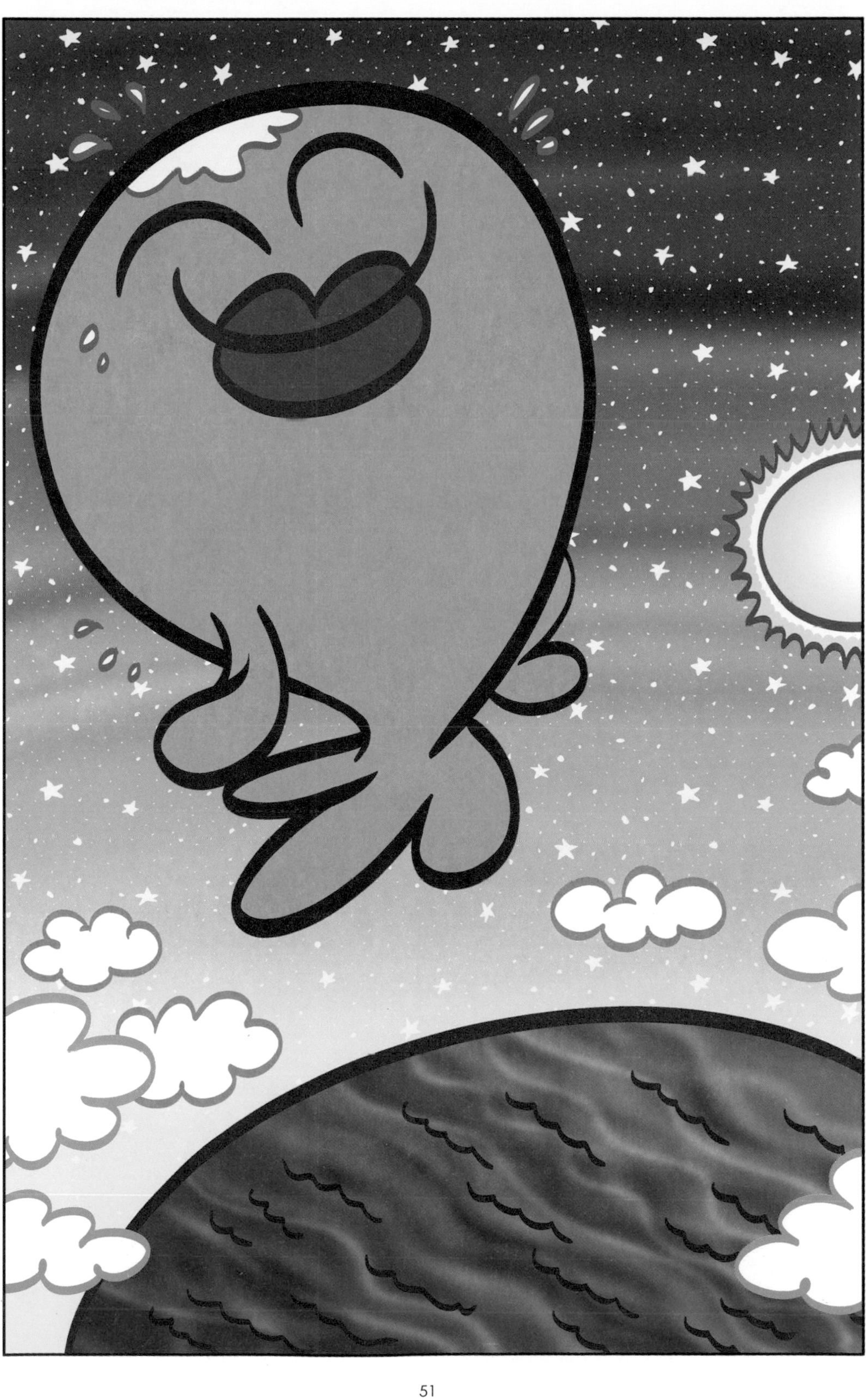

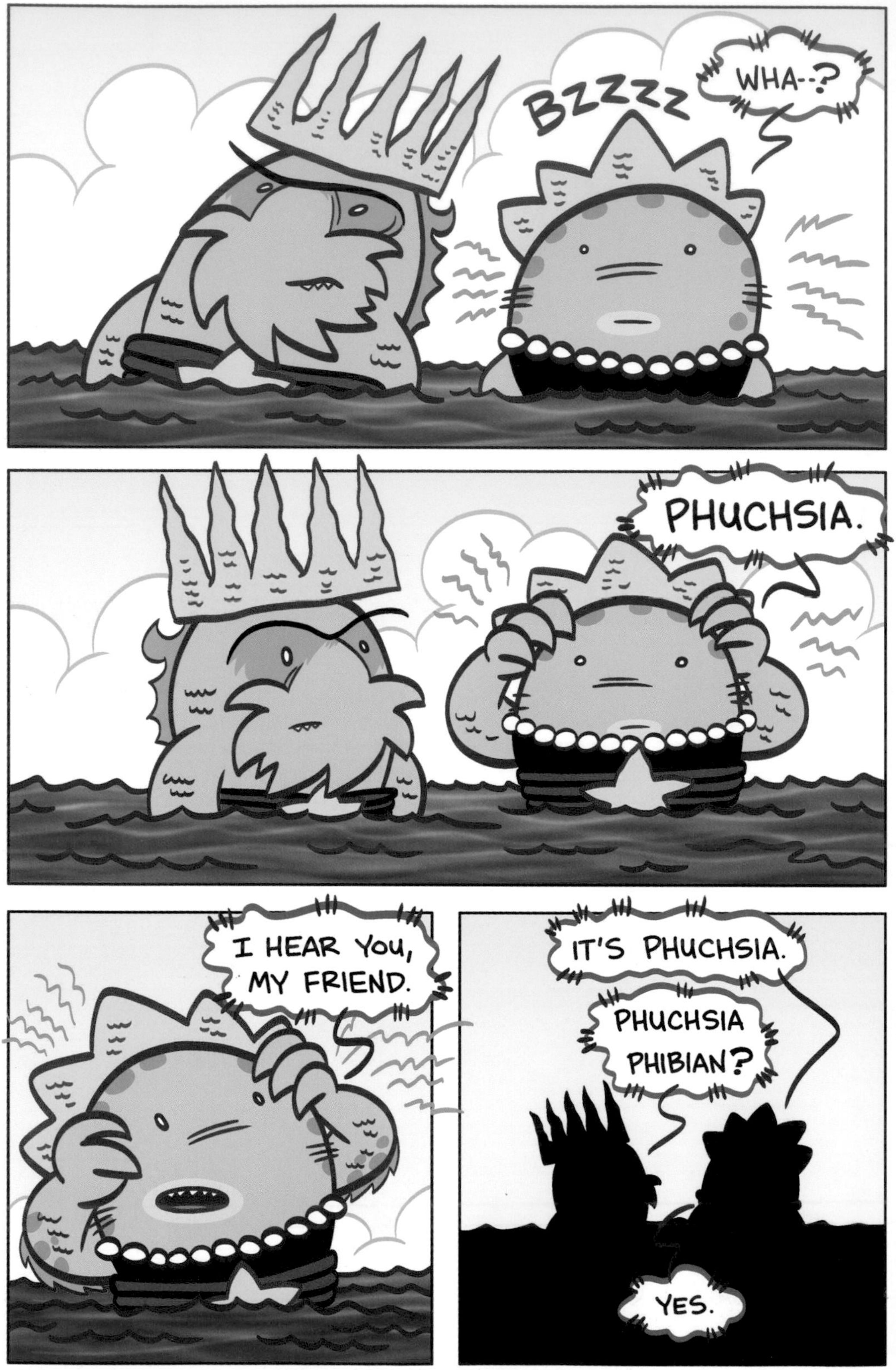
BZZZZZ
WHA--?
PHUCHSIA.
I HEAR YOU, MY FRIEND.
IT'S PHUCHSIA.
PHUCHSIA PHIBIAN?
YES.

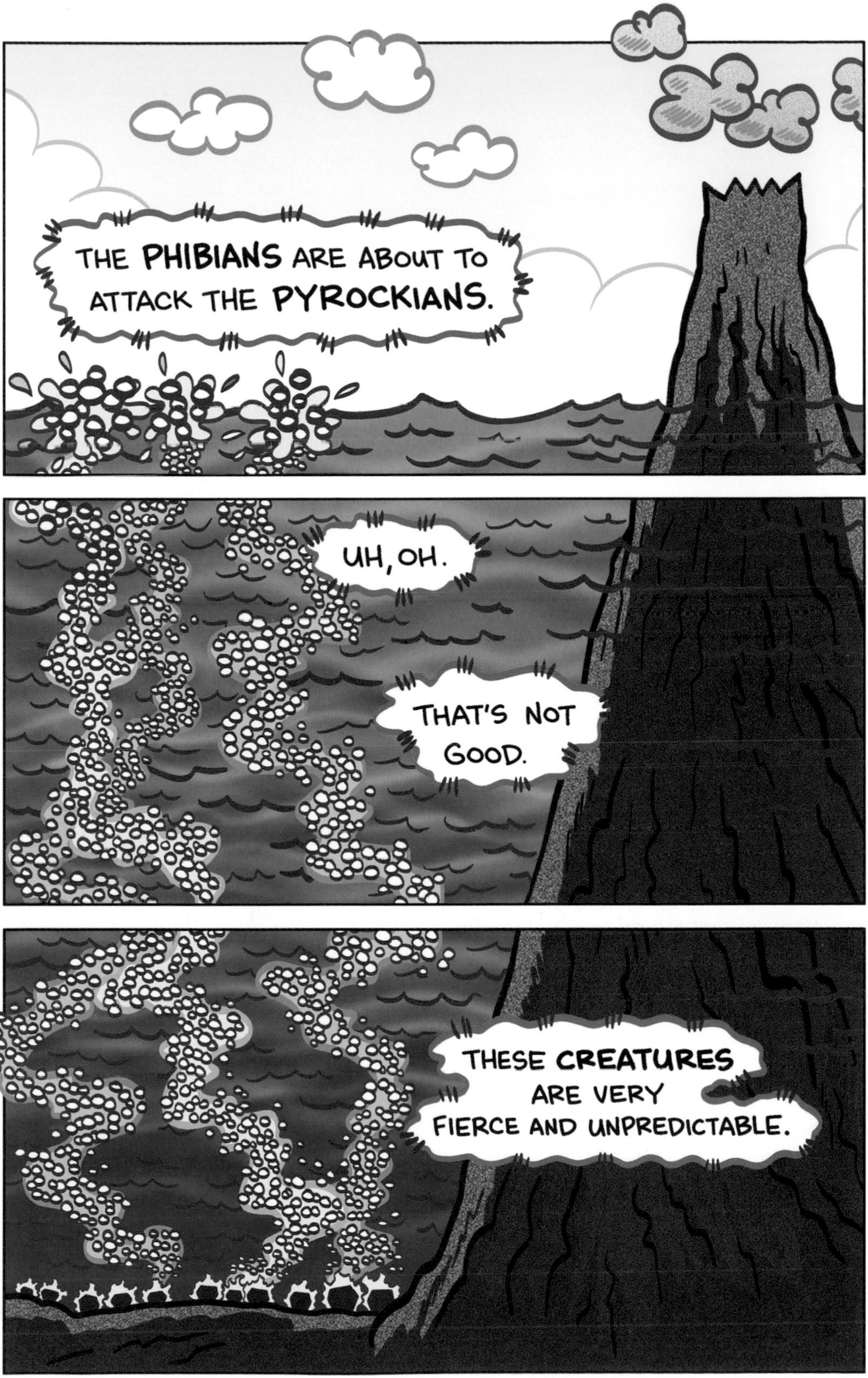
THE PHIBIANS ARE ABOUT TO ATTACK THE PYROCKIANS.
UH, OH.
THAT'S NOT GOOD.
THESE CREATURES ARE VERY FIERCE AND UNPREDICTABLE.

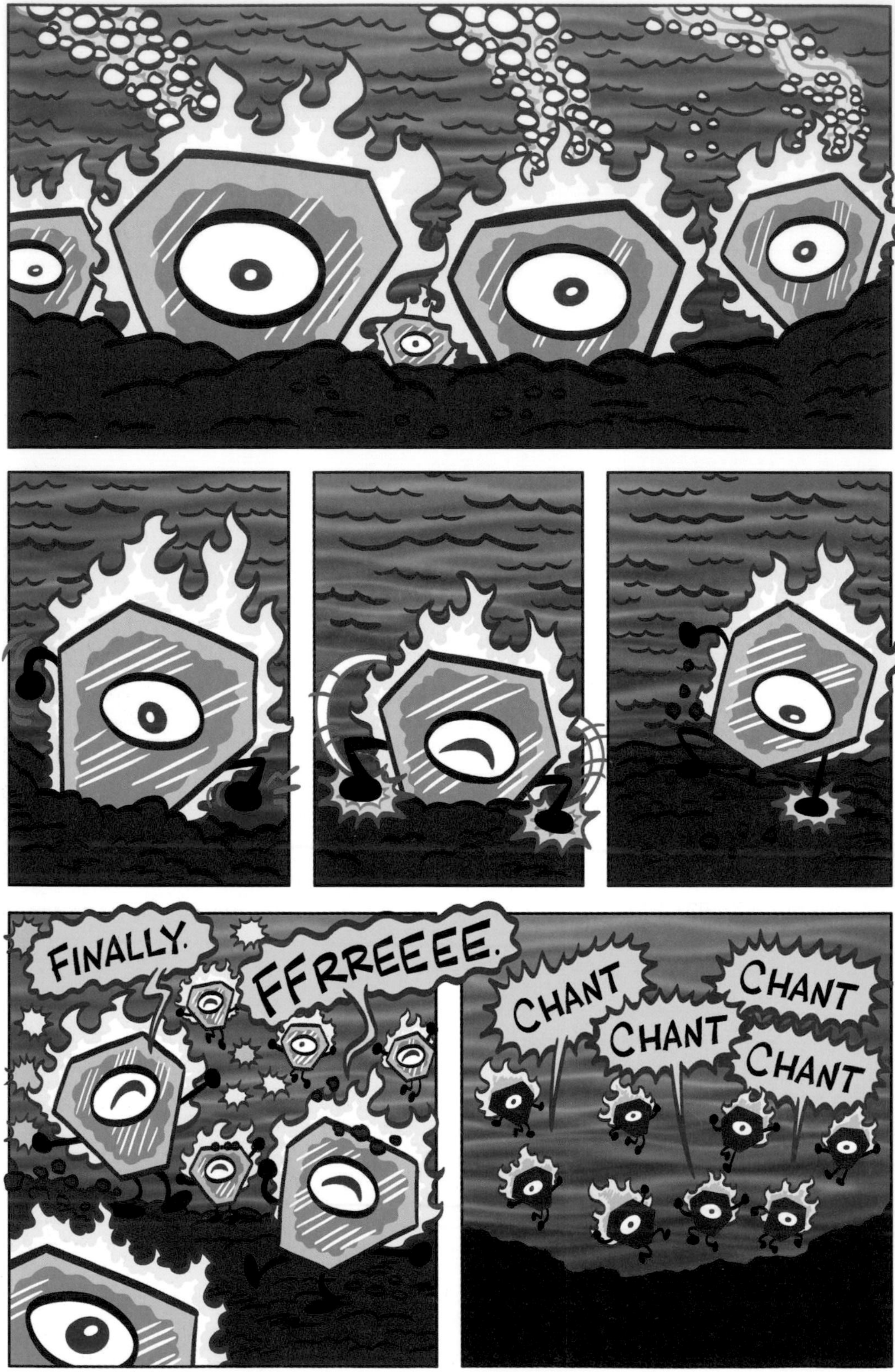
FINALLY.
FFRREEEE.
CHANT
CHANT
CHANT
CHANT

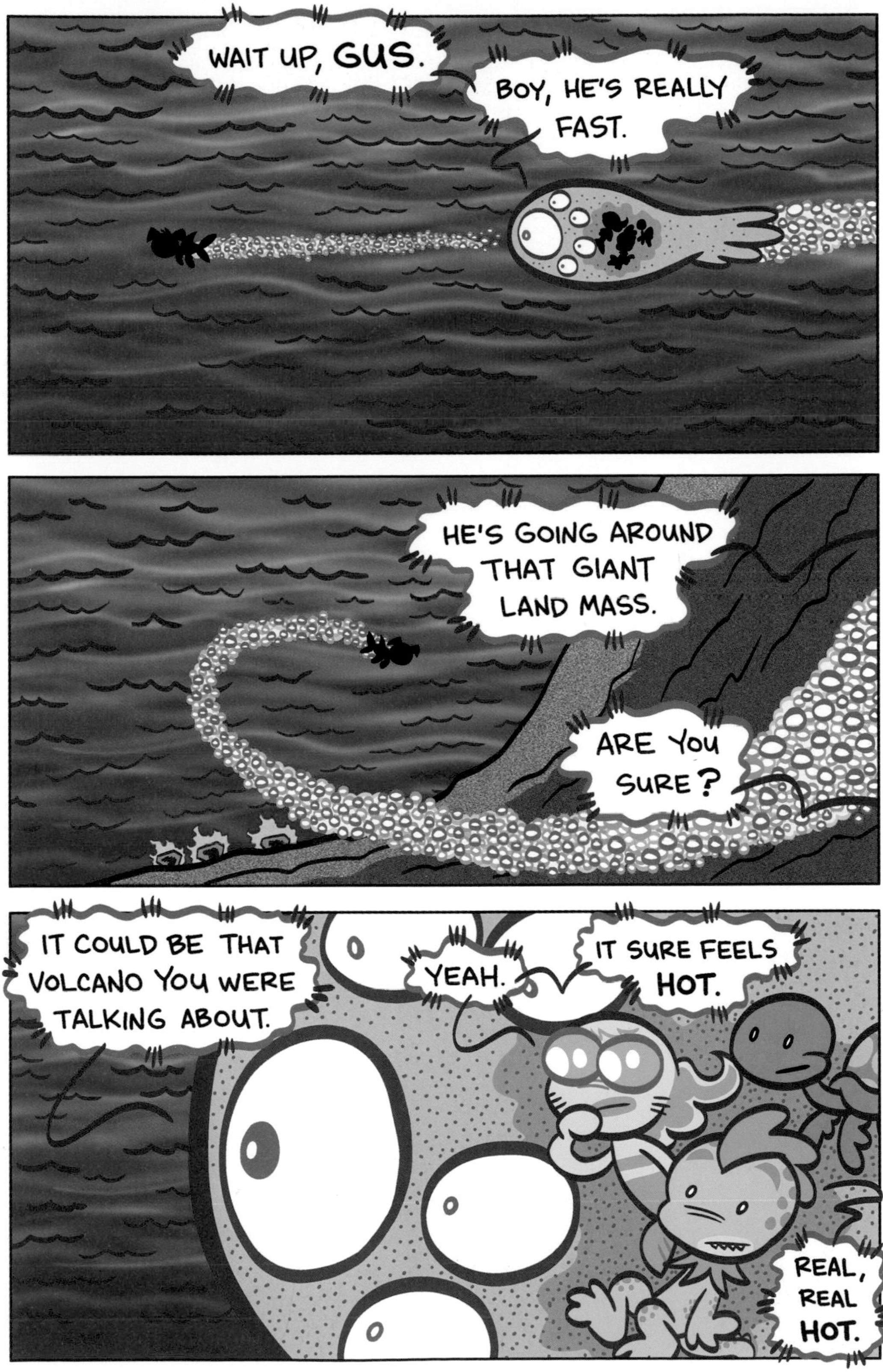
WAIT UP, GUS.
BOY, HE'S REALLY FAST.
HE'S GOING AROUND THAT GIANT LAND MASS.
ARE YOU SURE?
IT COULD BE THAT VOLCANO YOU WERE TALKING ABOUT.
YEAH.
IT SURE FEELS HOT.
REAL, REAL HOT.

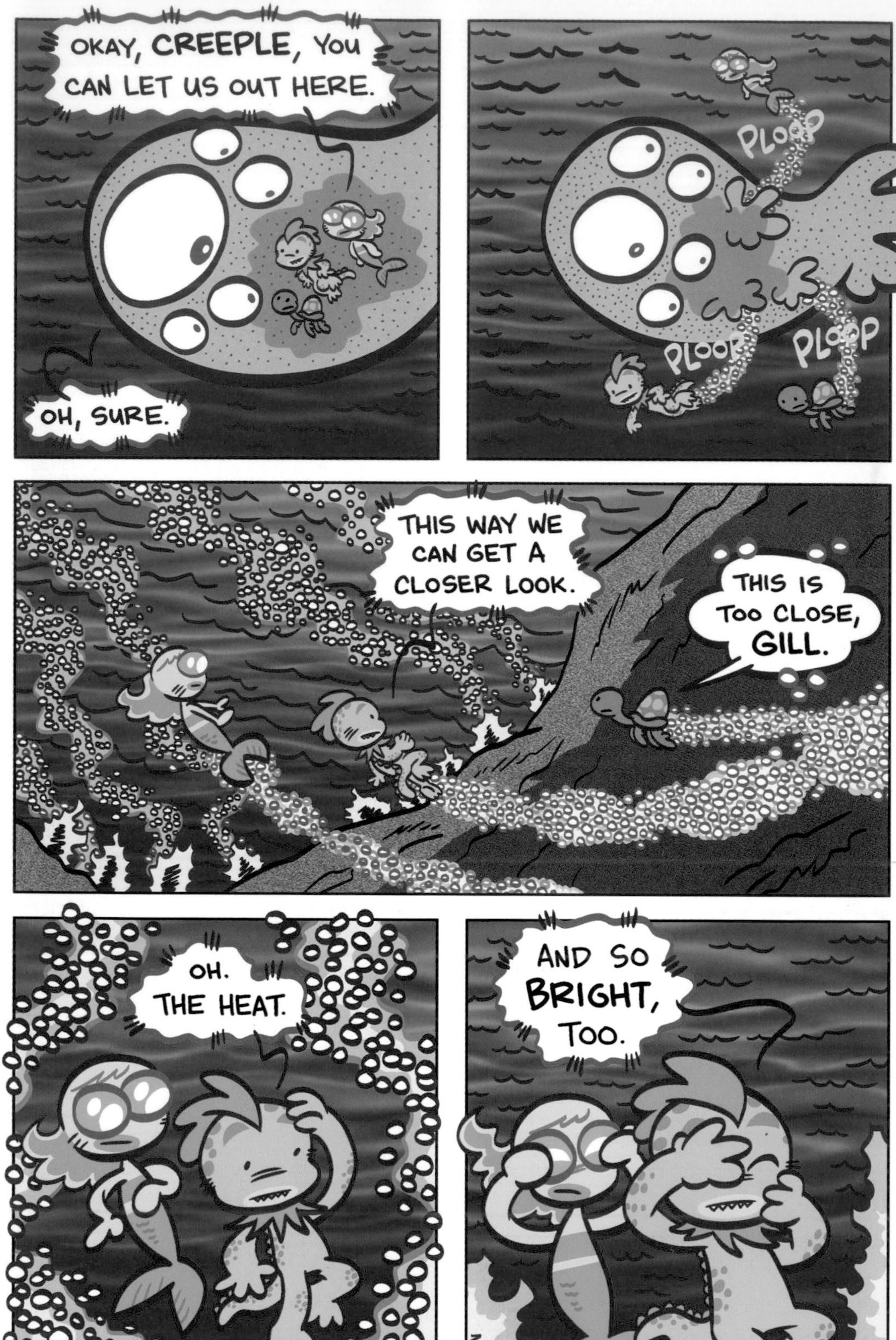
OKAY, CREEPLE, YOU CAN LET US OUT HERE.
OH, SURE.
PLOOP
PLOOP
PLOOP
THIS WAY WE CAN GET A CLOSER LOOK.
THIS IS TOO CLOSE, GILL.
OH. THE HEAT.
AND SO BRIGHT, TOO.

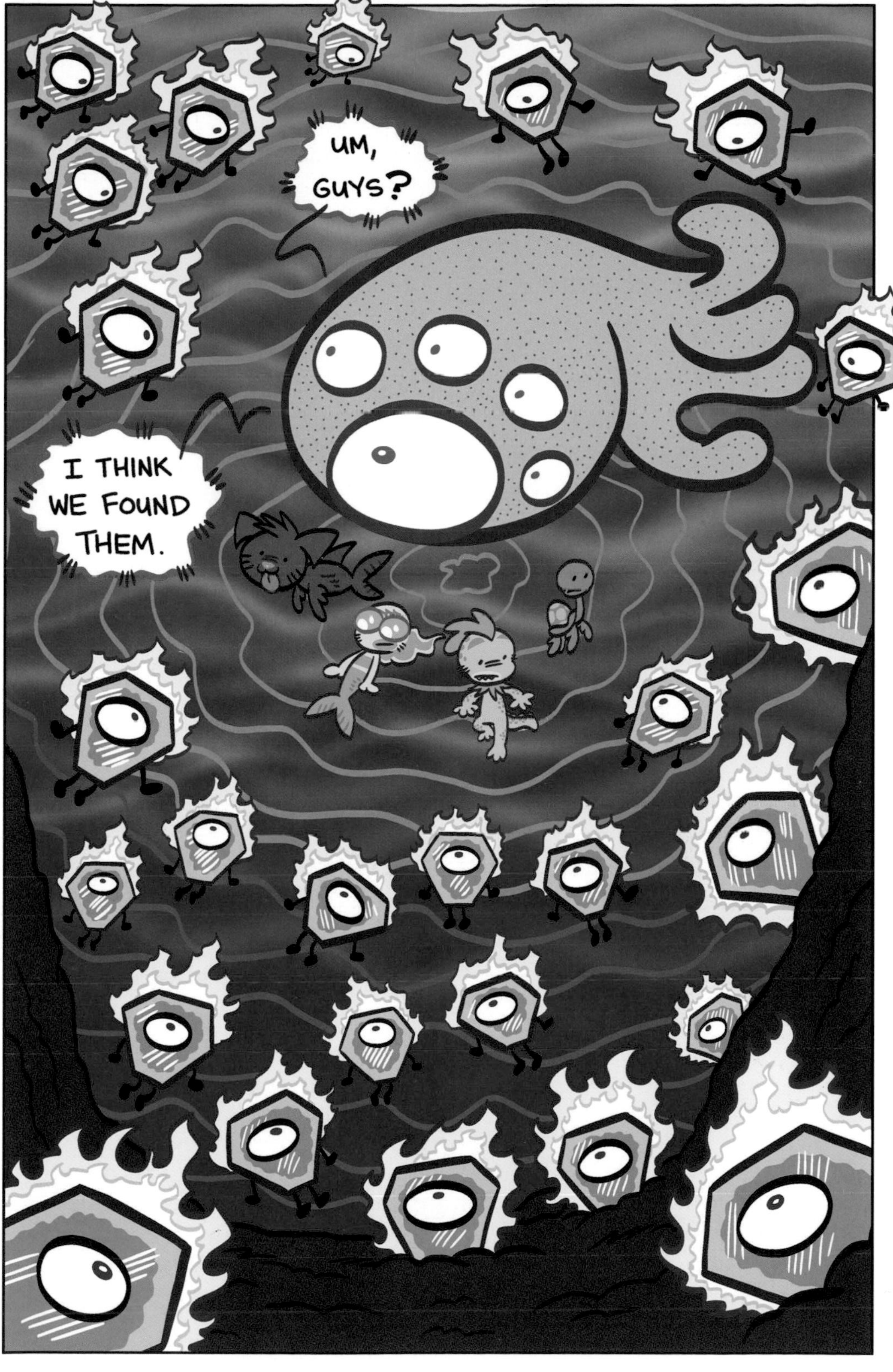
UM, GUYS?
I THINK WE FOUND THEM.

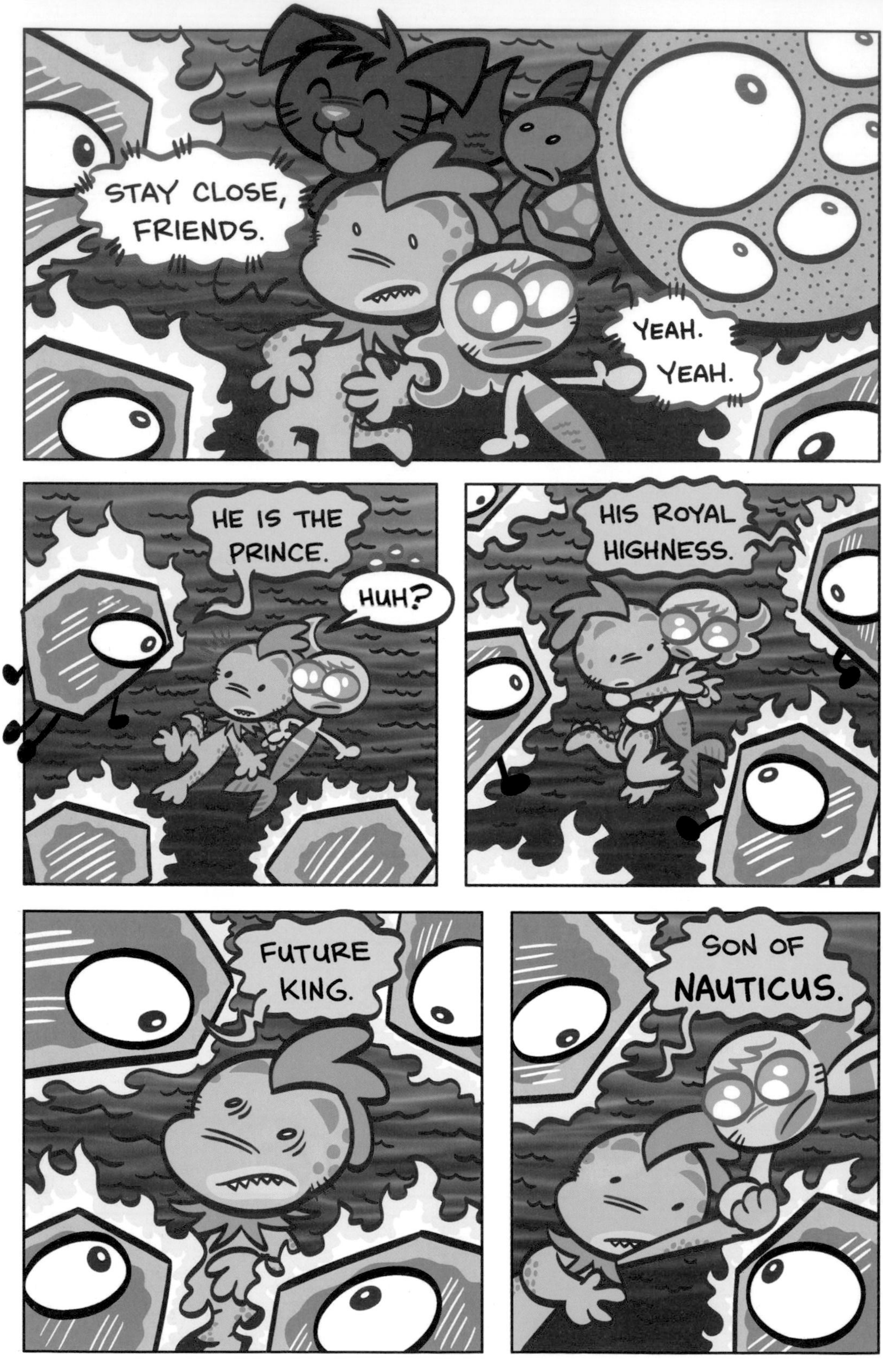
STAY CLOSE, FRIENDS.
YEAH. YEAH.
HE IS THE PRINCE.
HUH?
HIS ROYAL HIGHNESS.
FUTURE KING.
SON OF NAUTICUS.

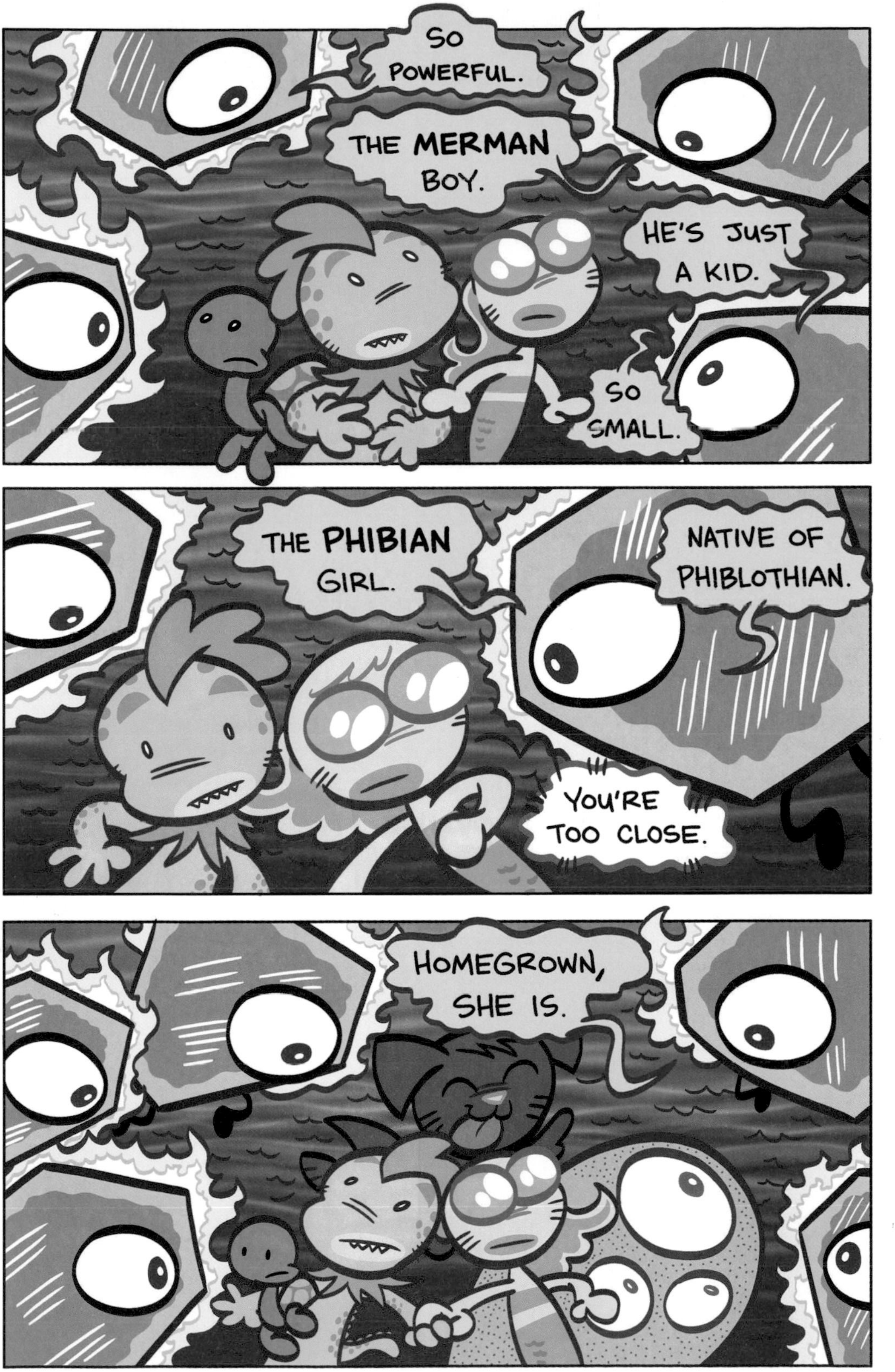
SO POWERFUL.
THE MERMAN BOY.
HE'S JUST A KID.
SO SMALL.
THE PHIBIAN GIRL.
NATIVE OF PHIBLOTHIAN.
YOU'RE TOO CLOSE.
HOMEGROWN, SHE IS.

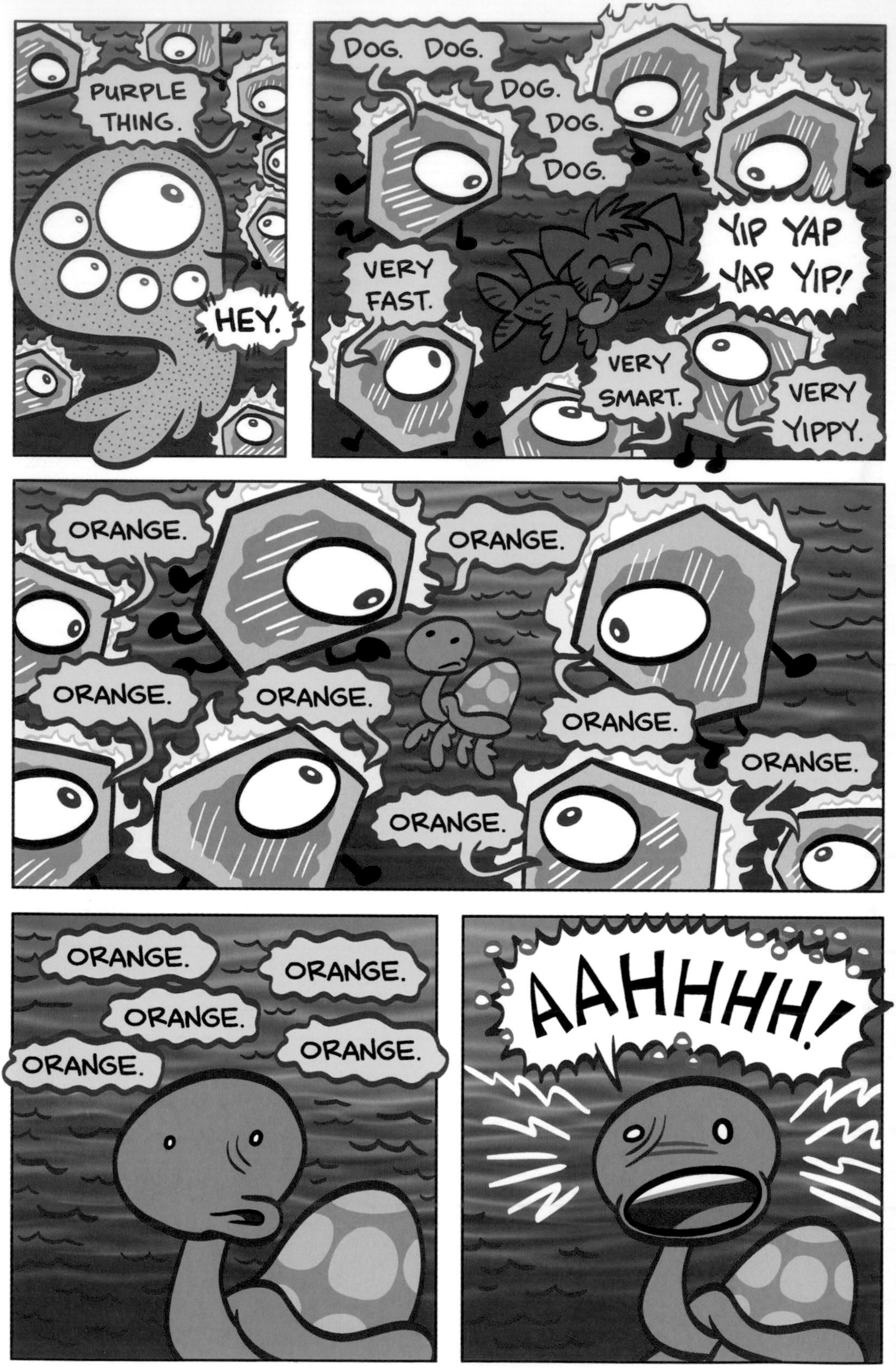
PURPLE THING.
HEY.
DOG. DOG.
DOG.
DOG.
DOG.
VERY FAST.
YIP YAP YAP YIP!
VERY SMART.
VERY YIPPY.
ORANGE.
ORANGE.
ORANGE.
ORANGE.
ORANGE.
ORANGE.
ORANGE.
ORANGE.
ORANGE.
ORANGE.
ORANGE.
ORANGE.
AAHHHH!

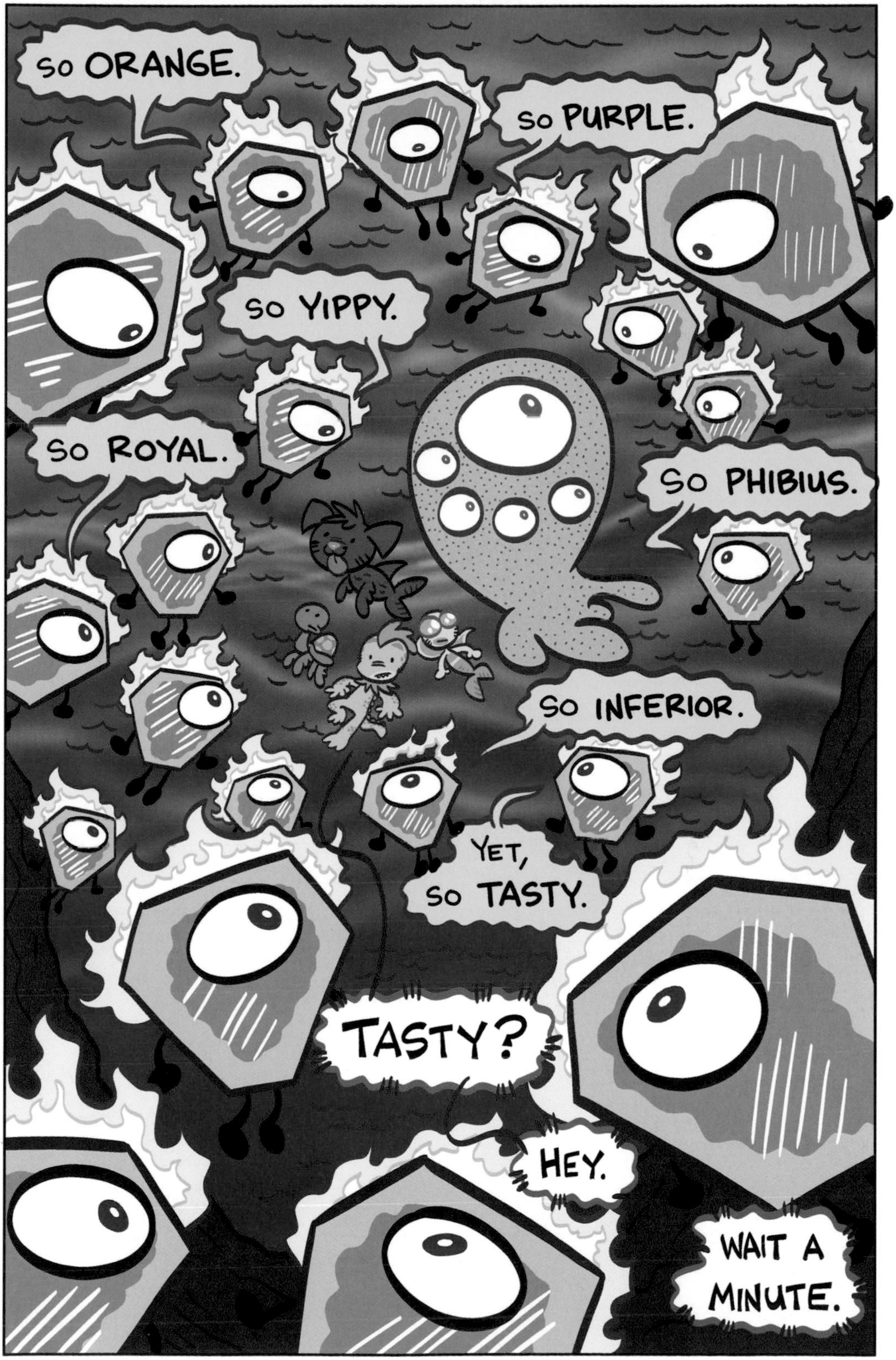
So ORANGE.
So PURPLE.
So YIPPY.
So ROYAL.
So PHIBIUS.
So INFERIOR.
YET, So TASTY.
TASTY?
HEY.
WAIT A MINUTE.

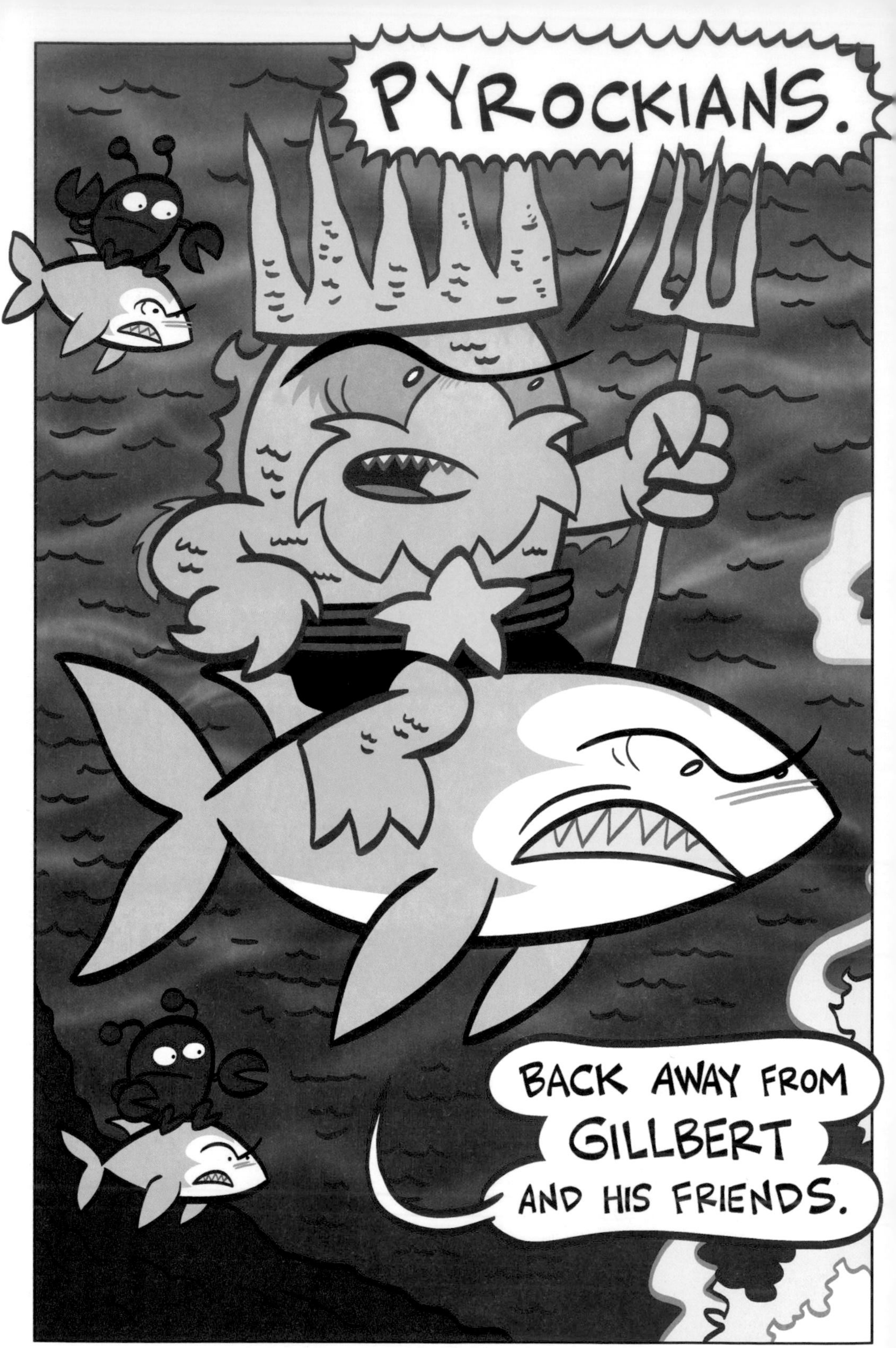
PYROCKIANS.
BACK AWAY FROM GILLBERT AND HIS FRIENDS.

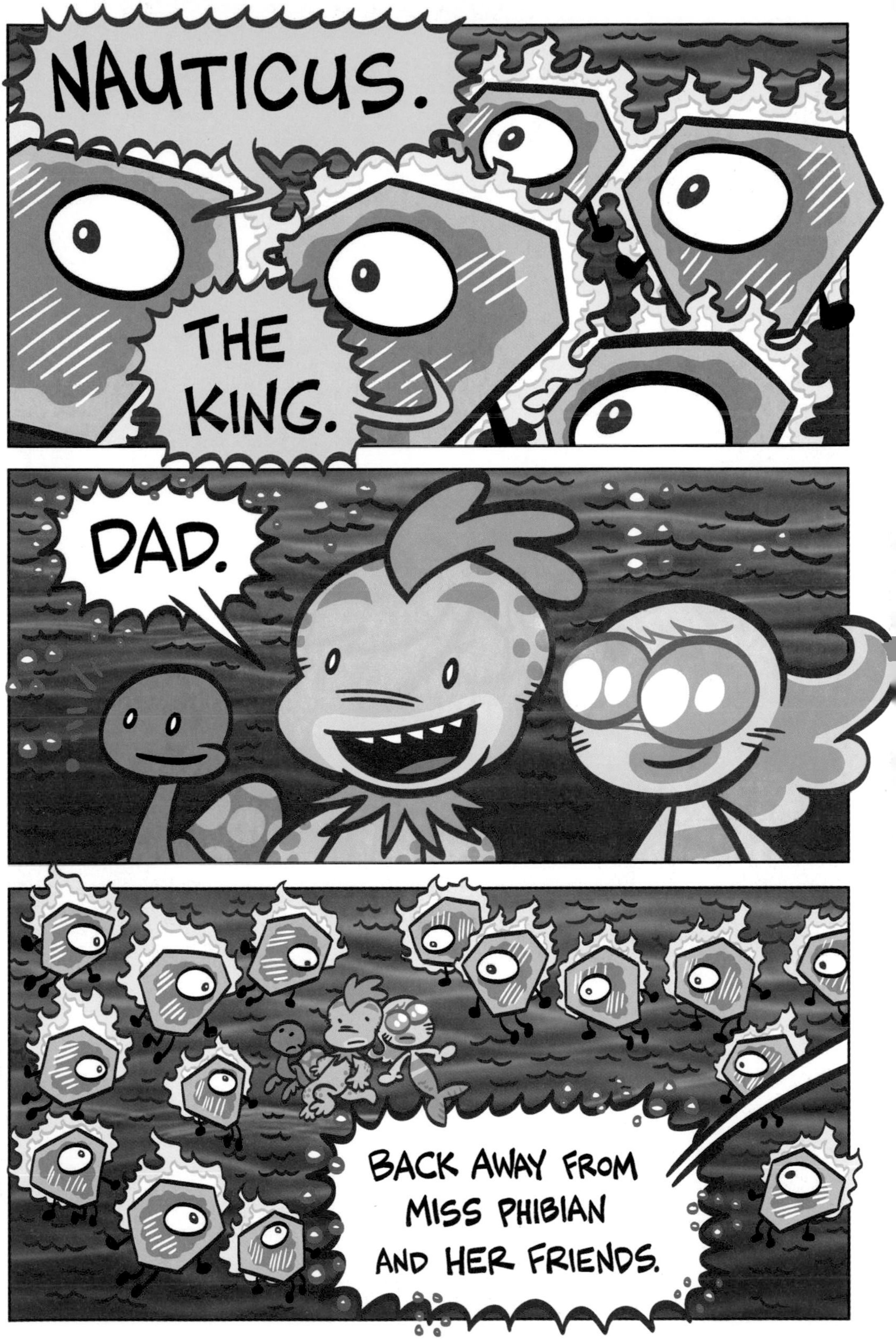
NAUTICUS.
THE KING.
DAD.
BACK AWAY FROM MISS PHIBIAN AND HER FRIENDS.

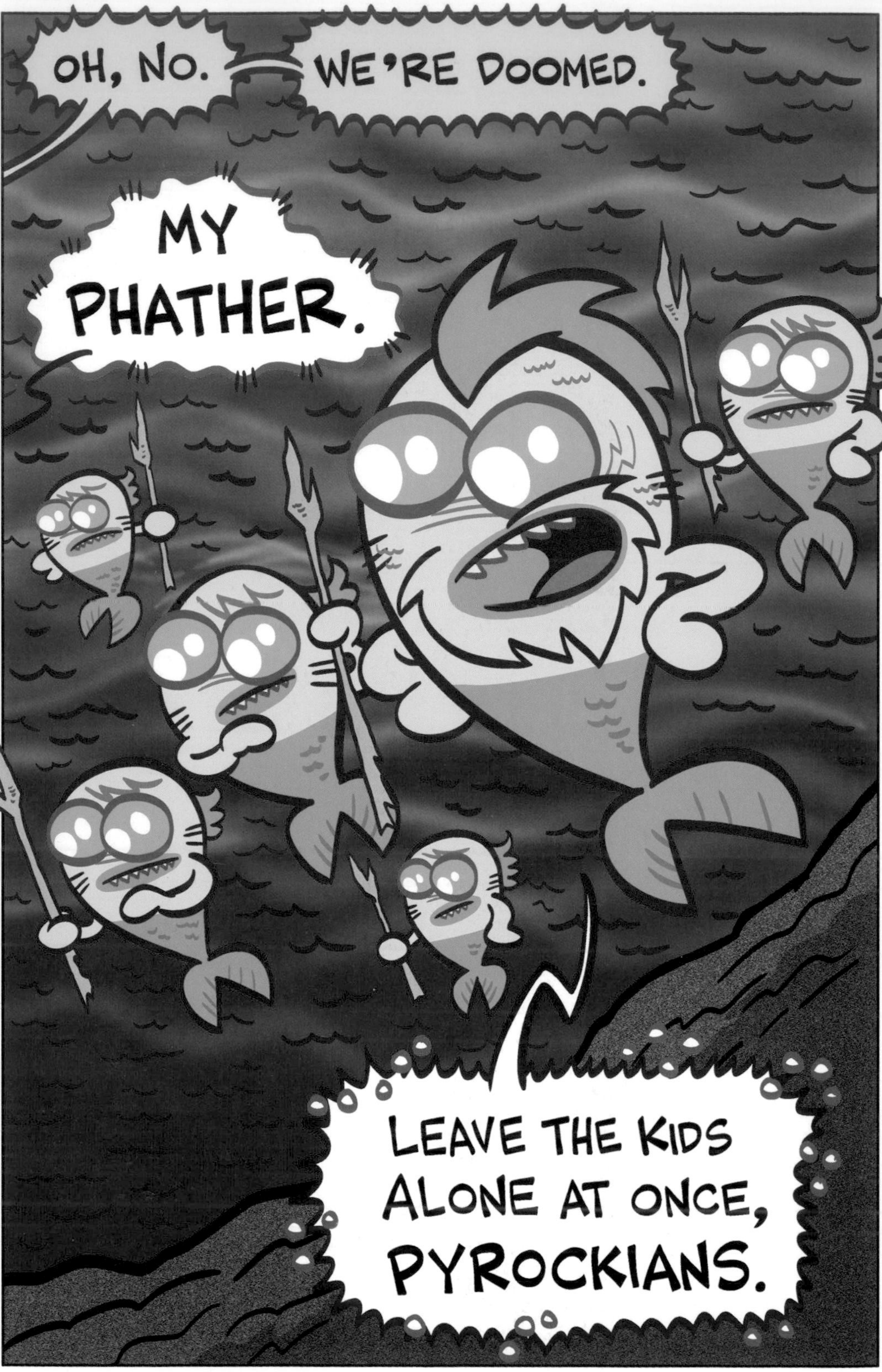

OH, NO.
WE'RE DOOMED.
MY PHATHER.
LEAVE THE KIDS ALONE AT ONCE, PYROCKIANS.

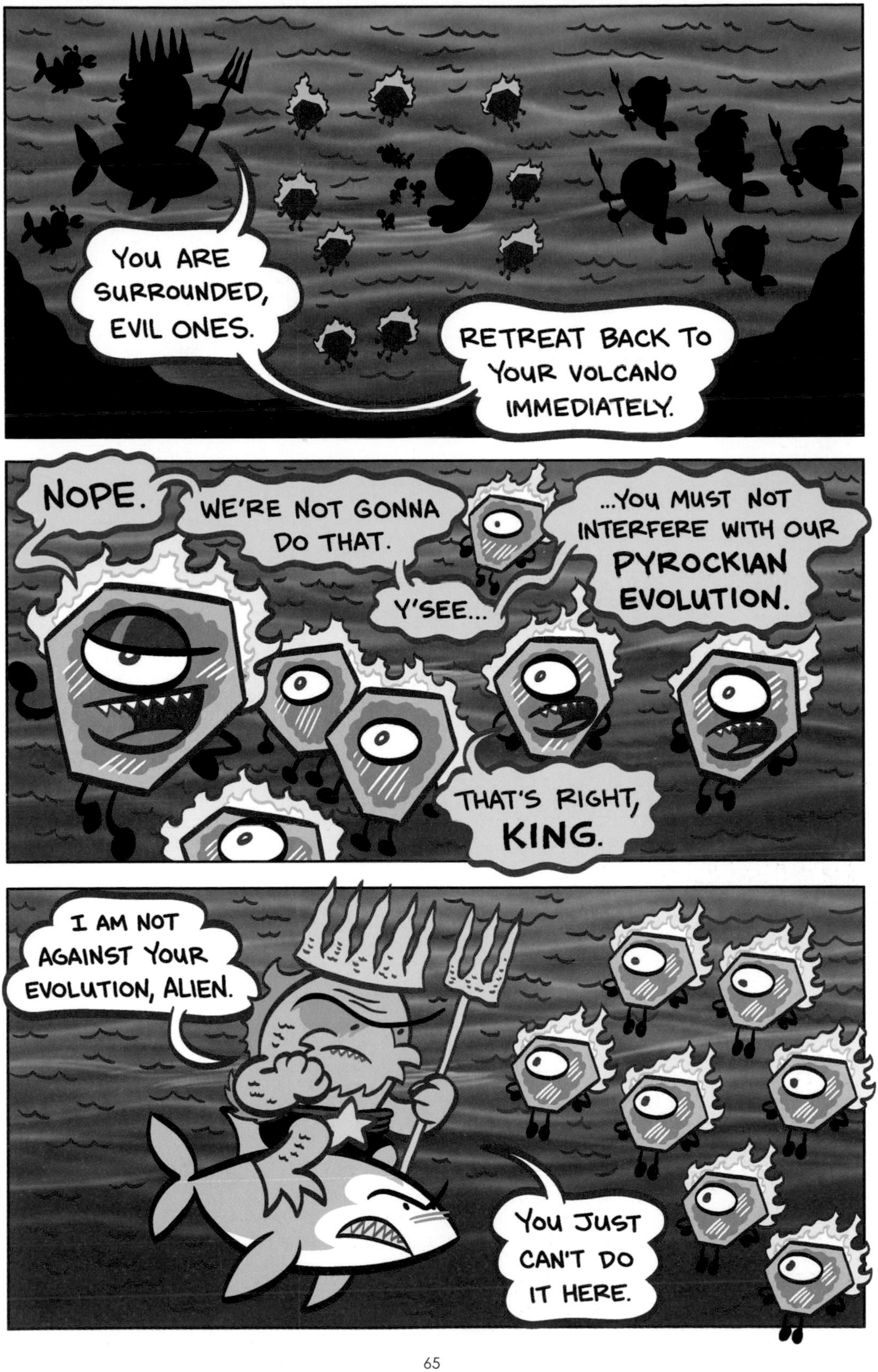
YOU ARE SURROUNDED, EVIL ONES.
RETREAT BACK TO YOUR VOLCANO IMMEDIATELY.
NOPE.
WE'RE NOT GONNA DO THAT.
Y'SEE...
...YOU MUST NOT INTERFERE WITH OUR PYROCKIAN EVOLUTION.
THAT'S RIGHT, KING.
I AM NOT AGAINST YOUR EVOLUTION, ALIEN.
YOU JUST CAN'T DO IT HERE.

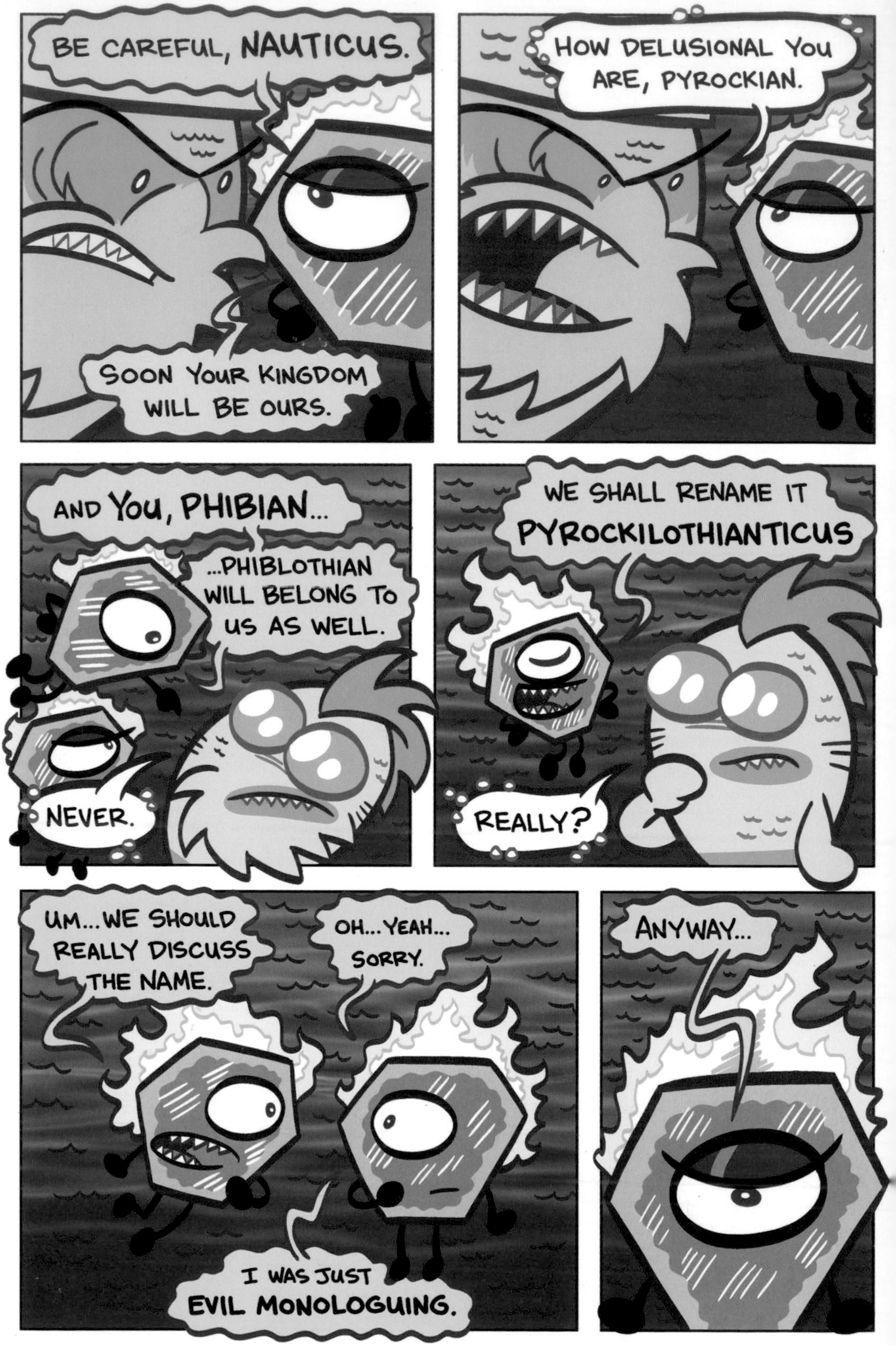
BE CAREFUL, NAUTICUS.
SOON YOUR KINGDOM WILL BE OURS.
HOW DELUSIONAL YOU ARE, PYROCKIAN.
AND YOU, PHIBIAN...
...PHIBLOTHIAN WILL BELONG TO US AS WELL.
NEVER.
WE SHALL RENAME IT PYROCKILOTHIANTICUS
REALLY?
UM... WE SHOULD REALLY DISCUSS THE NAME.
OH... YEAH... SORRY.
I WAS JUST EVIL MONOLOGUING.
ANYWAY...

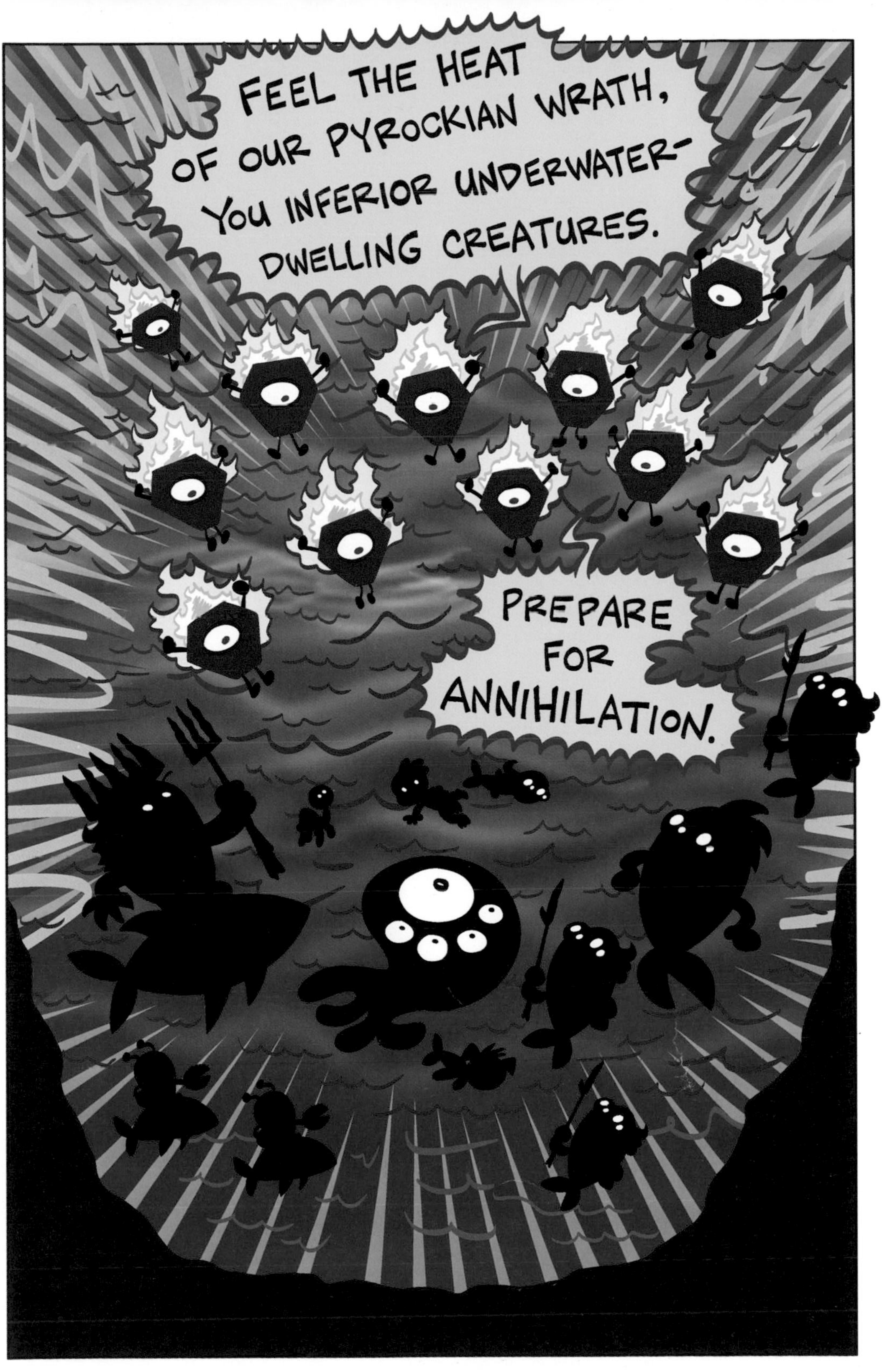
FEEL THE HEAT OF OUR PYROCKIAN WRATH, YOU INFERIOR UNDERWATER-DWELLING CREATURES.
PREPARE FOR ANNIHILATION.

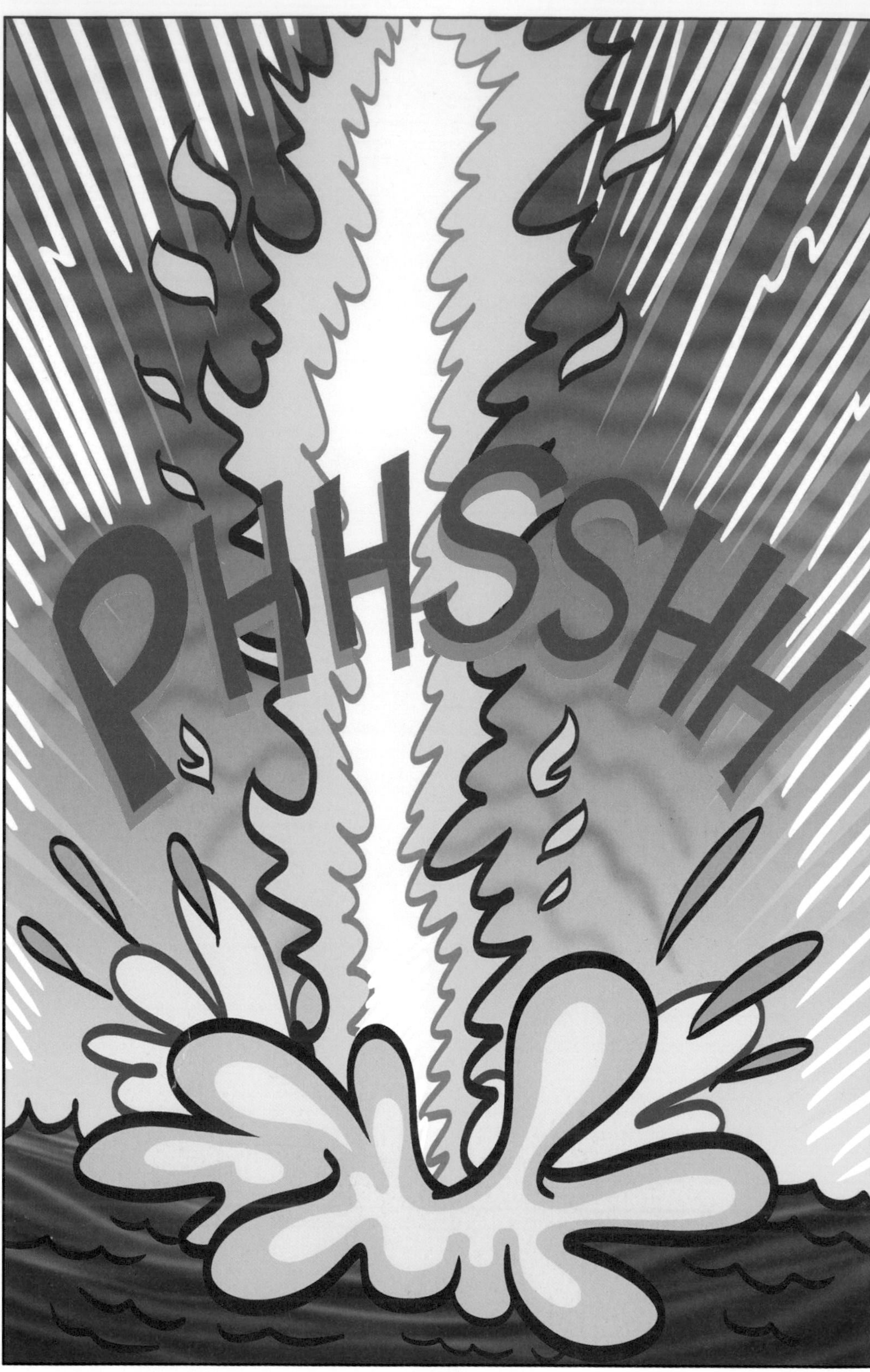
PHHSSHH

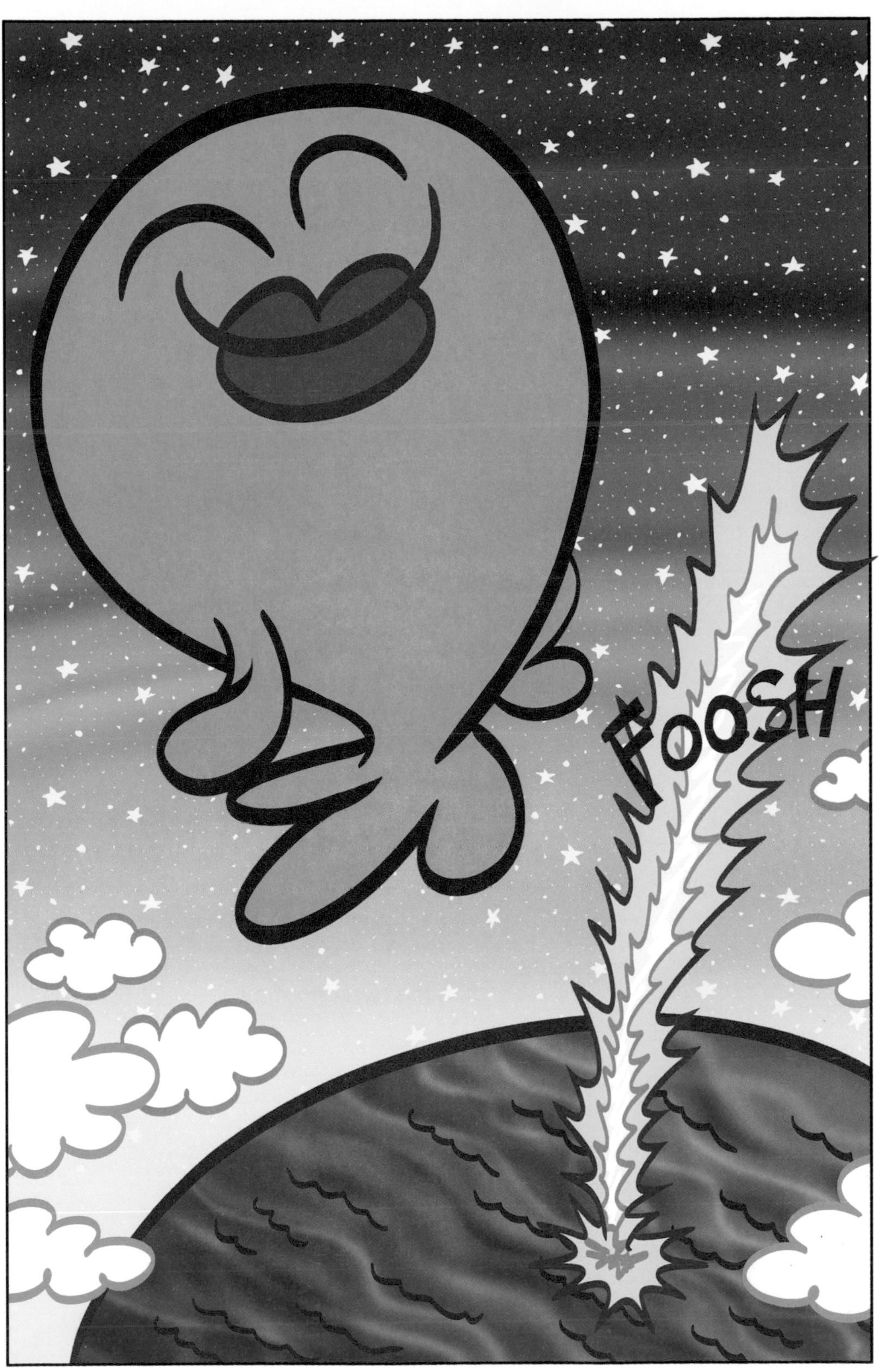
FOOSH

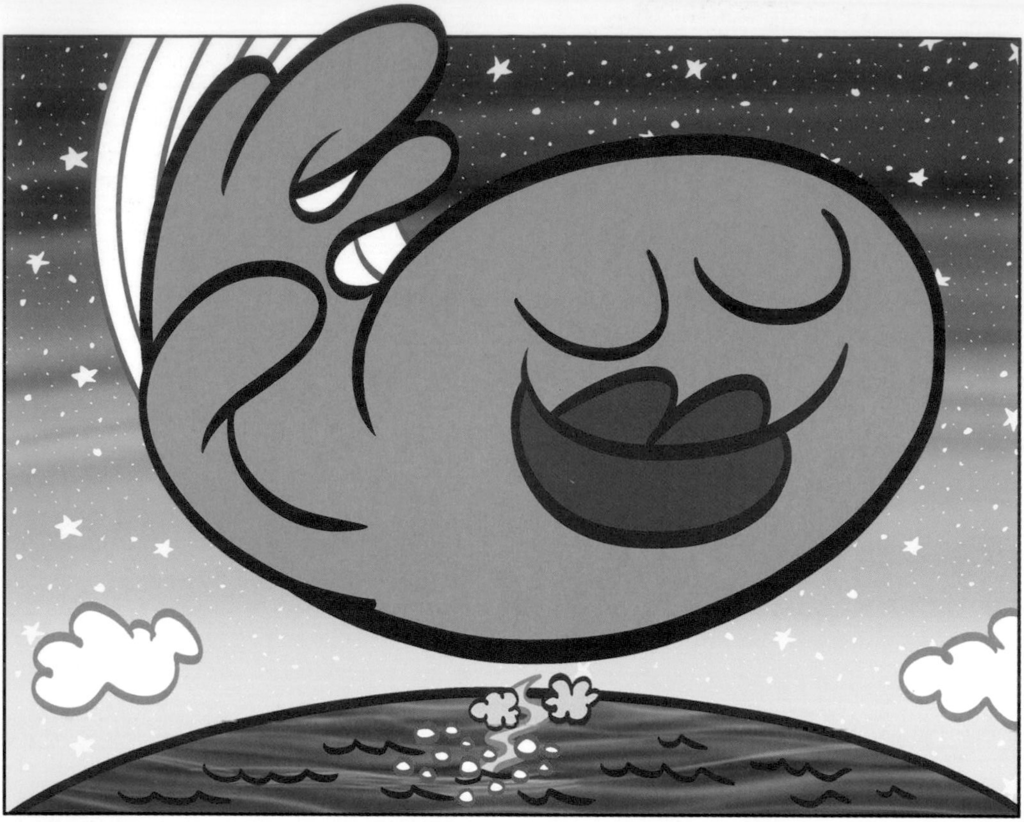

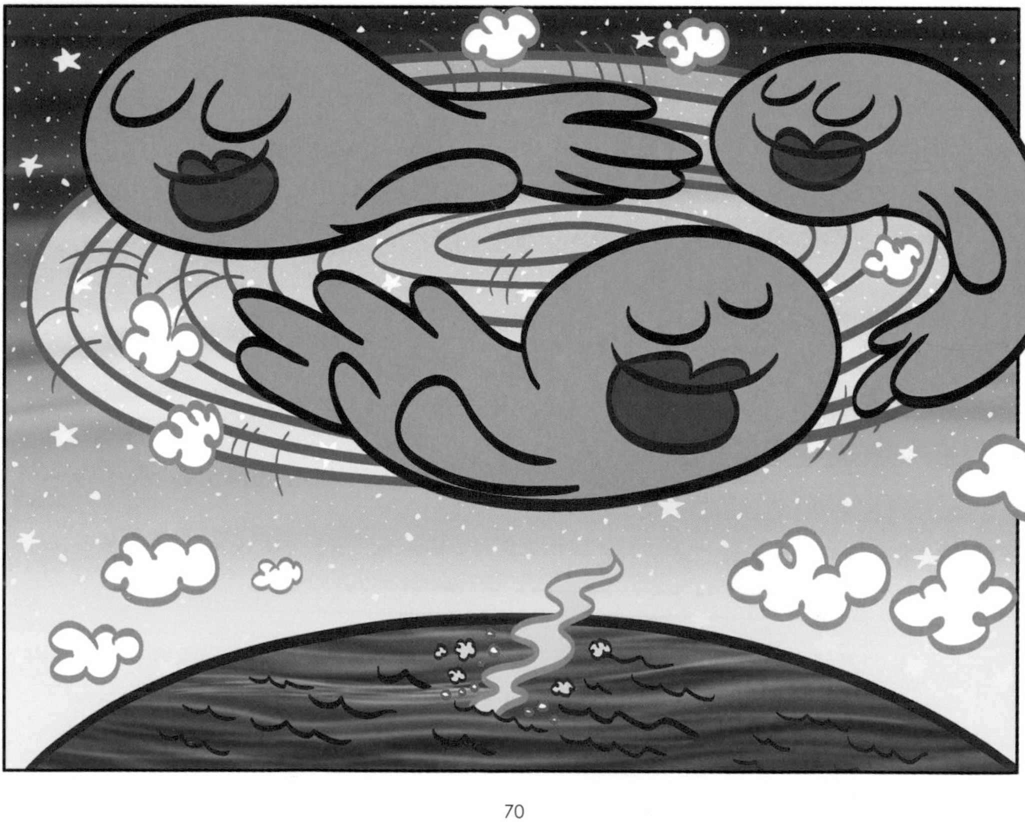

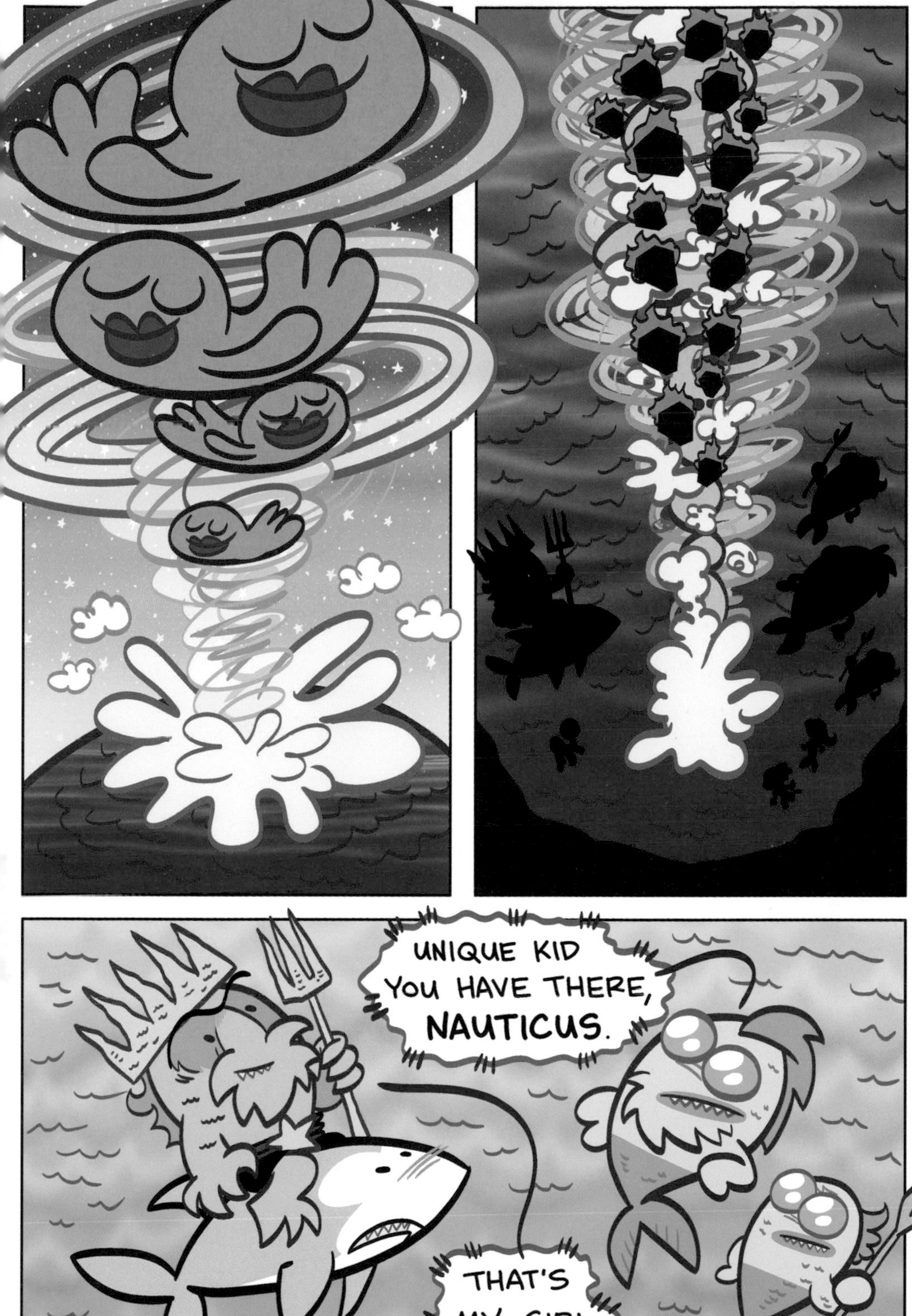
UNIQUE KID YOU HAVE THERE, NAUTICUS.
THAT'S MY GIRL.

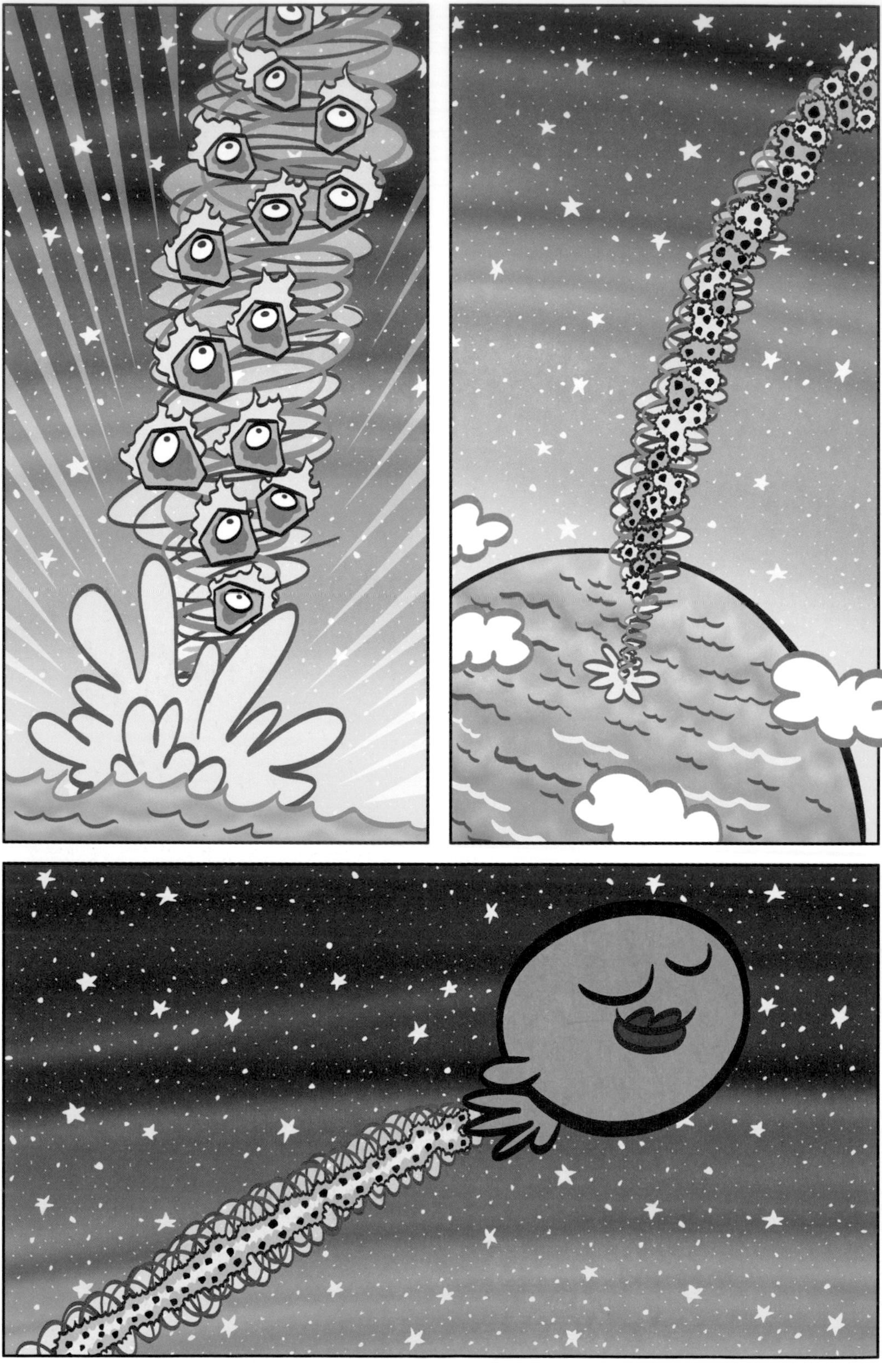

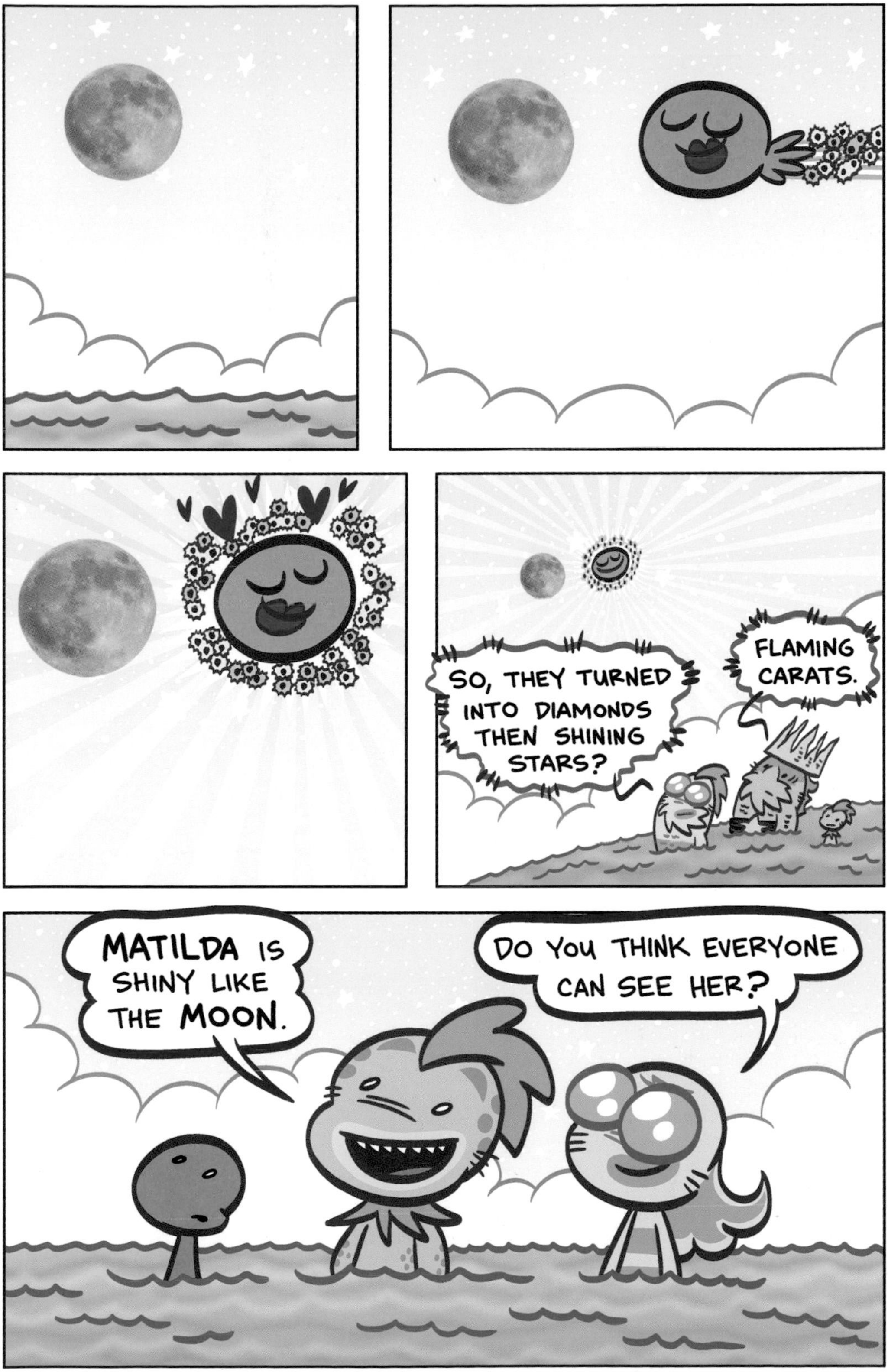
SO, THEY TURNED INTO DIAMONDS THEN SHINING STARS?
FLAMING CARATS.
MATILDA IS SHINY LIKE THE MOON.
DO YOU THINK EVERYONE CAN SEE HER?

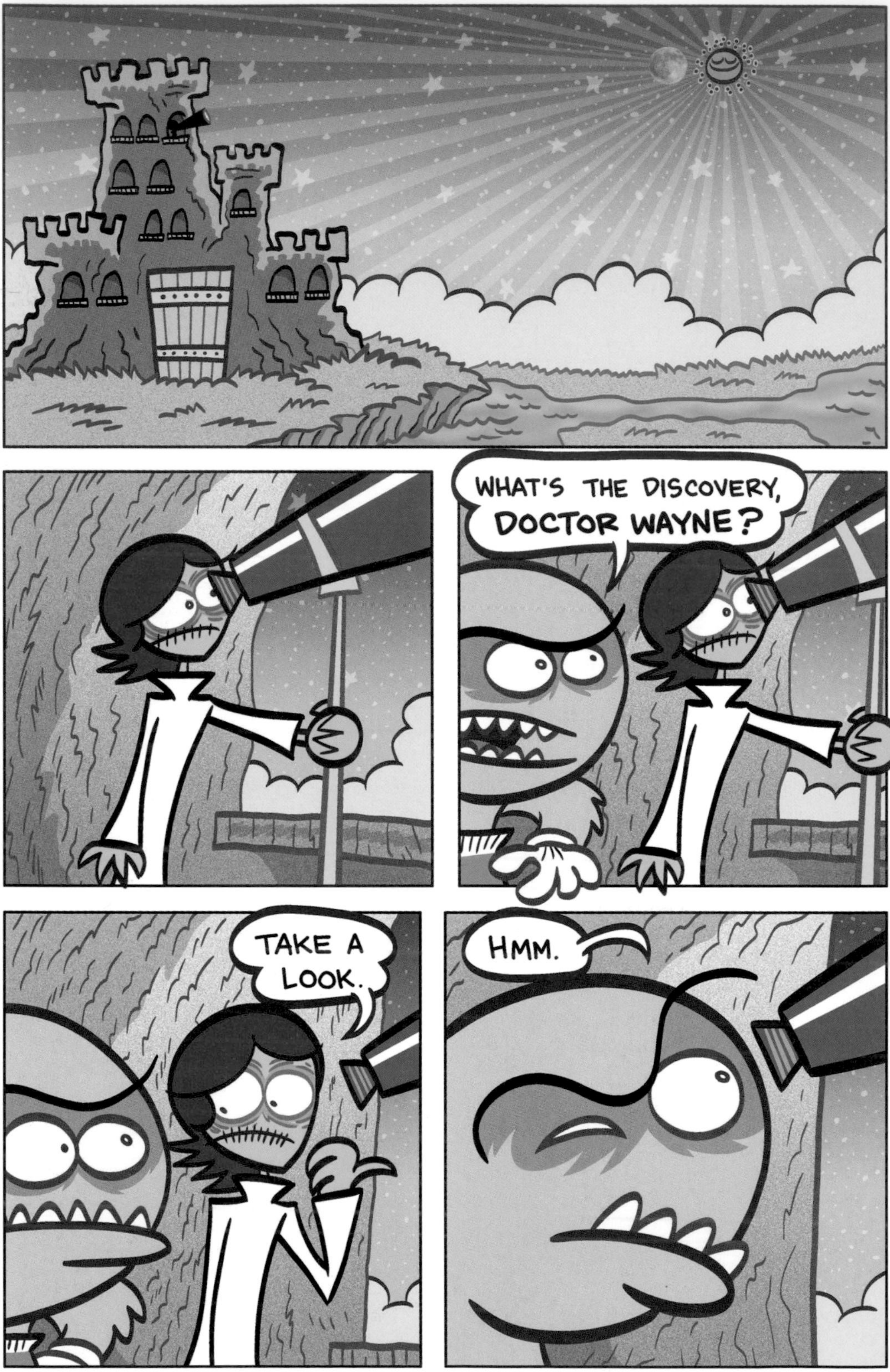
WHAT'S THE DISCOVERY, DOCTOR WAYNE?
TAKE A LOOK.
HMM.

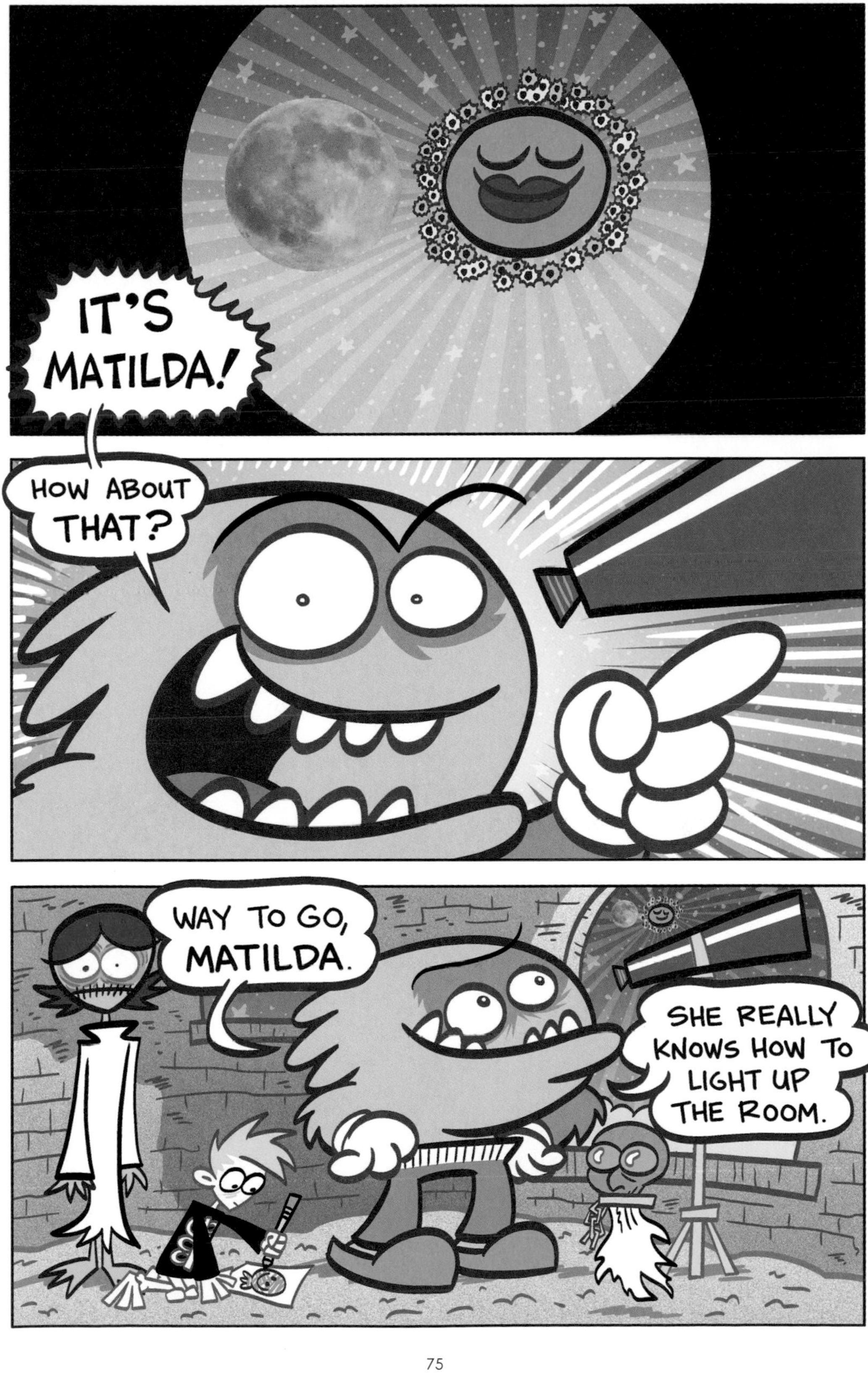
IT'S MATILDA!
HOW ABOUT THAT?
WAY TO GO, MATILDA.
SHE REALLY KNOWS HOW TO LIGHT UP THE ROOM.

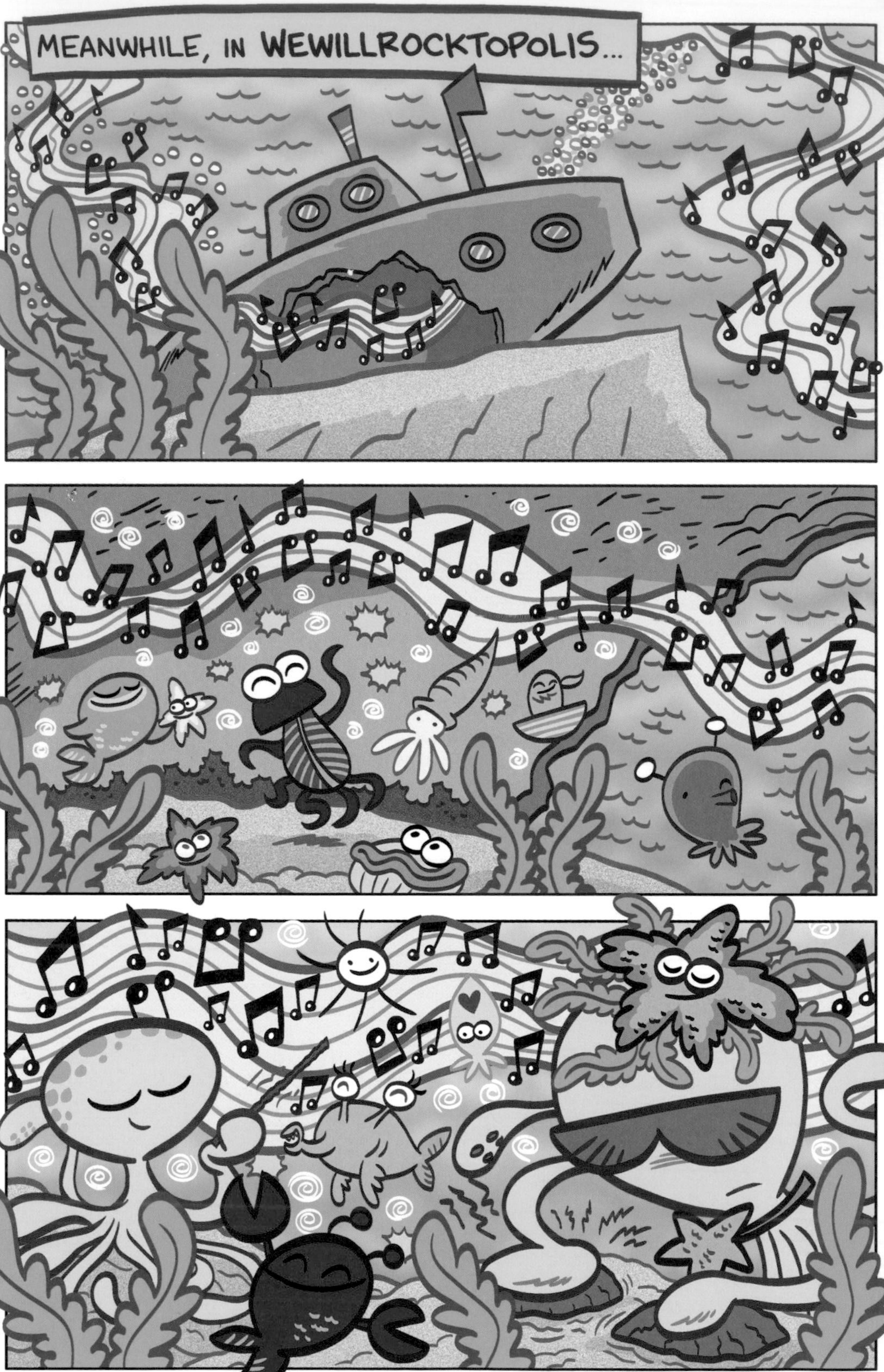
MEANWHILE, IN WEWILLROCKTOPOLIS...

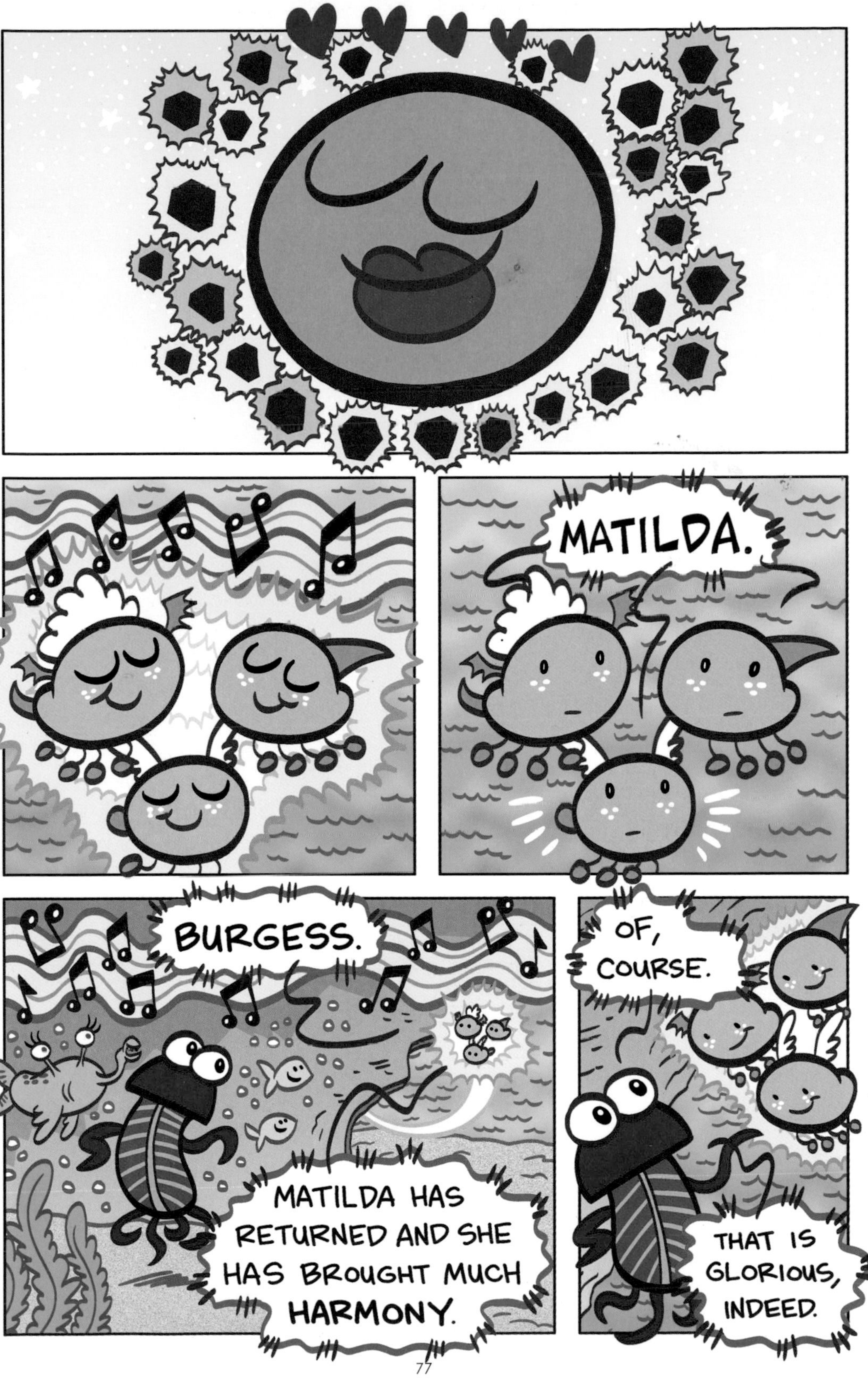
MATILDA.
BURGESS.
MATILDA HAS RETURNED AND SHE HAS BROUGHT MUCH HARMONY.
OF, COURSE.
THAT IS GLORIOUS, INDEED.

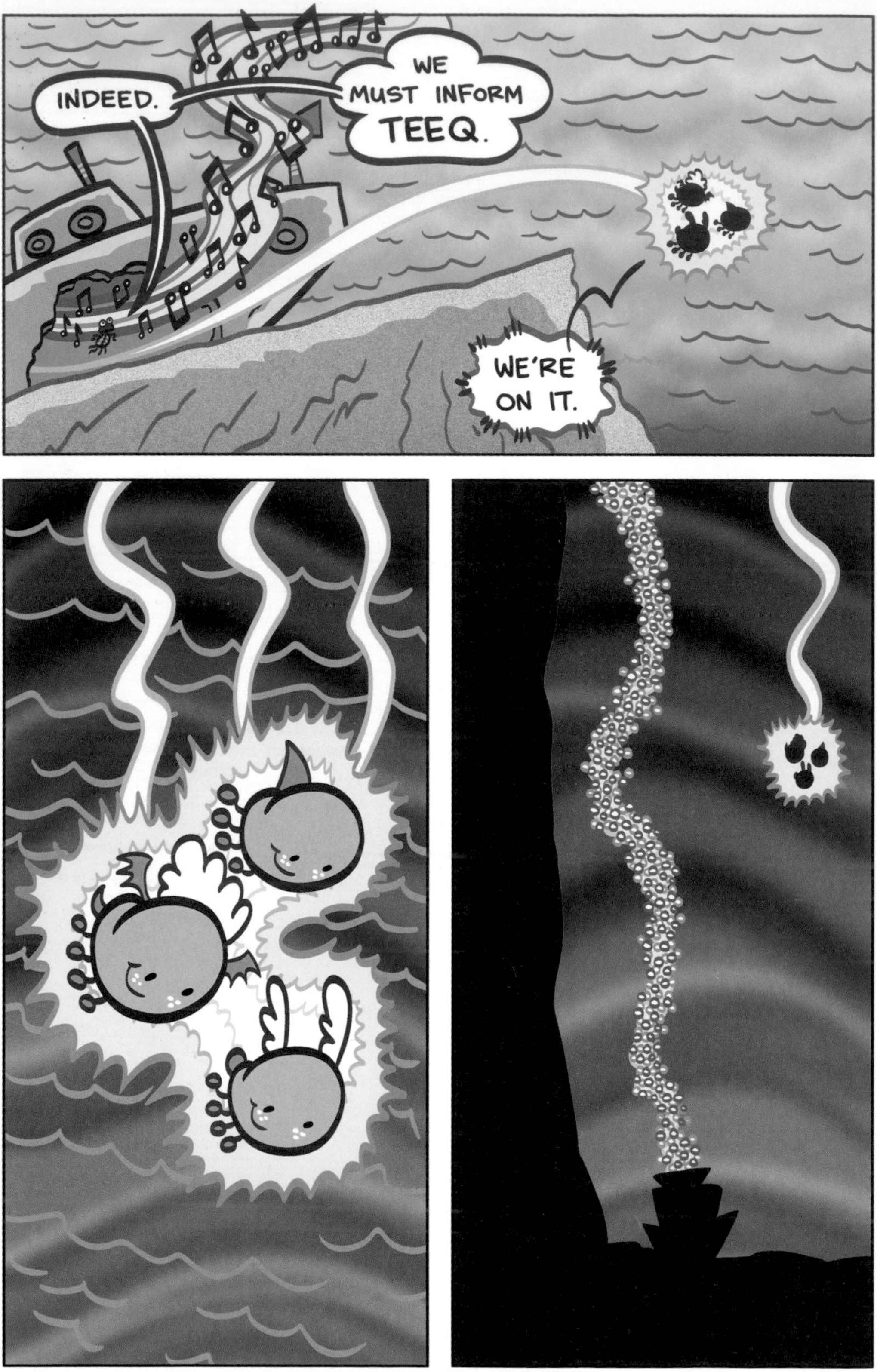
INDEED.
WE MUST INFORM TEEQ.
WE'RE ON IT.

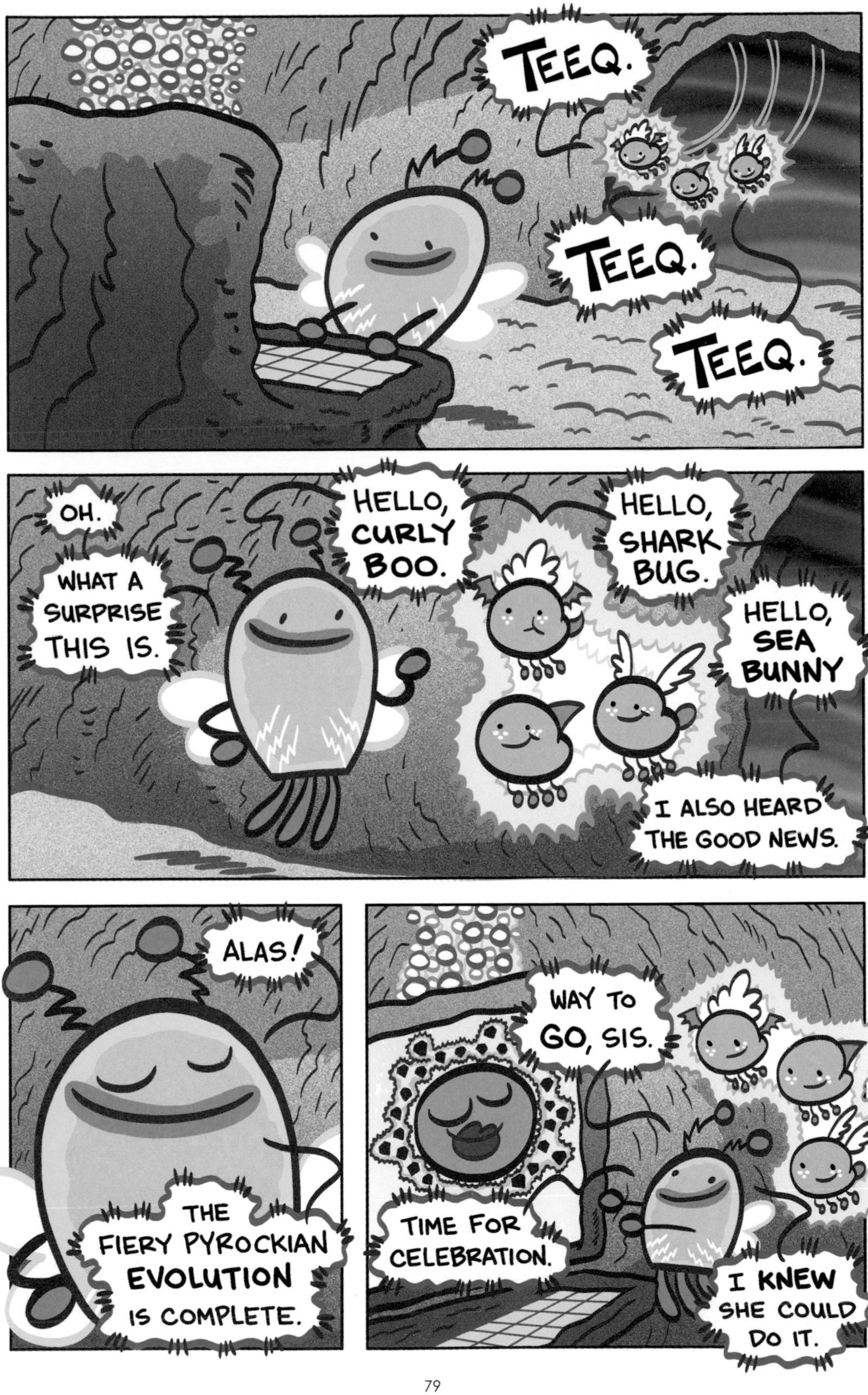
TEEQ.
TEEQ.
TEEQ.
OH.
WHAT A SURPRISE THIS IS.
HELLO, CURLY BOO.
HELLO, SHARK BUG.
HELLO, SEA BUNNY
I ALSO HEARD THE GOOD NEWS.
ALAS!
THE FIERY PYROCKIAN EVOLUTION IS COMPLETE.
WAY TO GO, SIS.
TIME FOR CELEBRATION.
I KNEW SHE COULD DO IT.

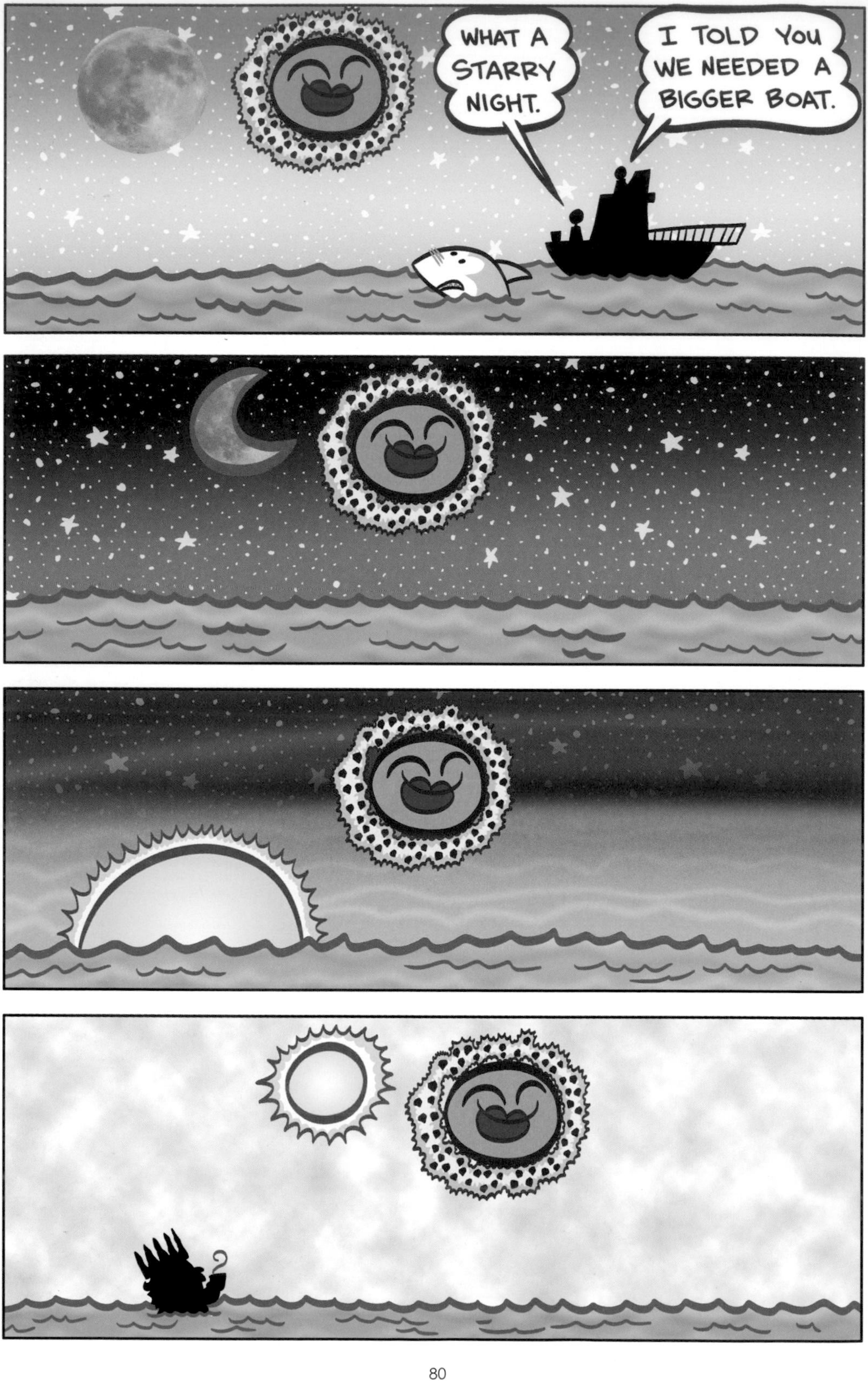
WHAT A STARRY NIGHT.
I TOLD YOU WE NEEDED A BIGGER BOAT.

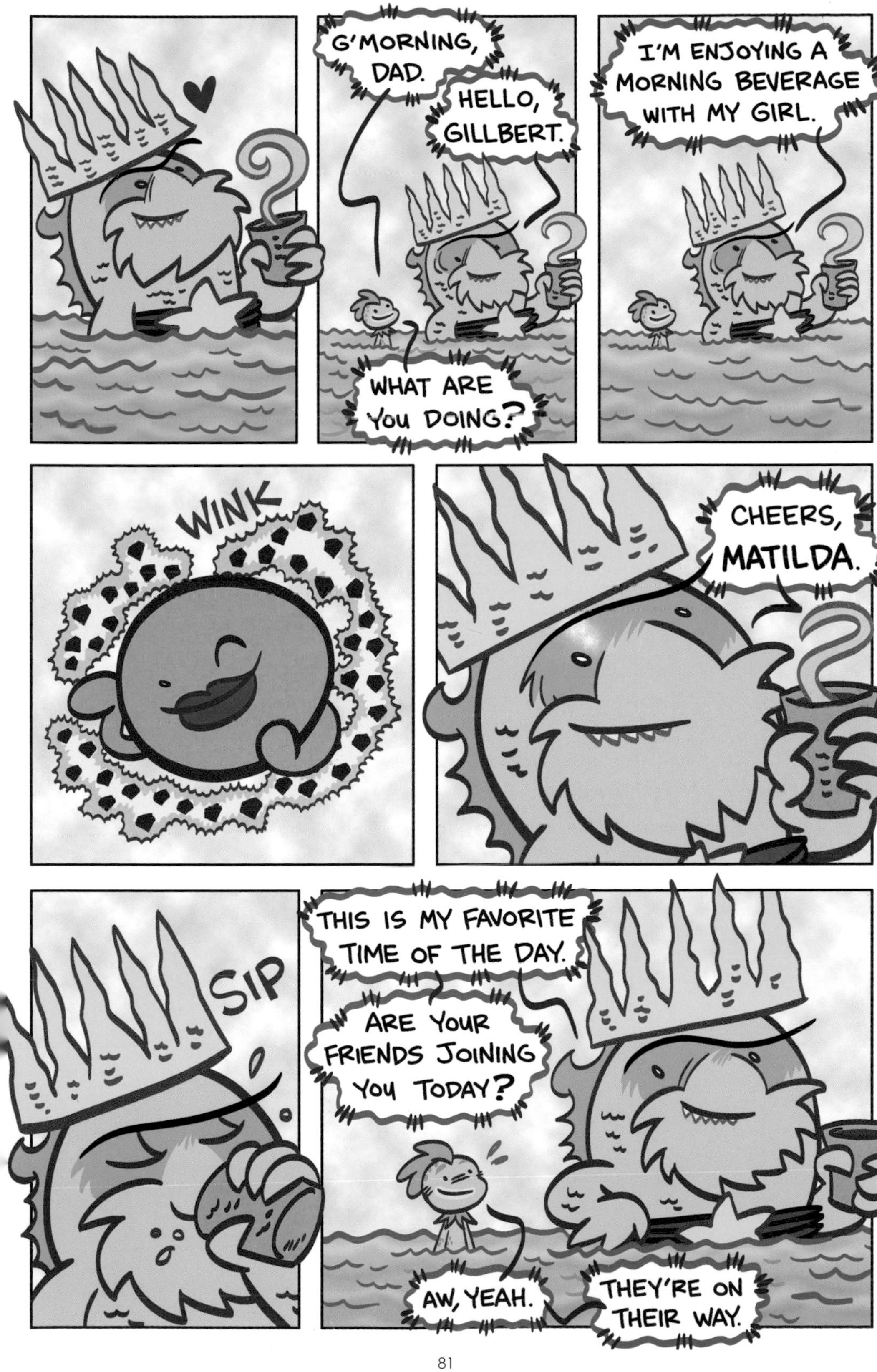
G'MORNING, DAD.
HELLO, GILLBERT.
WHAT ARE YOU DOING?
I'M ENJOYING A MORNING BEVERAGE WITH MY GIRL.
WINK
CHEERS, MATILDA.
SIP
THIS IS MY FAVORITE TIME OF THE DAY.
ARE YOUR FRIENDS JOINING YOU TODAY?
AW, YEAH.
THEY'RE ON THEIR WAY.

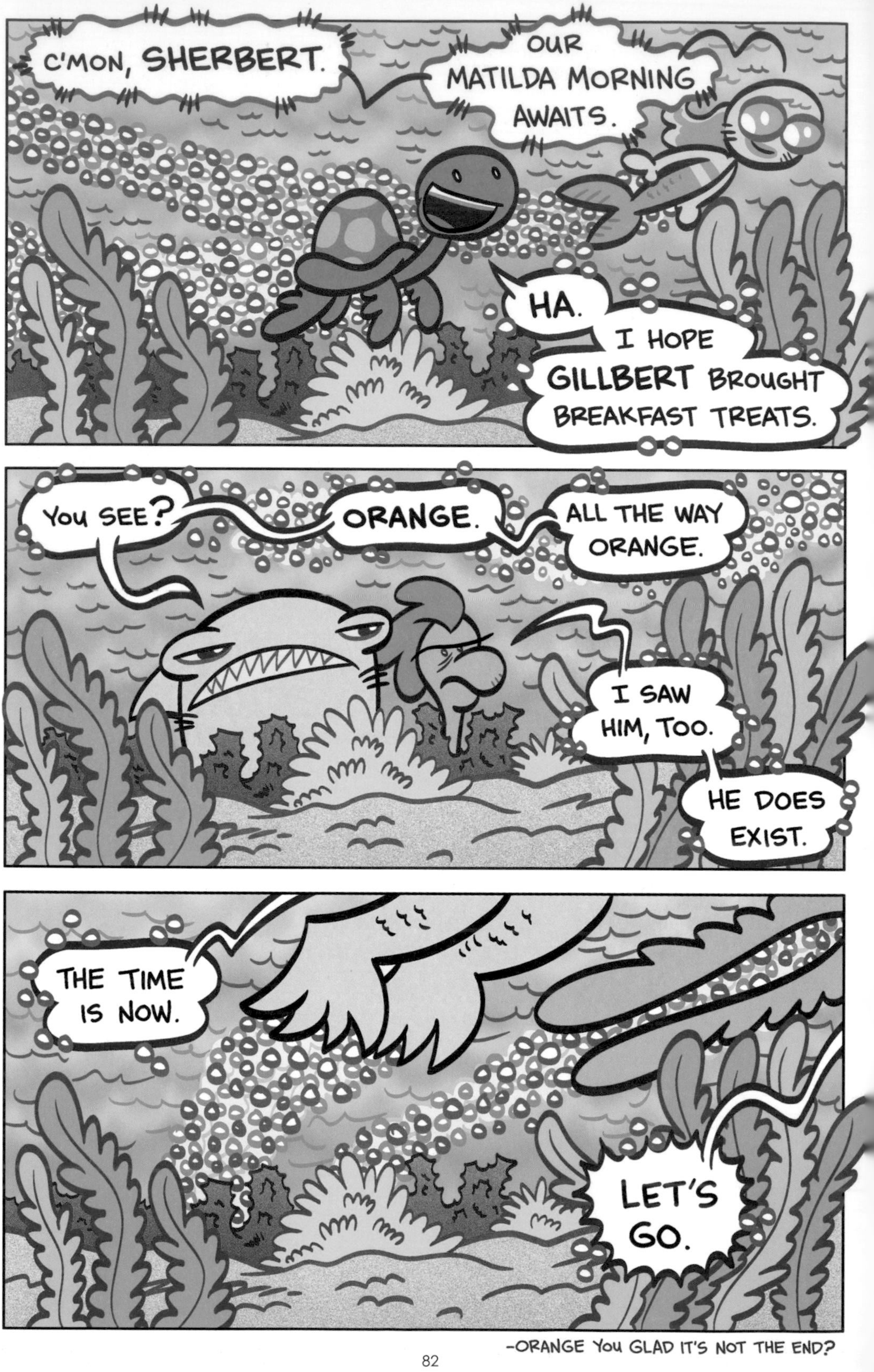
C'MON, SHERBERT.
OUR MATILDA MORNING AWAITS.
HA.
I HOPE GILLBERT BROUGHT BREAKFAST TREATS.
YOU SEE?
ORANGE.
ALL THE WAY ORANGE.
I SAW HIM, TOO.
HE DOES EXIST.
THE TIME IS NOW.
LET'S GO.

–ORANGE YOU GLAD IT'S NOT THE END?

WATCH OUT FOR PAPERCUTZ

Welcome to the third. totally-Pyrockian GILLBERT graphic novel "The Flaming Carats Evolution," from Papercutz, those deep-sea divers dedicated to publishing great graphic novels for all ages. I'm Jim Salicrup, Editor-in-Chief and Olympics-level non-swimmer, here to say a few things about sound…

As we all know, comics are a silent medium that attempts to create the illusion of sound by using "sound effects" and "word balloons." Gillbert and his friends communicate in sounds that can be understood underwater. That's what those little bubbles around Gillbert's word balloons imply. And Gillbert even learned how to communicate telepathically—from his mind into another's mind. That's when those little lines are coming out of the word balloons—to indicate mental communication. So, overall, the soundscape for a GILLBERT graphic novel, despite all the action, is fairly quiet. That got us wondering, which Papercutz series is the noisiest? You'd think it would be THE LOUD HOUSE, our graphic novel series based on the hit Nickelodeon TV series, but no matter how much chaos breaks out in their home, Linc, his ten sisters, parents, pets, and friends are not that noisy compared to other Papercutz titles. For example…

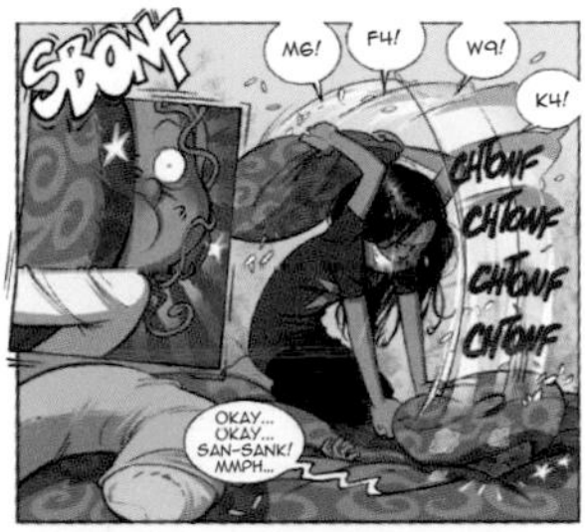
M6!
F4!
W9!
K4!
CHTONF
CHTONF
CHTONF
CHTONF
OKAY… OKAY… SAN-SANK! MMPH…

THE SISTERS (by Cazenove and William) are Wendy and her younger sibling Maureen. Even though their house is inhabited just by the two of them and their parents, they can get awfully loud. Here (top right) they are playing a friendly game of Battleship. You should see and hear them when they're actually fighting with each other.

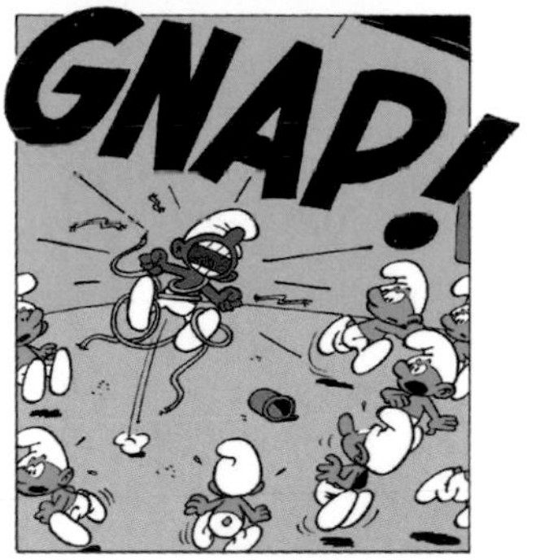
GNAP!

Things can get literally explosive in Papa Smurf's laboratory, when an experiment goes wrong, or when someone opens one of Jokey Smurf's presents. THE SMURFS TALES (by Peyo), can get raucous, especially when the Smurfs Village is invaded by Purple Smurfs (right)…In CAT & CAT (by Cazenove & Richez and Ramon), Catherine and her Cat, Sushi, and her dad, Nathan, are all far from being soft-spoken types. You wouldn't think one cat could cause so much calamity, but if you met Sushi, you'd know better. Sushi even has a noisy fantasy life (left)…

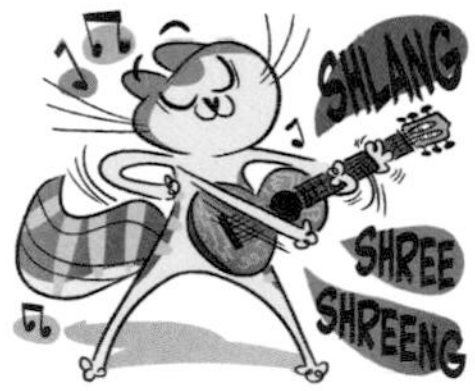
SHLANG
SHREE
SHREENG

Back in 50 BC, two warriors from a small village in Gaul, have been known to raise a ruckus while fending off the Roman Empire's legionaries. There's even a bard named Cacofonix and each book usually ends with raucous celebratory feast. Sometimes in ASTERIX (by René Goscinny and Albert Uderzo), Asterix and Obelix are overshadowed by the sounds of battle (left)…

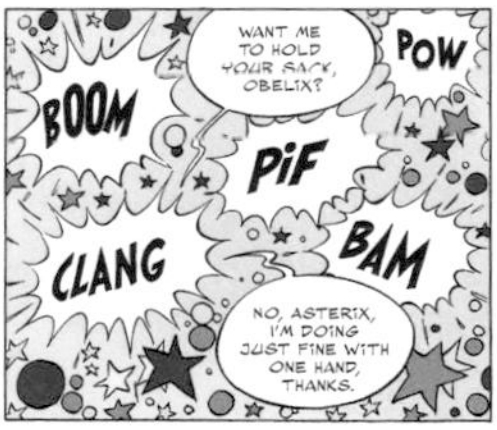
WANT ME TO HOLD YOUR SACK, OBELIX?
POW
BOOM
PiF
BAM
CLANG
NO, ASTERIX, I'M DOING JUST FINE WITH ONE HAND, THANKS.

But we have to go back even further in time to find the noisiest Papercutz graphic novel series of all—DINOSAUR EXPLORERS (by Redcode, Albbie, and Air Team). While there are moments of quiet for Sean, Stone, Rain, Emily, Dr. Da Vinci, Diana, and Starz, the DINOSAUR EXLORERS, once they're under attack by the prehistoric beasts there's a whole lot of shouting and screaming, not to mention roaring.

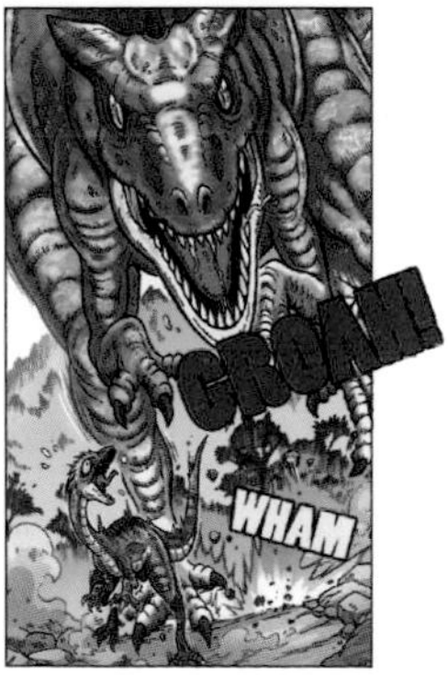
WHAM

After all that hubbub, you may want to seek out a quiet place. Our favorite quiet place, aside from the palatial Papercutz offices when almost the entire staff is working at home, is our friendly neighborhood library. While during these crazy times we can't hang out there much anymore, we can still borrow books. Even Papercutz graphic novels, such as GILLBERT #4 "The Island of the Orange Turtles," coming your way soon, are available at most libraries, not to mention booksellers everywhere. Just remember to be quiet at the library… you don't want to get shushed!

Thanks,

JIM

STAY IN TOUCH!

EMAIL:	salicrup@papercutz.com
WEB:	papercutz.com
TWITTER:	@papercutzgn
INSTAGRAM:	@papercutzgn
FACEBOOK:	PAPERCUTZGRAPHICNOVELS
FAN MAIL:	Papercutz, 160 Broadway, Suite 700, East Wing, New York, NY 10038

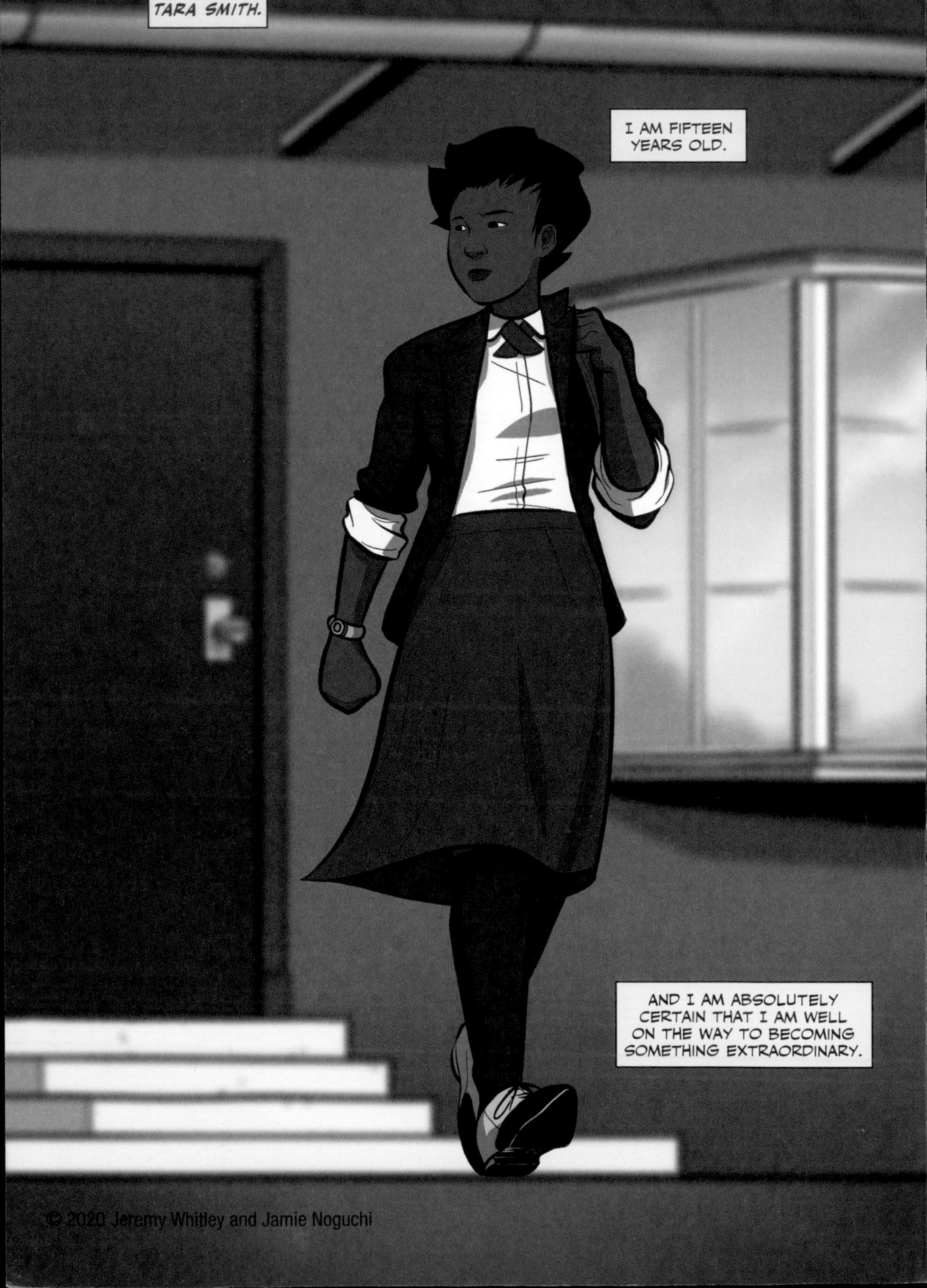
TARA SMITH.
I AM FIFTEEN YEARS OLD.
AND I AM ABSOLUTELY CERTAIN THAT I AM WELL ON THE WAY TO BECOMING SOMETHING EXTRAORDINARY.

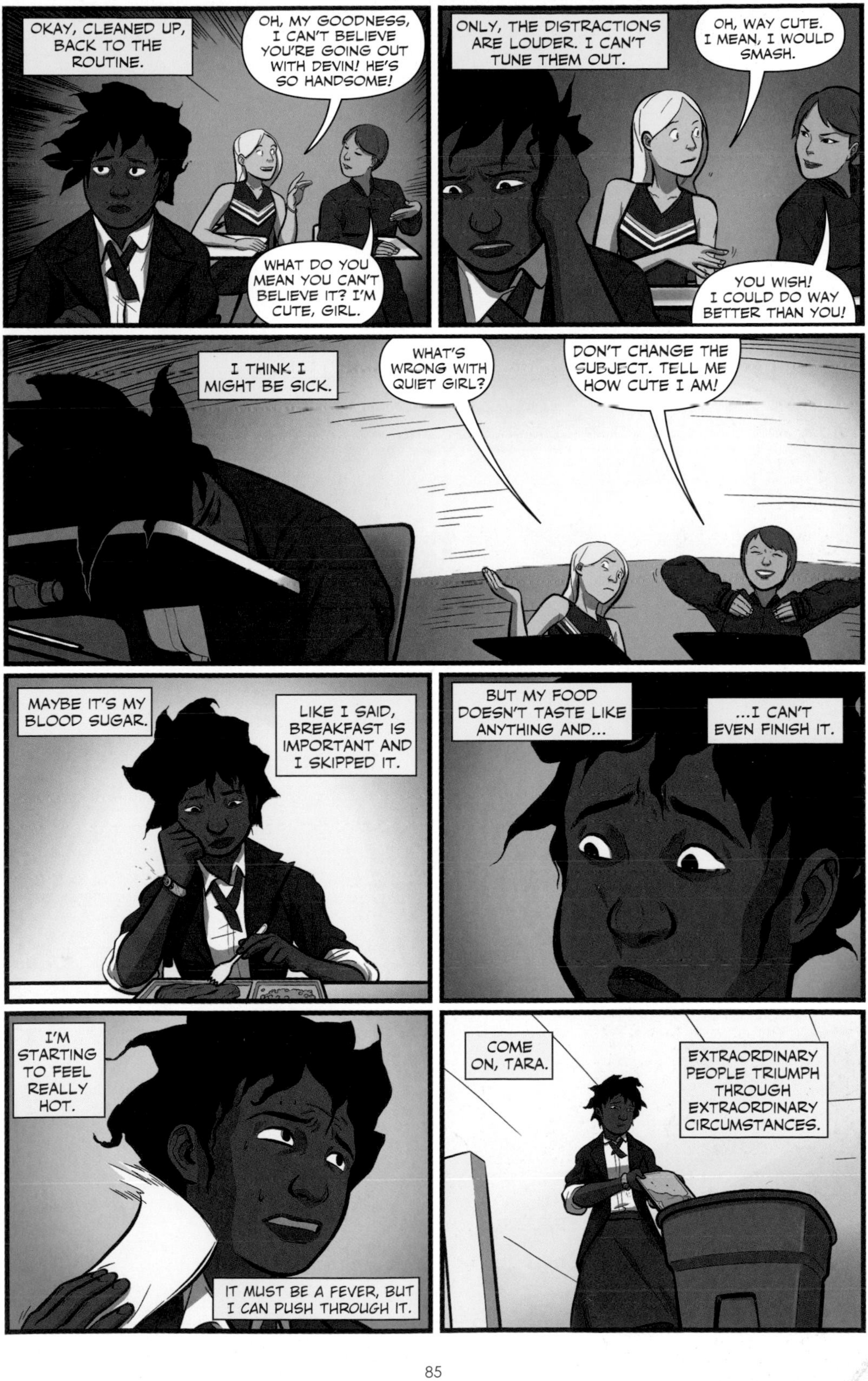
OKAY, CLEANED UP, BACK TO THE ROUTINE.
OH, MY GOODNESS, I CAN'T BELIEVE YOU'RE GOING OUT WITH DEVIN! HE'S SO HANDSOME!
WHAT DO YOU MEAN YOU CAN'T BELIEVE IT? I'M CUTE, GIRL.
ONLY, THE DISTRACTIONS ARE LOUDER. I CAN'T TUNE THEM OUT.
OH, WAY CUTE. I MEAN, I WOULD SMASH.
YOU WISH! I COULD DO WAY BETTER THAN YOU!
I THINK I MIGHT BE SICK.
WHAT'S WRONG WITH QUIET GIRL?
DON'T CHANGE THE SUBJECT. TELL ME HOW CUTE I AM!
MAYBE IT'S MY BLOOD SUGAR.
LIKE I SAID, BREAKFAST IS IMPORTANT AND I SKIPPED IT.
BUT MY FOOD DOESN'T TASTE LIKE ANYTHING AND...
...I CAN'T EVEN FINISH IT.
I'M STARTING TO FEEL REALLY HOT.
IT MUST BE A FEVER, BUT I CAN PUSH THROUGH IT.
COME ON, TARA.
EXTRAORDINARY PEOPLE TRIUMPH THROUGH EXTRAORDINARY CIRCUMSTANCES.

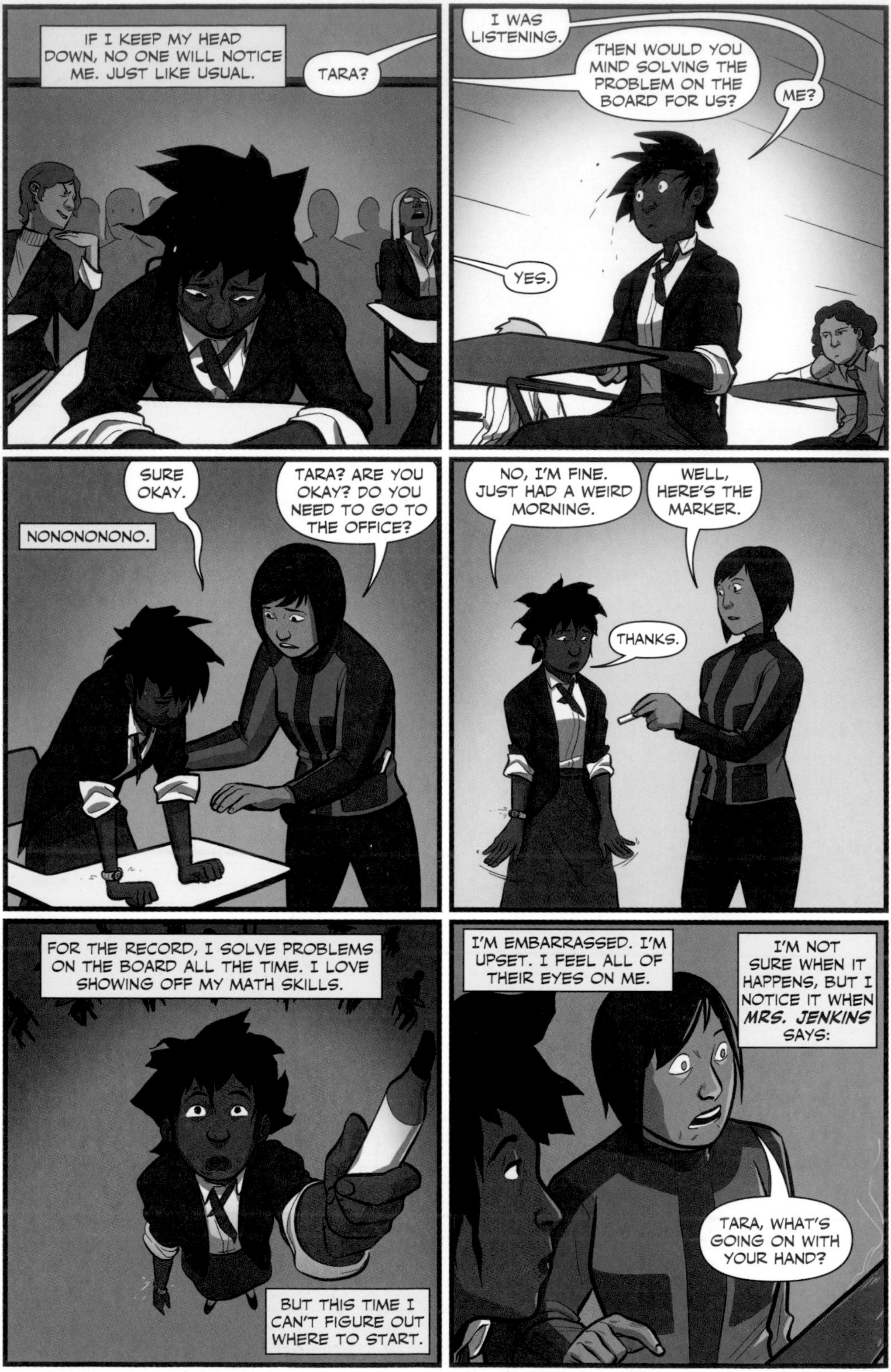
IF I KEEP MY HEAD DOWN, NO ONE WILL NOTICE ME. JUST LIKE USUAL.
TARA?
I WAS LISTENING.
THEN WOULD YOU MIND SOLVING THE PROBLEM ON THE BOARD FOR US?
ME?
YES.
SURE OKAY.
NONONONONO.
TARA? ARE YOU OKAY? DO YOU NEED TO GO TO THE OFFICE?
NO, I'M FINE. JUST HAD A WEIRD MORNING.
WELL, HERE'S THE MARKER.
THANKS.
FOR THE RECORD, I SOLVE PROBLEMS ON THE BOARD ALL THE TIME. I LOVE SHOWING OFF MY MATH SKILLS.
BUT THIS TIME I CAN'T FIGURE OUT WHERE TO START.
I'M EMBARRASSED. I'M UPSET. I FEEL ALL OF THEIR EYES ON ME.
I'M NOT SURE WHEN IT HAPPENS, BUT I NOTICE IT WHEN MRS. JENKINS SAYS:
TARA, WHAT'S GOING ON WITH YOUR HAND?

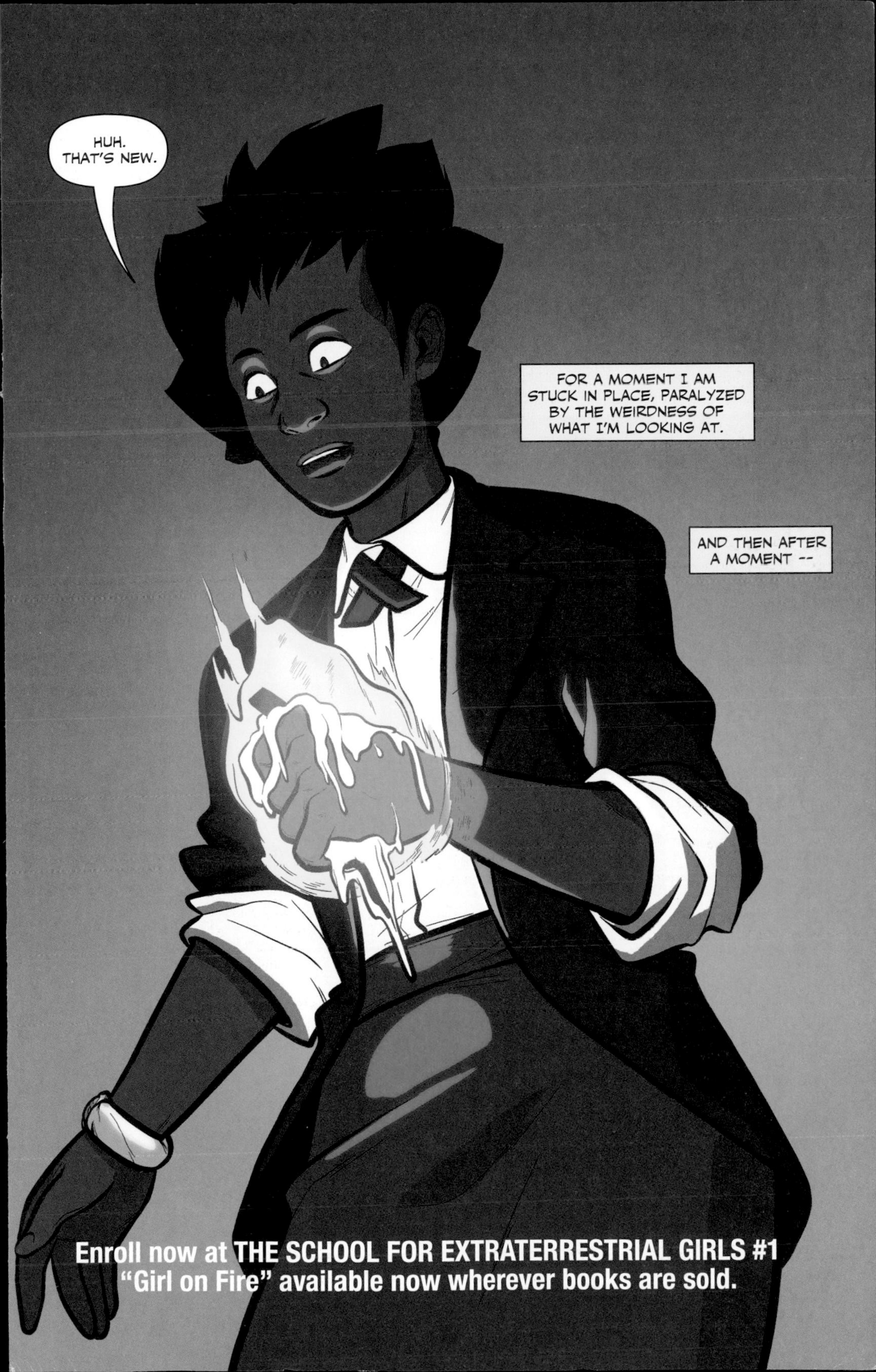
HUH. THAT'S NEW.
FOR A MOMENT I AM STUCK IN PLACE, PARALYZED BY THE WEIRDNESS OF WHAT I'M LOOKING AT.
AND THEN AFTER A MOMENT --
Enroll now at THE SCHOOL FOR EXTRATERRESTRIAL GIRLS #1 "Girl on Fire" available now wherever books are sold.

MORE GREAT GRAPHIC NOVEL SERIES AVAILABLE FROM

PAPERCUTZ™

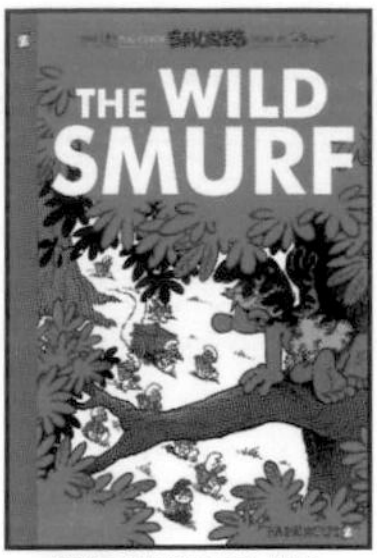
THE WILD SMURF
THE SMURFS #21

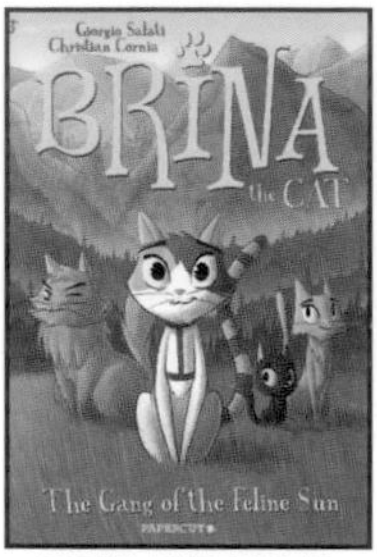
BRINA the CAT
The Gang of the Feline Sun
PAPERCUTZ
BRINA THE CAT #1

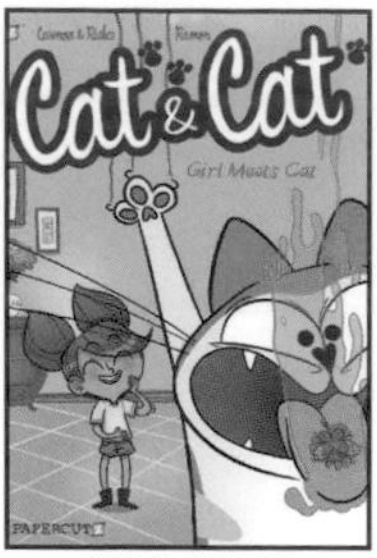
Cat & Cat
Girl Meets Cat
PAPERCUTZ
CAT & CAT #1

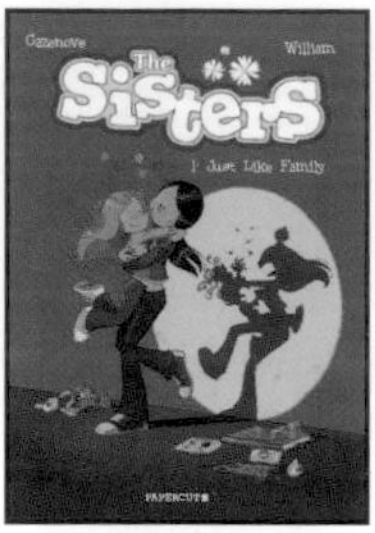
The Sisters
1. Just Like Family
PAPERCUTZ
THE SISTERS #1

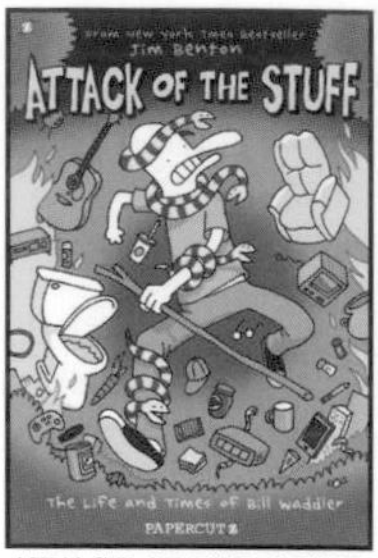
Jim Benton
ATTACK OF THE STUFF
The Life and Times of Bill Waddler
PAPERCUTZ
ATTACK OF THE STUFF

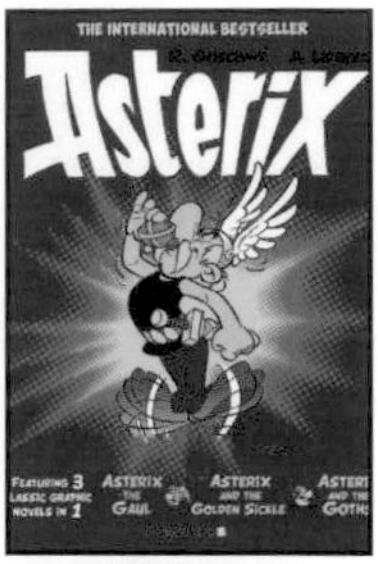
THE INTERNATIONAL BESTSELLER
Asterix
PAPERCUTZ
ASTERIX #1

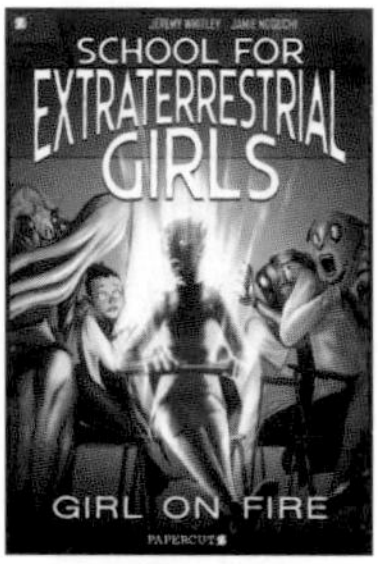
SCHOOL FOR EXTRATERRESTRIAL GIRLS
GIRL ON FIRE
PAPERCUTZ
SCHOOL FOR EXTRATERRESTRIAL GIRLS #1

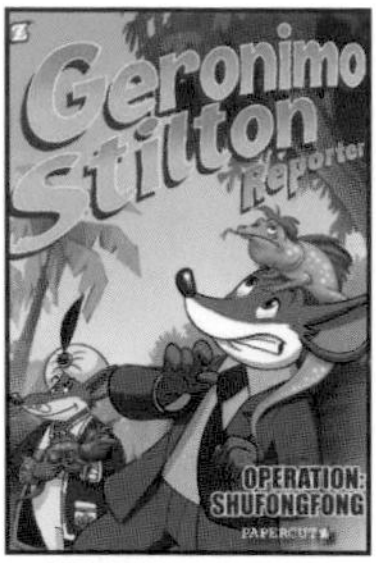
Geronimo Stilton Reporter
OPERATION: SHUFONGFONG
PAPERCUTZ
GERONIMO STILTON REPORTER #1

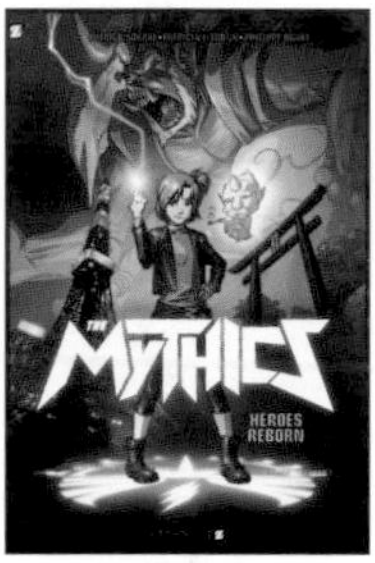
MYTHICS
HEROES REBORN
THE MYTHICS #1

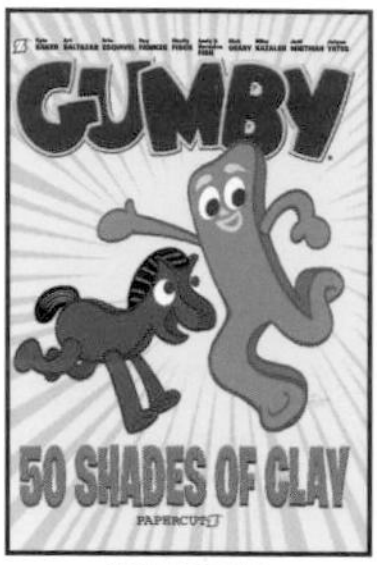
GUMBY
50 SHADES OF CLAY
PAPERCUTZ
GUMBY #1

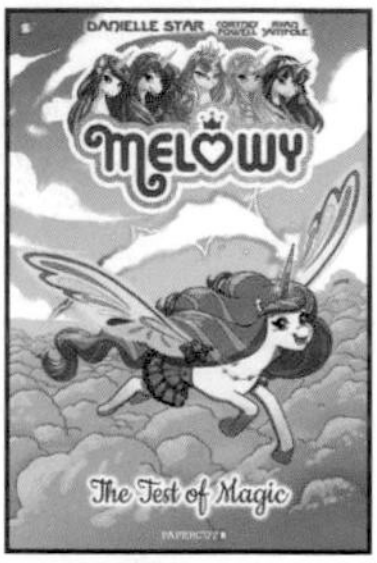
DANIELLE STAR
Melowy
The Test of Magic
PAPERCUTZ
MELOWY #1

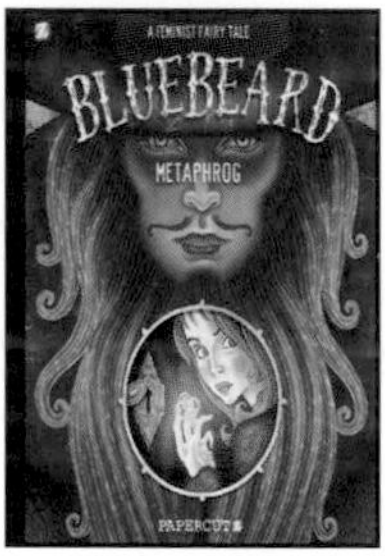
A FEMINIST FAIRY TALE
BLUEBEARD
METAPHROG
PAPERCUTZ
BLUEBEARD

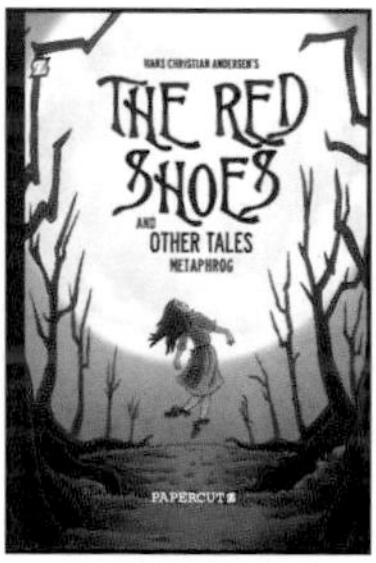
HANS CHRISTIAN ANDERSEN'S
THE RED SHOES
AND OTHER TALES
METAPHROG
PAPERCUTZ
THE RED SHOES

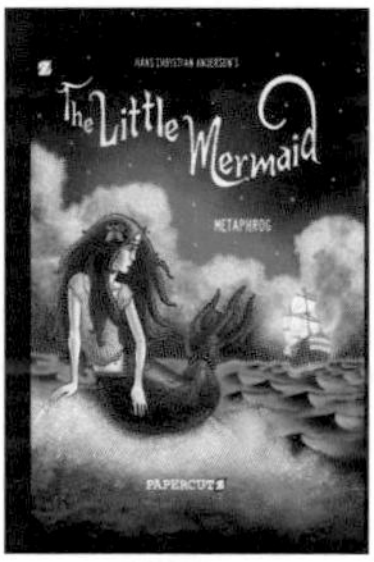
HANS CHRISTIAN ANDERSEN'S
The Little Mermaid
METAPHROG
PAPERCUTZ
THE LITTLE MERMAID

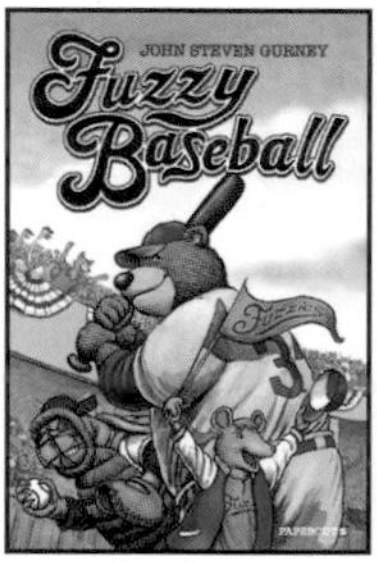
JOHN STEVEN GURNEY
Fuzzy Baseball
PAPERCUTZ
FUZZY BASEBALL #1

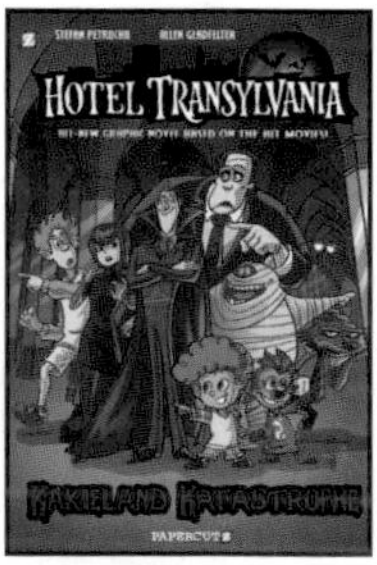
HOTEL TRANSYLVANIA
KAKIELAND KATASTROPHE
PAPERCUTZ
HOTEL TRANSYLVANIA #1

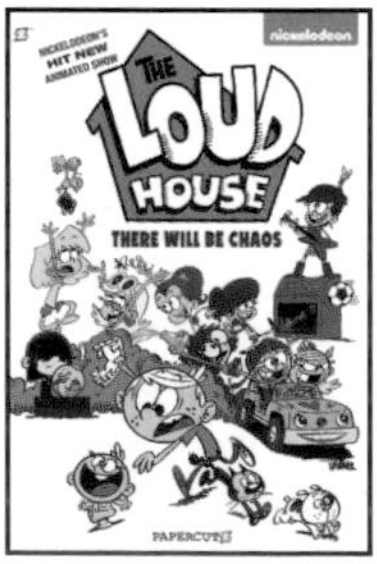
nickelodeon
THE LOUD HOUSE
THERE WILL BE CHAOS
PAPERCUTZ
THE LOUD HOUSE #1

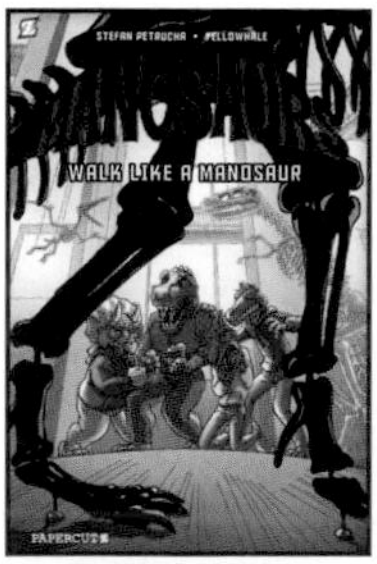
WALK LIKE A MANOSAUR
PAPERCUTZ
MANOSAURS #1

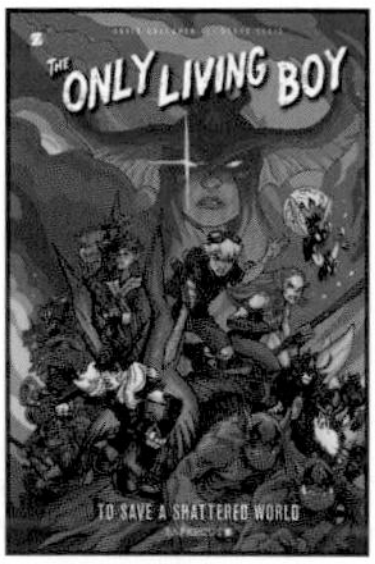
THE ONLY LIVING BOY
TO SAVE A SHATTERED WORLD
THE ONLY LIVING BOY #5

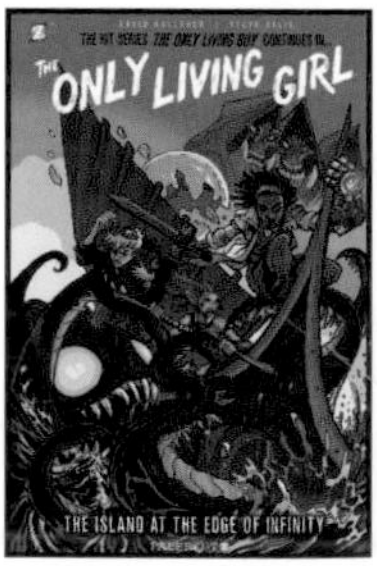
THE ONLY LIVING GIRL
THE ISLAND AT THE EDGE OF INFINITY
THE ONLY LIVING GIRL #1

papercutz.com

Also available where ebooks are sold.